"You think this lit

Cole stared at the profile of the child asleep on his aunt's shoulder. "That's a pretty serious charge. Do you have some kind of proof?"

Tessa let out a sigh, "None. But I have a DNA kit in my purse. And just to be clear, I'm not accusing you of anything."

He shook his head. "If your sister didn't tell you about me, how did you get my name?"

"Her diary. I brought it along and I'd be happy to show you the passage that put you at the top of my list. Later. After I get Joey in bed, maybe?"

Before he could answer, she said, "If I've made a mistake, we'll leave in the morning. No hassle, I promise. I'm not trying to pin Joey's paternity on anybody. I only want to do the right thing for my nephew. I know what it's like to grow up without a father."

Grow up without a father. Something he wouldn't wish on anybody—especially not a sweet kid like Joey who grabbed your heart with both fists and didn't let go.

Dear Reader,

I was born into a family of gamblers. My mother used to say that her father would have bet on whether or not the sun would come up the next day...if he could get the right odds.

When I was invited to participate in a series about a group of friends who get together for weekly poker games, I didn't hesitate to dust off my deck of cards and jump in. But I knew I needed a refresher course, so I turned to friends Dave and Sandra Meek—and the other players who make up their own kind of "Wild Bunch." Thanks for letting me leave a few dollars ahead. I also have many fond memories of my parents and their friends gathered around the kitchen table with stacks of red, white and blue plastic chips, the sound of cards being shuffled and the friendly razzing as fortunes rose and fell. I felt exactly the same when the "Wild Bunch" started to come to life. I love these guys, and, win or lose, they're there for each other.

The decision to set this series in a small town near San Antonio turned out to be most fortuitous for me, since that meant I could call upon friends Karen and Jim Hale for the inside scoop. Karen not only devoted several days to playing tour guide, but she made sure we ate authentic Tex-Mex and barbecue. Boracho beans and Shiner Bock—I can't wait to return. Karen also proved instrumental in helping me understand what went wrong in Cole's real estate deal. Thanks again for the grand, Texas-size hospitality.

While in San Antonio, I picked up a bunch of Texas goodies to share on my Web site, so please drop by www.debrasalonen.com and enter the TEXAS HOLD 'EM contest.

Debra
Romantic Times BOOKreviews' 2006 Series Storyteller of the Year

BETTING ON SANTA
Debra Salonen

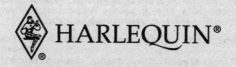

HARLEQUIN®

TORONTO • NEW YORK • LONDON
AMSTERDAM • PARIS • SYDNEY • HAMBURG
STOCKHOLM • ATHENS • TOKYO • MILAN • MADRID
PRAGUE • WARSAW • BUDAPEST • AUCKLAND

ISBN-13: 978-0-373-71452-0
ISBN-10:   0-373-71452-1

BETTING ON SANTA

ABOUT THE AUTHOR

As a child, Debra wanted to be an artist. She saved her allowance to send away for a "Learn To Draw" kit, but when her mother mistook Deb's artful rendition of a horse for a cow, Deb turned to her second love—writing.

Debra's first published romance novel was released in 2000. Since her first sale, she has tackled many challenging, provocative subjects in her stories: blended families, aging parents, the death of a spouse, catastrophic illness and divorce, child abduction, fertility issues and adoption. She was recently honored as *Romantic Times BOOKreviews'* 2006 Series Storyteller of the Year

Books by Debra Salonen

HARLEQUIN SUPERROMANCE

1003—SOMETHING ABOUT EVE
1061—WONDERS NEVER CEASE
1098—MY HUSBAND, MY BABIES
1104—WITHOUT A PAST
1110—THE COMEBACK GIRL
1196—A COWBOY SUMMER
1238—CALEB'S CHRISTMAS WISH

1279—HIS REAL FATHER
1386—A BABY ON THE WAY
1392—WHO NEEDS CUPID?
    "The Max Factor"
1434—LOVE, BY GEORGE

SIGNATURE SELECT SAGA

BETTING ON GRACE

HARLEQUIN AMERICAN ROMANCE

1114—ONE DADDY TOO MANY
1126—BRINGING BABY HOME
1139—THE QUIET CHILD

To my fellow TEXAS HOLD 'EM authors—
I knew from the start this wasn't a gamble,
because you're all the best!

And to Victoria—
for just the right hints at just the right time.

CHAPTER ONE

Thursday, November 29, 2007

"SMILE, SANTA."

Cole tried. It wasn't easy with Sally Knutson on his knee and her three cats wreaking havoc on his costume. The gray one was tangled in the glossy white beard, batting at the lush strands. The calico perched on his shoulder had every needle-tipped claw hooked solidly through the red velvet, his undershirt and his flesh. The slightest movement on Cole's part meant instant pain. The third—the "shy" one—was wedged between its owner's ample bosom and Cole's two-pillow padding.

His mother hadn't said anything about hazard pay when she volunteered him to fill in for Ray Hardy, the man who truly *was* Santa to most of the citizens of River Bluff, Texas. A fixture at the Congressional Church's annual holiday bazaar and toy drive, Ray hadn't missed a night—until he slipped in the shower that morning. Now the man was facing hip surgery.

"Look at the camera, Sugar Baby," Sally cooed.

Cole assumed she was talking to the feline on his

shoulder since Sally was his mother's age—and about forty pounds overweight, if his aching leg was any indication.

"Any time, Melody," Cole urged, a bead of sweat threatening to turn into a rivulet down the side of his cheek. Their Hill Country weather had become oppressively muggy thanks to the tropical moisture out in the Gulf. It was almost December, and Cole was ready for some cooling. Especially if he was going to be stuck in a Santa suit for who knew how long.

"Sorry," the high school senior said, looking up so quickly her green felt hat nearly fell off. "The battery is struggling to keep up. I should have had Dad bring the other rechargeables."

He wondered if Ray had these kinds of problems, and if so how the man had managed to survive all these years. Not only was Cole's patience exhausted, his butt was sore. The ornate chair that usually sat behind the pulpit wasn't made for comfort, he'd decided after the first half hour. But it looked impressive on the raised "snow-covered" dais situated in one corner of the church parking lot, which, with the help of hundreds of strands of twinkle lights, had been transformed into River Bluff's version of the North Pole.

"It's green," Melody said, moving into position. "Look at me, Sal. Say, 'catnip.'"

The only way to simulate a smile when you were wearing a one-piece beard and mustache was to flex your cheek muscles in an exaggerated grin. Unfortunately, this made Cole's beard rise, which made the cat on his lap pounce, which spooked the cat on his shoulder.

"Somebody moved," Melody accused, fiddling with the camera. "Stay put. We have to try another."

Sally shifted her weight to reposition the cat on his shoulder, and Cole's ankle twisted slightly. A shaft of pain radiated upward from his old injury. One that had never completely healed right—a legacy of a holiday he preferred to forget.

"Am I squishing y'all, honey?" Sally asked, apparently hearing his swallowed moan. "You need a bit more padding on your tushy, like Ray. Wasn't it a shame about his fall?"

"Terrible," Cole said through clenched teeth. "Mom said he's had a big crowd here every night since the bazaar opened." And the church's holiday festival ran through the middle of December.

Sally disentangled the tabby's paws from Cole's beard. "True. I was here last night and gave up after about an hour. The girls aren't patient."

He could tell. The "girl" on his shoulder was using his costume for a scratching pad. "Um, Sal, could you do something about this one, too?" he said, turning his chin to point.

The "shy" one suddenly took a swipe at his beard, pulling it down a good inch so the attached mustache covered his lip.

"Okay, everybody, let's try again," Melody called. "Say Merry Christmas."

"Murway Kwemat," Cole mumbled, eyes watering.

"Oh, this is cute, Sally," Melody exclaimed, studying her camera. "I think it's a keeper."

Sally got up, a cat under each arm. She adroitly hopped off the raised platform and walked to where Melody was standing. The third cat scaled the side of Cole's head, finding purchase in his beard, plush red hat and scalp.

"Ow!" he howled, reaching up clumsily in his oversize white gloves to try to dislodge the beast. "Sally, help."

She shoved the other two pets at Melody, who dropped the compact digital camera. Melody's cry was muffled by Sally's loud, "Ooh, poor Sugar, did you think Mama was going to leave you with the big, mean stranger?"

"*Mean?* What'd I do?" Cole complained, rubbing his head in a way that made his costume shift back and forth. He had to straighten his beard before he could spit out several cat hairs.

"You're not a cat person, Cole. Animals can tell."

He would have tried to defend himself but she didn't give him a chance, instead hurrying back to where Melody was kneeling over the remains of her camera.

Cole checked his watch. Fortunately, Santa's booth was due to close in ten minutes. He looked toward the candy-cane gate. Only one person in line. A stranger with a toddler on her hip. By the bemused expression on her face, she'd witnessed the entire spectacle. Cole was glad to have a fake beard to hide behind.

The woman looked to be about his age. Jeans, a belted leather jacket and an oversize purse apparently used to counterweight the toddler on her opposite hip. Cole guessed the boy's age to be about two.

Not that Cole knew a lot about kids, but he'd learned a great deal after just one night as Santa. For instance, he now knew there was a difference between teething and mere drooling.

"Um…sorry. We're experiencing technical difficulties," he said. "Santa left his other—more efficient—elves at the North Pole."

Melody suddenly burst into tears. Sally gave him a reproachful look that made him feel like a heel, and he lumbered off the dais. The toes of his size-fourteen boots—Ray's boots—were stuffed with newspaper, which made walking a challenge. Plus, his balance was off because of the lopsided padding across his middle.

"Aw, Melody, I'm sorry. I was kidding. You're doing great. It's not your fault the camera won't work."

Sniffling, the girl picked up the small silver digital. She pressed what Cole assumed was the On button. Nothing happened.

Melody shook her head. "It's shot, but luckily the photos I took tonight will be okay. I can take out the memory card and print them on my computer at home."

Cole said a silent thank-you before looking at the last customer in line. "Sorry about this. We could probably have a new camera by tomorrow. I'd like to tell you the *real* Santa will be back by then, but I doubt it."

The woman looked at her son, who didn't resemble her in the least. The child was a towhead with wavy hair that curled around the collar of his denim jacket. Even in the dim light of the Christmas bulbs looped around the poles, Cole could tell that the boy's mother was beautiful. Shoulder-length, dark auburn hair pulled off her face with a simple clip. Wide-set eyes that were blue or green—far lighter than he'd expect with her dark coloring.

When she turned to face him, he had a momentary sense of déjà vu. Had they met before? Was she from around here or maybe someone he'd sold a house?

No. He definitely would have remembered a face like hers.

"I have a camera. If you wouldn't mind, I could take Joey's photo with you and have a copy printed later. I'd still pay, of course."

He liked her. Firm, direct and businesslike, but feminine, too.

"Um…" He looked around for someone to ask if there were rules against do-it-yourself photography, but Sally had moved off to pack her cats into their lavish pink leather carrier. Melody was on her cell phone, no doubt complaining to her dad, Cole's poker buddy, Ed, about Santa's lack of empathy with her broken camera. Cole's mother was probably helping at the refreshment booth where a few stragglers still lingered. "Why not?"

The woman set down the boy—Joey, she'd called him—and dug a camera out of her bag. It was much more elaborate than the one Melody had been using.

"I'm going to take your picture while you sit on Santa's lap, sweetie," she said in a soft voice, as she led

Joey to the platform and waited while Cole climbed into his chair. "Can you do that for Auntie Tessa?"

Auntie?

Cole settled back against the wide, hard throne, subtly shifting his padding to make room for the boy, who didn't look too sure about this whole thing.

"Hi, there, Joey. How are you tonight?"

The boy's big blue eyes grew even rounder and he appeared to be holding his breath. Cole had wanted kids, had imagined raising a boy just like this one. But Crystal had insisted they weren't ready. "We need to establish ourselves financially first," she'd said.

What she didn't say was if that didn't happen she'd kick his butt to the proverbial curb faster than a Texas tornado could demolish a mobile home.

He refocused his attention on the child on his knee, his uninjured left one this time. The boy was a featherweight compared to Sally, and Cole bounced him reassuringly, picking up speed as the child's bottom lip started to curl outward.

"Um…what kinds of toys do you like, Joey? Trains? Bob the Builder? I'm a builder. Um, in the off-season," he added, feeling like a complete idiot. "How 'bout a bike? I mean, trike. Would you like a tricycle for Christmas?"

Joey opened his mouth but no words came out. Cole was just happy the kid wasn't bawling his expressive blue eyes out. Cole looked at the aunt for help and found her squatting a few feet away, snapping shot after shot.

"Smile, Joey. Your aunt looks like a real professional. I think she's done this before."

"Less bouncing, please."

Cole felt his cheeks heat up. Duh.

He used this gloved finger to turn Joey's chin his way. Giving the kid his most friendly, concerned smile, he said, "Just tell me what you want, Joey."

"Mommy," the little guy said.

Then, a second later, he threw up. All down the front of Cole's brilliant white beard, red suit and wide black belt.

Chaos ensued.

Women appeared out of nowhere. Like an old-time magician, Joey's aunt produced a plastic container filled with wet wipes from her purse and started cleaning the child up. Cole's mother, whom he hadn't seen since she helped him get into the bulky red suit, dashed to his side with a towel.

Joey sobbed.

"I'm so sorry, baby," the woman said, comforting Joey after thrusting a glob of wet towelettes into Cole's gloved hands. "It's okay, sweetie. It's not your fault. I should have known we were trying to squeeze in too much." She rocked the child back and forth.

As his cries subsided, she apologized to Cole. "I'm so sorry. The minute Joey spotted you he wanted to *see* Santa, and I thought it would be great to take a photo back to my mother. She's with my sister. Joey's mom. Who's in the hospital," she added under her breath.

"How sad," Cole's mother said. "There's no good time to be sick, but it's especially difficult during the holidays. Is it serious?"

The woman nodded, her lips pressed together as if

fighting any outward display of emotion. Big Jim would have approved. His ex-father-in-law had once advised Cole that the key to selling real estate was to never let anyone past the outer wall. "Never let people know you're emotionally invested. Show them your soft underbelly and they'll gut you."

Cole had been gutted—once.

He slid carefully off the chair and, as discreetly as possible, shook his beard into the towel his mother was holding.

The woman noticed, and immediately stooped to collect her purse, which she'd dropped to the pavement. "I'll pay to have the suit cleaned."

"Oh, don't fret," his mother said. "Don't think for a minute this sweet child is the first to ever throw up on Santa. Ray—our usual Saint Nick—could tell you stories that would curl your hair."

"I think I nailed him when I was six or seven, right, Mom?" Cole asked. "And I still got a train set that year."

Before she could reply, the jaunty jingle of a cellular ring tone chimed. The stranger reached unerringly into an outer pocket of her Coach bag—one of his ex-wife's favorite brands—and pulled out a high-tech-looking phone. Cole had always had the most up-to-date gizmos on the market when he'd been a Realtor. Connectivity meant opportunities. Opportunities meant money. Now, he didn't even have a landline to his house.

"Excuse us a minute," he said, nodding toward his mother to take their cleanup efforts behind the dais.

Tessa watched him amble away with a graceless gait that didn't match his youthful voice. She knew by the musical tone that the caller was her mother. She also knew what Autumn's question would be—"Did you find him? Did you find Cole Lawry?"

Tessa could have answered, "Yes, Mom, I'm looking right at him." But that would have revealed more than she was ready to discuss in such a public setting. She flipped open the phone. "Hi, Mom. How's Sunny?"

"The same as when you left. The doctor still hasn't been in and nobody will tell me anything, but that's not why I called. I wanted to tell you I'm sorry I lost my temper. I know you're doing what you think is best and maybe you're right. If that man is Joey's father, then I guess he should be informed about Sunshine."

For the second time in five minutes, Tessa had to fight back tears. *What's wrong with me?* A delayed reaction to everything that had happened, she figured, including the tense drive over the same road her sister had been traveling when she crashed her rental car and wound up in a coma.

"It's okay, Mom. We're both dealing with a lot."

Understatement of the year.

"Have you found him yet?"

"Yes, but we haven't had a chance to talk. Too much going on. He's playing Santa at a holiday bazaar."

"How did you find that out?"

"Joey and I stopped at a café and I asked our waitress about Cole Lawry. We left the car at the diner and walked the couple of blocks here."

"Must be a pretty small town if everybody knows everybody. So you talked to him? Do you think he's the one?"

Tessa glanced toward the ornate chair where she'd openly studied the man playing Santa Claus. "He's wearing a white beard and has a couple of pillows stuffed around his middle, Mom. It's kinda hard to tell what he looks like. But he has blue eyes."

Intriguing blue eyes.

"Oh," Autumn said. "Where is he now?"

"Probably changing clothes. Joey threw up on his lap. Too much excitement, I think, although he might be coming down with something." She put the back of her hand to her nephew's forehead. "He feels slightly feverish."

"Oh, my poor bubba. Can I talk to him?"

Tessa lowered her purse to the ground again, then stood Joey on his feet. She knelt in front of him. "Grams is on the phone, sweetie. Wanna tell her good-night?"

He nodded and took the phone from her.

Knowing how short his attention span was and that he tended to drop things he no longer wanted, Tessa hovered over him. The tiny respite gave her mind a chance to weigh the pros and cons of continuing her plan or trying to come up with an alternative.

She looked around the church parking lot. The people who had been wandering among the booths when she and Joey first arrived were mostly gone. Only a few cars and trucks remained. A dozen or so women chatted in small groups, some calling out to each other as they carried stock to their minivans. Tessa couldn't see any children.

That made her realize how late it was. She looked up and saw that the stars were out. "Damn," she muttered.

Her rental car was three blocks away and the town didn't look as though it had made streetlights a priority.

"O…kay," Joey said in the singsong way that meant he was done with whatever it was he'd been doing. He opened his hand.

She caught the cherry-red phone inches from the pavement, her heart racing. This was her most immediate and tangible connection to the real world. The flight to Texas had been awful—made worse by the fear that her sister wouldn't be alive when they got here; spending hours in a hospital watching Sunny confined to a bed, wires and machines attached to her body, was too scary to be real. Her cell phone, laptop and BlackBerry were Tessa's touchstones of normalcy.

She decided not to call her mother back to say goodbye. Instead, she'd phone from the motel. She'd booked the place online and used her credit card to pay for it, so hopefully they were holding a room even though she was late checking in. Pocketing the phone, she stood and held out a hand. "I guess we'd better head back to the car, pal. It's getting dark. Maybe we can see Santa another time."

Joey looked toward the dais just as a lean man with sandy-blond hair and broad shoulders emerged from behind the curtained area. Santa's changing room, she assumed. Instead of a red suit, he wore jeans, thick-soled work boots, a gray T-shirt and zippered sweatshirt with the sleeves pushed back on his well-muscled forearms. The sweatshirt bore a logo she couldn't make out.

"Oh, good, you're still here," he said, jogging toward them. His smile struck her as friendly and real. He seemed nice. Too nice to be the recipient of the news she was there to deliver.

"We were just leaving. It sure gets dark fast around here."

"Yeah, I know. Mom said she thought she saw you walk up. Are you staying nearby?"

"The Trail's End Motel. But we walked here from the diner. The waitress said it was only a couple of blocks away, but they were really big blocks."

He gave her a rueful grin. "Yep, this is Texas. Everything's bigger. I'm guessing you're not from around here."

"Oregon," she said, watching for some kind of reaction.

"Wow. Long way from home. Can I give you a lift to your car? River Bluff isn't exactly famous for its sidewalks."

A voice in her head warned against hopping into a car with a stranger, but she made a snap decision. "Sure. Thanks." He was the man she'd come here to find. Although he didn't know that or he might not have been quite so kind and generous. "I take it you're off duty?"

"Till six-thirty tomorrow. The regular you-know-who broke his hip. I'm a last-minute replacement."

Tessa was touched by his acknowledging Joey's presence, although she could tell Joey wasn't paying attention to either of them. When the little boy ran out of steam, he had a tendency to drop, wherever he was.

"Is your car nearby?"

He pointed to a dust-coated silver Forerunner parked a couple of yards away. It was one of the last vehicles left in the lot, which was probably quite big when it wasn't filled with a holiday bazaar and a fake North Pole.

"Hey, Joey, can I carry you? Your aunt looks like she's ready to call it a day, too." He looked at Tessa before holding out his arms to her nephew. "Um…not that you aren't beautiful. Just tired," he stammered. "I'll shut up now. My sister, Annie, says I only open my mouth to switch feet."

Tessa laughed. "It's okay. I'm not offended. Joey, sweetheart, can this nice man carry you?"

He shook his head and plastered his body to her leg. Tessa leaned down and picked him up. Joey shyly buried his face in the crook of her neck, refusing to even acknowledge Cole.

"No problem. I'll open the door for you." He started away, then stopped and reversed direction. He held out his hand. "I'm Cole Lawry, by the way."

She couldn't quite manage to shake his hand, but she wiggled her fingers. "Tessa Jamison. This is my nephew, Joey Barnes. His mother—my sister—is Sunny Barnes."

He repeated the name, his expression thoughtful. "Why does that sound famil—" His eyes widened. "Do you mean the same Sunny who used to work at BJM Realty?"

Tessa nodded.

"Are you kidding? I haven't seen her in a couple of

years. And you said she's in the hospital? What happened? Is she going to be okay?"

Too many questions to answer while holding twenty-five pounds of dead weight. "Can we talk in the car?"

"Oh, of course," he answered. "I'm sorry. You just took me by surprise." As he hurried ahead of her, she noticed a slight hitch to his gait. A few seconds later, he was helping her into the four-wheel-drive vehicle.

"Can you hop up on the seat with him in your arms? How 'bout if I hold your purse?"

She shifted Joey to the right so she could extend her left arm. The relief was tangible as he slid the strap from her shoulder. "Thanks."

"No problem. What do you have in here? Gold bars?" he asked, jiggling the bag with exaggerated effort.

"Spoken like a true nonparent. I was the same until Joey came along. Now, I have a standing appointment with a chiropractor every two weeks."

He wedged the bag on the floor behind the seat. "Good to know. I'm going to be an uncle in a few months. My sister is expecting her first child."

"Will this be your mom's first grandchild?"

He nodded. "She's over the moon."

"That was my mother on the phone a minute ago. She and Joey are really close. She's with Sunny at the hospital."

He moved in to steady her as she settled into the passenger seat. She could smell peppermint on his breath. From the candy canes he'd been giving out, she guessed.

"Thanks," she said, pulling up her legs. The interior of the truck appeared much cleaner than she'd expected.

He grabbed the door but didn't close it. His sandy brows came together in a pensive frown. "Just out of curiosity, how'd you happen to wind up in River Bluff tonight?" Before she could answer, he said, "Oh wait, you're probably headed to the commune. That's where Sunny was living when I met her. What's the name of her friend? Andrea… Emily…"

"Amelia," Tessa supplied.

"Right. It's only a few miles south of here. I could draw you a map."

Tessa looked at him. She was too tired to get into this, but putting things off had never worked for her in the past, so she took a deep breath and said, "I do want to see Amelia to tell her about Sunny, but that's not the reason I'm here. I came to River Bluff looking for you."

"Me. Really? Why?"

"Because I need to know if you're Joey's father."

CHAPTER TWO

COLE STRUGGLED TO make sense of what she was saying. *Me? A father? To Sunny's kid?* But in order for that to be true, he and Sunny would have had to make love. Which they never did. Right?

He shivered as a thought occurred to him. There was that one night when he and Sunny had bumped into each other at the bar. A low point in his life when he'd tried to drown his troubles. He'd been too drunk to drive home. Sunny had been a friend, she'd put him up for the night. But nothing happened. He was sure of it. Almost positive.

"You think this little boy is mine?" he asked, staring at the profile of the child asleep on his aunt's shoulder. "That's a serious charge. Do you have some kind of proof?"

She let out a long sigh and shook her head. "None, but I have a DNA kit in my purse. And, just to be clear, I'm not accusing you of anything. Sunny came back to Texas to confront Joey's father, but before she could talk to him—or tell me the man's name, she rolled her car. She's in the hospital in San Antonio in a coma. Her prognosis is…guarded."

He didn't like the flat, defeated way she said the word. "I don't know what to say. Your sister was so bright and bubbly. The hospital…a coma…." He shook his head. "Wait. If she didn't tell you about me, then how did you get my name?"

"Her diary. I brought it along and I'd be happy to show the passage that put you on the top of my list. Later. After I get Joey in bed, maybe?"

Cole hesitated. He wanted this cleared up as soon as possible and was curious as hell about what Sunny had written, but he hadn't been kidding when he said she looked exhausted.

She took a deep breath and let it out then said, "If I've made a mistake, we'll leave in the morning. No hassle, I promise. I'm not trying to pin Joey's paternity on anybody. I only want to do the right thing for my nephew. I know what it's like to grow up without a father."

Grow up without a father. Same as Cole. Something he wouldn't wish on anybody. "Where'd you say you were staying?"

"The Trail's End Motel. We haven't checked in, but they should be holding a room. I paid for it online with my credit card."

"You should be okay. Things are slow this time of year and I know the desk clerk, Barney. How 'bout if I drive you there, then go after your car?"

He closed the door without waiting for an answer. By the time he started the engine, she had her eyes closed. Her chin brushed the top of her nephew's head when they hit a pothole.

Even driving slowly, it only took a few minutes to reach the small, cottage-style motel across the street from the Medina River. He pulled up to the office and parked.

Tessa lifted her head.

"Wait here," he said in a low voice. "I'll get you registered." He opened the door and got out but returned a second later. "I'm sorry, Tessa. I forgot your last name."

"Jamison."

"Got it. I'll be right back."

He dashed into the overly heated reception anteroom. As expected, the man behind the counter was hunched over his computer and barely glanced up—until it hit him that the person resting his elbows on the counter wasn't a tourist.

"Cole. What the heck are you doing here?" Barney asked. "You know we don't rent rooms by the hour."

"You're quite the joker, man, but no, that's not why I'm here."

"Are you gonna invite me to the poker game? You could have called. You didn't need to stop by."

Cole glanced out the window at the woman who was watching them. "You're holding a room for a friend. Tessa Jamison. She said she put it on her credit card. If you give me the right price, then I'll guarantee you a spot at the table."

Barney returned to his computer. "I was wondering what happened to her. She's a friend of yours?"

"Yep. Her and her boy. They stopped by the holiday bazaar and we got talking."

"Is she staying just the one night?"

Cole had no idea. She'd suggested they talk in the morning, but he had to work. Maybe she planned to stick around, but with Sunny in hospital, more than likely she'd be heading back to the city right away.

"She'll let you know in the morning. Her kid is asleep and I told her people in this town don't stand on protocol. That's not a problem, right?"

Barney frowned. "Are you trying to get me fired?"

"Your mother wouldn't do that to you, Barn, and you know it. Besides, it's almost Christmas."

Barney snickered. "I heard about you playing Santa. Not exactly type-casting, was it?"

"I'm gonna be an uncle in a few months. I'm thinking of this as on-the-job training. Come on, Barney, what's a little paperwork among friends?"

It took some more wheedling, since Barney insisted he needed her photo ID and vehicle license number, but Cole finally got a room key. He hurried back to the car and hopped in. "Straight ahead. Number five. I'll pick up your car while you put Joey to bed."

"Are you sure? We can walk to it in the morning. You seem to favor one foot. I hate to put you out."

Shit. She'd noticed his limp. *I must be more tired than I thought.* Usually, his ankle only bothered him after a long day of carpentry. Of course, today he'd worked all day then bounced little kids on his knee for a couple of hours. "I'm fine. Occupational hazard."

He parked in front of the small cabin. A rustic overhead fixture gave off just enough light for him to see the lock. He opened the door then stepped inside to turn on the light. He waited while she laid the sleeping child on the double bed.

She carefully removed the toddler's jacket and shoes before pulling the covers over him. Standing, she arched her back slightly and let out a sigh. "I didn't realize how heavy he could get. I'm not sure I would have made it if we'd had to walk. And he's a real bear when you wake him up to put him into his car seat."

"No problem. If you give me your key, I'll run after your car. Make and color?"

She sat on the bed closest to the door and opened her purse. "White Toyota Camry. With a baby seat in the back. Please don't wreck the car. I had to sign a waiver that said only I would drive it."

"It's five blocks. I guarantee it'll be fine."

"But they're big, Texas blocks," she said, dropping the keys into his outstretched palm.

He saw a sparkle of humor in her eyes that surprised him—and made him even more curious about her. He was beginning to see a bit of Sunny in her.

He pocketed the keys and left. His ankle was sore—he could tell it was swollen— but he needed this time to think.

Sunny. A sweet kid who drifted through his life right at the exact moment when the proverbial shit hit the fan. He'd helped her out of an uncomfortable situation, found her a job and a place to live. She'd repaid the favor by listening to his ridiculously stupid tale of love, loss, greed and corruption. She'd seen him at his lowest.

She'd offered friendship and a shoulder to cry on one night. That was all he remembered them sharing—even if he had woken up in her bed the next morning.

"Why didn't you talk to me about this, Sunny girl," he muttered, trying to coax a clear memory from the haze. He'd blocked out a lot about that time.

The memories scattered the instant his phone rang. He fished it out of his pocket, pausing to check the caller ID. Annie. Two years his senior. Friend, mentor, nag, sister.

"Hey, Anster. Everything okay with junior or junior-ette?"

"Yes, the baby is safely on board. That's not why I called."

Annie and her husband, Blake Smith, who was one of Cole's closest friends, had overcome separation, a miscarriage and Annie's second marriage. Finally, things seemed to be working in their favor. She was happily—healthfully—pregnant.

"Good. Then I'll get back to you later. I'm busy."

"Oh, please. How busy can you be? Mom said you just left the bazaar. This isn't San Antonio, where you actually have to deal with traffic. Although it doesn't sound like you're in your truck. Where are you?"

"Getting gas," he lied. "Why'd you call?"

"I saw Jake today. When I asked him about the Card, he kinda gave me the brush-off. Have you heard any more about what he intends to do with the place?"

The Wild Card Saloon had never been the most popular bar in town as far as local women were concerned. Partly because the original owner, Lola Chandler—Jake's mother—had been beautiful, independent and seemingly content to raise her son on her own.

Sadly, Lola passed away when Jake and Cole were in junior high. Her brother, Verne, stepped in to take over the bar and give Jake a home—of sorts—but Jake took off as soon as he turned eighteen. No one had heard from him again until Blake tracked him down to break the news Verne had died and to invite him to the wedding in Vegas. Now he was back in town riding a pricey Hog.

"Are you asking as a reporter for the paper? What makes you think I'd know anything?" Cole asked, unable to keep the bitterness from his voice. Annie wasn't the only one Jake had snubbed since his return.

"Because the two of you were thick as thieves in school."

"Yeah, well, times change, as they say."

Annie made a huffing sound. "Men. What's so hard about sitting down face-to-face and starting a dialogue? Maybe he's waiting for you to come to him."

"Yeah? Then he can wait till hell freezes over." Cole had reached Main. Only one car was parked on either side of the street for three blocks. A white compact. Clearly a rental. "In the meantime, I don't give a damn what he does with the Wild Card. I'm hosting next week, in case your husband didn't mention it."

Between Verne's death and the big storm that took off part of the roof, the regulars had been forced to find other places for their weekly poker game.

·"You don't even have a table."

"I will by then. Listen, Spunky, if that's all you wanted, I gotta go. See you later." He knew she hated that nickname. Which was why he used it. Gave her something else to stew about.

He turned off the phone and picked up the pace as he headed toward the Longhorn Café. At least Tessa had had the good sense to pick Ed Falconetti's place for dinner. For a guy from New Jersey, Ed was one heck of a cook—even if his hot dog dinner hadn't appeared to settle well with Joey, Cole thought with a smile.

Joey. Was there even a remote chance he was Cole's child?

His ankle gave slightly and a shaft of pain radiated upward, making him stumble. His recovery was graceless, but Tessa's rental car was close enough to grab, so he didn't go all the way to the ground. As much as he would have liked to blame his sore leg on Sally and her cats, he knew the underlying cause.

He pushed himself upright and used the key to unlock the driver's-side door. The sooner he got back to the motel and had a talk with Tessa Jamison, the sooner they could clear up this matter. He had a feeling once she heard his story—and learned about his father—she'd pack up her genetics test and leave.

TESSA PACED about the room the way she did the night before a big presentation. Her business partner, Marci, liked to tell prospective clients that Tessa lived and breathed planning and organization. True. But what had proven a boon to their thriving consulting firm wound up being something Alan, her boyfriend of two years, apparently had felt threatened by.

"Marci may let you run the whole show, and Lord knows your sister and mother never complain about you micromanaging their lives, but I'm a man, Tessa. At least throw me a token bone before you plan every detail of our life."

She'd considered therapy after they broke up, but ultimately decided there was nothing wrong with wanting to be successful and working hard for fixed goals. Her long-range planning included a college fund for Joey and retirement security for her mother, not something Autumn was likely to create for herself. If a man felt threatened by Tessa's drive and ambition, then she didn't need him in her life.

Some people probably considered her materialistic, but Tessa refused to apologize for surrounding herself with nice things, name brands and designer clothes. She loved driving her BMW SUV into her reserved parking space and taking the elevator to her apartment…fourteen floors above the street where she'd once panhandled for change while her stepfather played his guitar. Until he became too sick to hold a chord.

Maybe Alan would have understood if she'd told him the whole story, but there were parts of her past she didn't talk about. To anybody.

She hadn't dated since Alan. The idea seemed so pointless. Men either didn't get her or felt threatened by her drive and success. She imagined she'd scare the wits out of Cole Lawry. Not that he was someone she'd ever consider dating. From what she'd learned about him on the Internet, he was a man who had had it all, then lost it.

"How does someone go from successful business-man to part-time carpenter and volunteer Santa?" she murmured, conscious of her nephew asleep a few feet away. "Honestly, Joey, I hope he's not your father. You deserve better. He seems like a nice guy and all, but what kind of role model would he be for you? Not as bad as Zeb, of course."

She pushed the thought of her stepfather away.

"Focus. Focus on the task at hand," she ordered. "If Cole Lawry isn't the one, then what next?"

At a soft knock on the door, she hurried across the room to unlock the extra bolt and open the door. "That was fast."

"Small town. I'd have been here sooner, but my sister called to talk about one of my poker buddies who's back in town and might be reopening his mother's old bar."

"Poker?"

The word tripped something in her memory. When Sunny first returned home from Texas, she went on and on about how much fun she'd had playing in a bar tournament. "I won fifty bucks my first time out," she'd bragged.

When Tessa asked how much it cost to enter the game, Sunny had admitted the fee was twenty-five. "But I still came out ahead, Tess. And I had a lot of fun playing. So don't give me a hard time about something you've never tried."

Never would try.

He dangled her keys from the end of his index finger. She couldn't help noticing how rough and callused his hands looked. "I locked the car. Do you need anything out of it? Your suitcase or diaper bag?"

"I'll get it later." She motioned at the small round table near the window. "Tell me about poker," she said, stalling. Why? She didn't know. Unless he had a gambling problem that might play a factor in Joey's future, if he turned out to be the one. "Sunny came home hooked on the game. She made it sound like an organized sport."

He pulled out the lone chair and sat. "I'm not surprised. Texas Hold 'Em is pretty popular around here. Some friends and I have had a game going since high school. My sister labeled us the Wild Bunch because we used to play in the back room of the Wild Card Saloon."

"And you still get together?"

"Once a week. Although now Annie calls us the Not-So-Wild Bunch."

She smiled because he smiled, but she couldn't get her head around the dedication and commitment required to keep a game going for so long. A card game, of all things. "What about after high school? Didn't some of you go to college? Or get jobs out of the area?"

"Yeah, that happened, of course. Brady had a football scholarship and played in the NFL until he got injured. Luke was career military. They're both home now, but even when they were gone, the game went on. Since I was living in San Antonio, I usually managed to come back once a week to play with some of the old-timers."

"Why?"

He shrugged. "I take it you don't play."

"You mean gamble? No. I work far too hard for my money to just throw it away."

"Too bad. New blood is always welcome."

His tone was light but the arch of his brow suggested he was put off by her statement, which had probably come off as judgmental. She sat on the edge of the bed and pulled her purse onto her lap.

"Okay, let's get this over with." She dug into the main compartment until she found the plastic bag that contained her sister's diary. "I should warn you up front that my sister has a unique way of journaling. It's hit-and-miss. Kinda like reading a jigsaw puzzle," she said, holding up the bulging book.

"Then how did you decide to contact me?"

She removed the well-worn journal from the plastic bag. The cover was faded black silk with a Chinese design of white and pink lotus flowers in gold thread. All four corners were frayed, the stitching along the binding tattered and torn. Bits and pieces of paper stuck out at odd angles. "I've marked a couple of spots. If I can find them."

"What's all the other stuff?"

"Junk. A horoscope here. Fortune-cookie proverb there. Recipes ripped from a magazine. Photos of people I've never met. Even a grease-stained menu from a fast-food restaurant. Things that mean nothing to me but probably have some significance to Sunny." She couldn't help seeing her sister, small and lifeless.

She swallowed the lump in her throat and frantically flipped pages until she found the spot she was looking for. "Here it is. The entry isn't dated but it says, 'I met my first real-life Texas hero today. His name is Cole Lawry. I have a feeling he's going to play a huge role in the story of my life.' Then she drew four curlicue hearts beside your name."

"Four hearts? Let me see." He took the book from her and studied the page she'd marked with a newspaper clipping Sunny had saved that showed Tessa and Marci opening their new office. Small-business Consultants Go BIG, the headline read.

He read the passage, which continued on from what she'd read aloud with a dozen or so lines filled with flowery words like *magnanimous* and *gentlemanly*. The first time she'd read the excerpt, Tessa had wondered if her sister had copied them from a thesaurus.

He let out a soft whistle. "Well, that's weird. It doesn't exactly say anything about having sex, does it?"

She got up and leaned close enough to point out the last line. It was written in teal-colored ink, where the rest of the passage was in black. "I believe she added this later. It references your giving new meaning to the word *friendship*."

He frowned. "That could mean anything. No attorney

in the world would base a paternity suit on something this flimsy. Did my ex-wife put you up to this?"

"I beg your pardon?" She pulled back sharply, bumping into the bed.

He ran a hand through his hair with an air of frustration. "Crystal's convinced I have some hidden assets stashed away that she somehow managed to miss when she was taking me to the cleaners. Maybe if I rolled over at the threat of a paternity lawsuit, I'd—"

She snatched the book out of his hand and pointed to the door. "I want you to leave. Now. Forget the DNA sample. Joey doesn't need a man like you for a dad."

He blinked. "What's that supposed to mean?"

"It means I made a mistake by reading more into those four little hearts than my sister intended. She's never been a very good judge of character, but she definitely blew it with you."

"Hey. Wait. Back up. I'm sorry. I lost it there for a minute. You're not working for Crystal, are you?"

"I have no idea who you're talking about."

"Of course you don't." He shook his head. "God, I am such an idiot. My sister says I tend to think the world spins for my benefit. She blames herself because she babied me after our dad commit—died. I apologize."

Tessa took a deep breath to get her temper under control then she walked to the door. "No. You were right the first time. The mistake was mine. My mother tried to warn me. We argued before I left the hospital today. She said this was Sunny's business and I'd only make things worse by sticking my nose in it. But I'm not the kind of person who can just stand around doing nothing." She closed her eyes and without meaning to, added, "Watching my baby sister slowly slip away."

Cole's ankle began to throb—the way it did when he was upset or pissed off. And at the moment he was thoroughly disgusted...with himself. He had nothing but good memories of Sunny—even though, at the time she worked in his father-in-law's office, his life had been in chaos.

He stood up but didn't move to leave. "I'm sorry, Tessa. I blew it a minute ago. My only excuse is that my ex-wife is a piece of work and I could see her doing something like this right before the holidays. Can we start over?"

She shook her head. "There's no reason to talk about this. Unless you actually were involved with my sister."

He gently urged her back to the bed. Once she was sitting, he returned to his chair. "Sunny and I were friends. I helped her out of a tight spot when she was staying at the commune up the road. She wasn't happy, and she didn't seem to have any options. I gave her some."

"What kind?"

"A job. A place to live. I advanced her some money, which she paid back. Your sister was—is—a nice person. I hope she pulls out of this."

"Thank you. I appreciate that, but I guess I need to be blunt. Did you or did you not have sex with my sister?"

CHAPTER THREE

"SHE WHAT?" Annie shouted. "A complete stranger shows up at your Santa gig and accuses you of fathering some kid you've never seen or heard of? That's, like, the most insane scam I've ever heard."

Cole looked at his sister and wished he'd listened to his gut and gone home instead of swinging by Annie's house. They were sitting on cheap plastic lawn chairs on her front porch, with a citronella candle burning on the low table between them. "It wasn't like that, Annie. She's not a scam artist."

"You're right about the artist part. That would imply she was good at this, but she *is* a scammer, Cole. That's a person who tries to take advantage of someone else. Someone good and kind and sweet. That's you, Cole. A born sucker."

He stood up. "I am not."

She had that know-it-all big-sister look on her face that he hated. She held up her index finger. "One word—*Crystal*. Now, *there* was a player. She took you for nearly everything you worked your ass off to get."

He dragged the chair a foot or so away and sat again.

His sister was too good at reading him. "She was my wife. Trust is one of your marriage vows, remember? Okay, forget it. I didn't come here to talk about me and Crystal. I thought you might have some suggestions on how to help Tessa and her nephew. If I'm not the boy's father, then she still needs to find out who is."

Annie looked at him shrewdly. "There was something in your voice when you said the word *if*. Is there a possibility you *could* be the kid's father?"

"Like I told Tessa…almost none."

She barked out a laugh. "That's like being almost pregnant. Speaking of which, want to go inside for my latest craving? Bananas and capers on saltines." He made a gagging sound. "No? Well, go on then. What happened?"

"A month or two before Sunny left, I got drunk at the Oasis. Remember that bar down the street from the office? It's also right around the corner from the apartment building Sunny was managing. She found me crying in my tequila."

"Over Crystal? Damn, that woman had her head screwed on backward. All she ever cared about was looking beautiful and being seen by all the right players as she drove around in her fancy car. You are so lucky to be done with her. So, anyway, this Sunny chick shows up and…"

"We talked. And she tried to dance with me…. Until it was obvious I couldn't walk, much less dance. She took me back to her place."

"Her one-bedroom apartment."

"I slept on her couch."

Annie looked at him, but didn't say anything for a minute. "Well, someone doesn't get pregnant by association. If you have any doubts about what happened, there must be more to the story."

"I woke up the next morning in her bed. Alone. She was at work. I don't remember getting into her bed. I don't remember having sex with her—I'm sure I didn't. You know me, Mr. All About the Vows."

She went over and put her arm around him. "I do know you, and I'm sure you're right. Sharing a bed isn't the same as swapping genetic material. So, there really isn't a problem, right? You told the Oregon sister that you weren't the daddy and sent her back to San Antonio—where she should be, by the way. I mean, who leaves the bedside of her comatose sister to hunt down some lead from a diary?"

Cole gave her a look he knew she'd understand.

"What? You think I'm being judgmental?"

"She's doing what you would do. She and her mother can't both be in Sunny's room, because one of them has to keep the kid busy. How do you entertain a toddler in a strange town?"

Annie's eyes went wide. "You like her. And feel sorry for her." She stepped back, a hand at the small bulge in the waistline of her brightly flowered cotton pajama bottoms. "No, Cole. No. This isn't a hawk with a broken wing. Or a three-legged cat. Or a cowardly dog who barks at his own shadow. You've got the biggest heart in Texas, but you can't save everybody who falls into your life with a sad story. Didn't you learn your lesson with Crystal?"

"I learned a lot of lessons from Crystal, but this isn't the same. Tessa doesn't want anything from me but a little swab of DNA, and frankly, I'm not worried about that. If it turned out the kid—Joey, his name is Joey—is mine, then I'd be okay with that. Your baby would have an older cousin."

"That's not how it works, Cole. You don't just open your mouth and give them spit because they ask. First, you protect yourself. You call a lawyer and—"

"My lawyer won't talk to me until I pay off my bill."

"Oh, stop. You're being obtuse. This is your future, Coley-boy, and I'm not going to let some stranger trash it when you're just now getting back on your feet. I'll go see her in the morning and—"

Cole recognized that particular tone. He called it her crusader voice. He took Annie's shoulders in his hands and made her look at him. "No, you won't. She's going back to San Antonio in the morning, and I told her I'd come see her at the motel where she and her mother are staying. I want to visit Sunny. Let's not lose sight of the fact that there's a beautiful young woman who might be dying. The rest of this will shake out. Got it?"

Annie closed her mouth in a pout that her husband claimed to find endearing but Cole knew meant trouble. "I'm going home now, Annie. Leave it alone. Promise?"

He squinted at her sternly until she nodded, but he had an uneasy feeling she was going to spend the rest of the night figuring out a way around her promise.

"Where's Blake, by the way?"

"Had an early meeting. Decided to stay in the condo."

Annie and Blake were still working out the logistics of their complicated lives, but Cole had no doubt they'd figure it out eventually. They loved each other and that was what counted.

"Your ankle's bothering you again, isn't it?"

"Nothing an ice pack and a couple of painkillers can't handle."

She frowned. "Cole. When are you going to see that orthopedic specialist I recommended?"

Never. "I'm busy. I have to work, remember?" He could tell from the concern in her eyes that she didn't buy his excuse for a minute. She knew the circumstances around the injury. She knew too much. "I'm leaving now."

She followed him to the edge of the porch and watched him walk to his car. "You have a right to live without pain, Cole. Dad would hate it if he thought you were suffering because of him."

He pretended not to hear. Nobody could say what Tim Lawry thought, and the man sure as hell wasn't here to set the record straight.

TESSA AWOKE at dawn and managed to work a good hour at her laptop before Joey woke up. She and Marci had rewarded themselves with a month's vacation each to celebrate A.R.E. Consulting's successful year. Marci and her husband had spent November in Scotland and England. Tessa had planned to use a few of her abundant frequent-flier miles to head to Hawaii the first week in December then return home to paint her spare bedroom. That had been before she got the call about Sunny.

Autumn and Tessa had had to pack up and leave so quickly Tessa hadn't been able to clear everything off her calendar. She'd rescheduled her final couple of follow-up appointments during an extralong, weather-related layover in Denver, but she hadn't gotten a chance to firm up her first-of-the-year contact list before she left town.

A.R.E. was an acronym for what Tessa and Marci believed was an ongoing process needed to keep any business—big or small—solvent, growth oriented and viable. Assess, Reassess and Evaluate. Their partnership was a perfect model. Every quarter, they set aside one afternoon to go over their records and reports.

As she often told clients, "Taking a cold, hard look at your company can save a lot of heartache down the road."

Tessa and Marci had already set the date for their fourth-quarter review. December twenty-sixth. The day after Christmas. Tessa had planned to have her January clients in the queue, contracts in hand, but now it appeared Marci would have to handle January.

The least Tessa could do was provide a nice, neat contact sheet, complete with payment schedule. If each of these potential jobs panned out, she and Marci would be looking at doubling their income over the year before.

Unfortunately, the contact list was quite spread out geographically. Las Vegas. Baltimore. Anchorage. Houston.

"Houston." She closed her eyes and tried to picture a map of the state of Texas. She'd been to Dallas twice, once to attend a small-business seminar and a few years later to teach a workshop at the same seminar. She had a vague recollection that Houston was farther south and east.

"I wonder how far Houston is from here—"

Why? Because if she were in the state on business, she'd have an excuse to look up Cole Lawry again?

Her eyes blinked open and she quickly closed her program and logged off. Ridiculous. Wouldn't happen. Ever.

She stood up and stuffed her lightweight VIAO into its carrying case. She'd already wasted way too much time going over every aspect of their meeting. The compassionate way he'd handled Joey's vomiting. His pique when he thought she was a stooge working for his ex-wife. The dichotomy of his upper-body strength juxtaposed with his slight limp.

He was intriguing, but so not her type.

"Stop it," she muttered. "I don't do intriguing, remember?"

She didn't normally talk to herself, either.

She nestled the computer in a spot in her suitcase and zipped the bag shut, not caring how noisy she was. It was time for Joey to wake up. After she got him dressed, she would settle her bill then they'd walk someplace for breakfast. Maybe the same diner they'd eaten in the night before. With any luck, they'd be on the road by ten.

"Joey—" She gently touched the child's shoulder. Some mornings he woke up swinging, duking it out with imaginary villains. Sometimes he'd cry for five or ten minutes, as if his whole world were ending. When he woke up on his own, he tended to be happier.

"Mommy," he cried, eyes squeezed tight, arms out.

"Oh, honey boy, I'm sorry. It's me, Auntie Tessa. Come here, love. Let me hold you till you wake up."

He sobbed against her shoulder, but only for a few seconds. Blinking sleepily, he mumbled, "Brecky?"

Sunny's word for his favorite honey-sweetened cereal. Tessa had learned not to leave home without it. It dawned on her that he must be famished since he'd lost his dinner on Santa's lap. She fished a small bag out of her purse.

"Sure. You can nibble on some while I get you dressed, then we'll go have some pancakes. Or eggs. You can pick, okay?"

The morning sped past, the way time does when you're dealing with a toddler. The older woman behind the desk of the motel had been perfectly agreeable with Tessa leaving her car while they went to breakfast. The slight overcast of early morning had given way to bright sunlight and Tessa regretted leaving her sunglasses in the rental.

By the time they got back to the motel, her head was pounding. Fortunately, whatever had caused Joey's upset stomach the night before hadn't returned. Still, she bought an extra package of wet wipes at the drugstore, just in case.

"Come on, sweets, we have to get going. Grandma is waiting for us."

"Uh-uh. Play more."

She'd promised him ten minutes in the sandbox at the playground across the road from their motel. That had been a good half an hour ago.

Not that she blamed him. She wasn't in any hurry to get back in the car, either. There was something very peaceful and uncomplicated about this town, she decided, staring at the leafless trees standing guard over the aquamarine-colored stream. The Medina River, the motel woman had called it, but it wasn't a river like the ones in Oregon.

Oregon. A world and a half away.

Home.

But was it home without her mother and sister? There had been times growing up when they hadn't had a roof over their heads, but Tessa had always had her family.

"Okay, sweets, time's up. We gotta go see Grandma."

Joey let out a squeal and took off running as fast as his pudgy little legs would carry him. Laughing, Tessa chased him, stealthily herding him closer to the parking lot. When he realized his mistake, he started to pitch a fit, but Tessa scooped him up in her arms and tickled him until he was laughing again. "Grandma, Grandma, Grandma," she repeated as she tucked him into his well-cushioned car seat.

He wiggled like a newly caught fish as she tried to clip the two ends of the belt together. "Hold still, kiddo. You've already broken most of my nails. There," she exclaimed triumphantly. "Here's your juice cup and your tractor."

Once he seemed content—for the moment, at least—

she closed the door. Her purse and the bag from the pharmacy were on the front passenger seat. She reached through the open window to get her sunglasses. As she searched for the case, she heard a horn honking and glanced up to see a woman with long curly hair round the corner on a bicycle.

The driver of the car yelled something Tessa couldn't make out then kept going as the bicyclist careened into the motel parking lot.

"Goodness. Automobiles think they own the road, don't they? Oh, hello. I was hoping I'd catch you," the stranger hailed as she came to a stop a few feet away. She quickly hopped off the bike and engaged the kick-stand. With an efficiency that bespoke years of practice, she whipped off her backpack and snatched out a slim, lined notepad before approaching Tessa with her free hand extended. "I'm from the local paper. I thought maybe we could do a piece to rally some support for your predicament."

Tessa shook her hand, but not because she wanted to. "My predicament? You mean my sister's accident? Well, thank you for the offer, but I'm not interested. How'd you hear about us?"

"Small town. Strangers in our midst. Word gets around." She held up her notepad. "This won't take long. I promise. Just a quote or two. People tend to be generous at this time of year."

Tessa was definitely put off by the woman's persistence, plus Joey wasn't a patient waiter. "Thank you, but no. We're doing fine. Sunny's hospital bills are being covered by health insurance and there's really nothing anyone can do at the moment."

"Are you religious? We could organize a prayer chain. My mother's church would be all over that."

Religious? Does going to sleep at night praying that you'll have food to eat the next morning count? "I appreciate the thought, but we're not members of a church. We're private people, and I'm sure my mother would be uncomfortable with anything intrusive."

That seemed to have the desired effect. The reporter stopped scribbling and lowered the pad to stare at Tessa a moment. Then, in a stern, serious voice, she said, "You don't think accusing a person of fathering a child he's never heard about qualifies as intrusive?"

Tessa looked at her more closely, noticing details she'd missed. Like the subtle bulge at her waistline that said she was several months pregnant. "You must be Cole's sister."

"You're right. I am. My name is Annie Smith. Cole came to see me last night. He told me about your accusation."

"Well, get your facts straight. I didn't accuse him of anything. I'm just trying to find out the truth—for Joey's sake." At that moment, a loud wail emanated from the car. Tessa turned to the backseat window. Joey had kicked off his shoes and was jamming his feet against the passenger-seat headrest. Obviously, he was fed up with being locked in his car seat while his aunt was standing around talking.

She felt Annie's presence and turned to face her.

"We have to go. I promised my mother I'd be back in San Antonio for the second shift of visiting hours. The nurses have been extremely conscientious, but it's exhausting for one person to be there 24-7."

Annie moved closer to the window and Tessa had to restrain herself from pushing Cole's sister away. What if he was Annie's nephew, too? The idea made her lightheaded. She'd honestly never extrapolated the family factor. Joey's father would have a family of some kind, maybe even additional children who would be Joey's half siblings.

"What a cutie." Annie wiggled her fingers against the window. "Look at that blond hair and blue eyes. I used to know a kid with the same blond hair and blue eyes."

Tessa took that to mean her brother.

"Well, if you ever met my sister, you'd know Joey looks just like her. Now, if you don't mind, we need to leave. When you see your brother, tell him…never mind. I'll tell him myself."

She got in the car and drove out of the parking lot without looking back, her heart beating double time, palms damp against the steering wheel. She didn't appreciate having Cole's sister imply that she had some kind of ulterior motive.

She remembered all too well what it was like to have people make assumptions about her—assumptions that were only true because of circumstance. Once she'd been old enough, she'd been able to change circumstance.

Annie Smith was wrong. Tessa didn't want anything

from Cole. Not his money, if his ex-wife had left him any. Not his busybody sister publicizing their plight. And definitely not his DNA.

She had one stop to make before returning to San Antonio. Sunny's friend Amelia had been responsible for inviting Sunny to Texas in the first place. According to Sunny's journal, Amelia had been there when Sunny met Cole Lawry for the first time.

With luck, Amelia would not only provide third-party confirmation that there was no way in hell Cole could be Joey's father, but she'd be able to give Tessa a lead on the other two names that appeared in the journal. Mr. Big and someone Sunny called the G-man.

CHAPTER FOUR

COLE GLANCED AT his watch. Time seemed to be crawling. He'd come to work two hours early to make up for an afternoon of wages he planned to miss, but even so, the morning just wouldn't end.

Maybe he was tired. After leaving Annie's, he'd worked around his place until nearly one. His mind had refused to shut off thanks to the minute-by-minute replay of his encounter with Tessa. And sleeping pills weren't an option. He'd relied on them too much when he lived in San Antonio and had thrown out every OTC package and prescription before moving back to River Bluff. Instead of tossing restlessly until dawn, he'd turned his attention to hooking up the sink in the guest bath.

One more thing to check off the list, he thought, grabbing his tape.

He measured the placement for the next stud then reached for the precut two-by-four. He had to use his hammer to knock it into place, then he grabbed the pneumatic nail gun.

Carpentry had been his first job out of high school. On-the-job training with a framing company working on custom homes for BJM Reality. That was how he met his future wife. Big Jim McNally's daughter, Crystal. Hot. Gorgeous. Spoiled.

But for reasons he never completely understood, she picked him and the whirlwind began. He should have known better. He knew better now.

"Yo, Cole," Ron said, tapping Cole on the shoulder. "Your phone is ringing. Third time in ten minutes."

Cole turned to face his boss. Ron Hayward, whose red hair, freckled nose and boyish grin had earned him constant comparisons to a certain child actor growing up, now looked more like a young Andy Griffith than Opie. He pointed to Cole's Carhartt vest on a stack of wallboard.

Cole dropped his hammer handle-first into its holder on his tool belt and tugged on the plastic tie that kept him from losing his earplugs when they weren't in his ears. "Sorry, boss," he said.

Who? he wondered. *Tessa?* He'd left her his cell number the night before in case anything changed in Sunny's condition.

Frowning, he picked up the phone and scrolled down to view his missed calls. Brady Carrick, NFL wide receiver turned cardsharp turned horse trainer. Luke Chisum's number came up second. Cole was relieved to have his friend, career army, back and out of harm's way. The last number belonged to Blake Smith, his brother-in-law. Three of the five Wild Bunch brethren all calling within fifteen minutes of each other?

"What the hell could be so important?" he muttered, hitting Blake's number first.

"A kid, Cole? You have a kid?"

Cole's expletive made all of his fellow workers stop what they were doing and look at him. Muttering, he walked down the plank ramp to the ground. "She promised to keep that between us."

Blake laughed. "Your sister is a reporter, Cole. It's in her blood. And, for what it's worth, I'm pretty sure she hasn't told your mother."

But she would. Eventually. Cole swore again. The problem with living in a small town was nobody respected your boundaries.

"So, you called to give me a hard time about this?"

"No, actually. I just did that for fun. I called because I heard something I knew would interest you. It's about Jake. Turns out you're not the only one with a secret."

"This particular secret isn't mine. At least, I don't think so. Although Mom would point out that this is the season for immaculate conceptions."

His brother-in-law roared. "Well, until we learn otherwise, can I call him Cole Jr.?"

"Tell me why you called or I'm hanging up."

"Spoilsport. Okay. You know Jake's been low-key about what he's been doing since he left town, right?"

Yeah. So low-key he'd never even found time to drop by and say, "How y'all doing?" "You're not going to tell me you found out he's been in jail the whole time, are you?"

"Nope. Just the opposite. I bumped into a guy at a meeting yesterday who said he knew Jake from his dealings with a West Coast company called

TellMell.com. I checked on the Internet last night and sure enough, Jake's name is at the top of the masthead of one of the hottest stocks on the market."

"You're shittin' me. Why wouldn't he say something?"

"Ask him. I called the company this morning figuring there might be more than one Jake Chandler in San Diego, and the receptionist said Mr. Chandler was on an extended leave of absence. Apparently, he's taking care of personal business in his old hometown in Texas."

Cole couldn't believe it. And he was pissed.

A voice in the distance called Blake's name.

"I gotta run. Big meeting. Talk to you later. Let me know what Jake has to say. If he's not strapped for cash then why the hell won't he fix up the bar? The game just doesn't feel the same at someone's house." He paused. "Have you got a table yet?"

"I'm working on it."

"Work fast. The game is Wednesday."

They said goodbye and hung up. Cole stood for a moment trying to digest the news. Jake. Rich. Successful. The freakin' Harley he was riding should have been their first clue, Cole thought, disgusted.

Was he upset because his former best friend didn't bother telling him he'd beat the odds and come out on top? Damn right. But considering the way Jake left town—under a cloud of suspicion, accused of setting a mysterious fire—he supposed he couldn't blame his friend for not being in a hurry to talk about his life.

Still, they'd shared a lot back then. Apparently not so much anymore.

"Everything okay?" Ron asked when Cole went back inside.

"Yeah. Just some of the guys checking to see if I was still hosting the poker game next week."

"Right," Ron said. "Bet that means you'd like the table delivered ASAP. How 'bout after work?"

Ron's wife was getting a new dining room set for the holidays and she'd offered to give Cole her old one. "Can't today. I'm filling in for Ray Hardy at the North Pole tonight, and I have to run to town first. Do you mind my taking off after lunch?"

"Sure. No problem. Wanna do it tomorrow?"

Saturday. He'd planned to get up early and try hanging a door in the bathroom. "Perfect."

"I'll even deliver it, if you're sure I get to play."

Cole cringed inwardly but kept a smile on his face. He liked Ron. He was an okay boss but a lousy poker player. The last time he'd joined the game, he'd walked away the big winner. From foolish bets spurred on by too much alcohol…on hands that should have gone bust. His poker pals didn't suffer fools gladly, but sometimes this was the price you paid having an open game in a small town. "Absolutely."

"So, now that you're getting into this Santa gig, you're gonna be looking to find a nice girl and have some kids of your own, huh? My wife's cousin is available. Not bad. Got some extra junk in her trunk, if you get my drift, but she can cook."

Cole called upon his Realtor-speak to distract Ron and end the conversation. He wasn't looking for a new wife. He wasn't in the market for a family. If a child suddenly landed in his life, he'd deal with that. But at the moment he had his hands full just taking care of himself and his dog, a one-bark wonder who was afraid of his own shadow, but did a whole-body wag when Cole pulled into the driveway. He made a mental note to be sure Pooch had food and water before heading into SA.

"AMELIA, IT'S SO GOOD to see you. You look wonderful."

The young woman threw open the door of the small, white, box-shaped home.

"Tessa," she exclaimed. "What a lovely surprise. Come in."

From the outside, the house appeared identical to the other five homes grouped around an open common area where a wooden swing set and bright plastic slide shared space with a dozen or so trees no taller than Tessa.

"I hated to drop in without calling first, but…"

"No phone. I know. The price we pay to live apart," Amelia said, ushering Tessa into the living room. Two curious little faces peeked around the cased opening leading to the kitchen.

Tessa shifted Joey on her hip and looked at the young woman who had been Sunny's closest friend in high school. Amelia looked older. Matronly almost. Her drab brown linen skirt reached midcalf and was topped by a bulky knit sweater that hid any hint of her figure. Angled across her torso, an African batik-print cloth held an infant, barely visible near her breast.

"You have a new baby," Tessa exclaimed.

"A week old today. I wrote Sunny. Didn't she tell you?"

Clearly Amelia hadn't heard. "Amelia, Sunny's been in an accident."

Amelia let out a small cry. "Is she okay?"

Tessa sat down on the worn, brown-and-gold plaid couch and set Joey on her lap. Hugging him lightly, she said, "Sunny flew to Texas last week and her rental car went off the road. It flipped several times and, although she was wearing her seat belt, she still suffered serious head trauma. She's in a coma at the University Hospital in San Antonio."

"Oh, dear heaven, no."

At their mother's cry, two young children, probably three and five, rushed into the room. Joey pushed her arms away to stand up. He hadn't known many playmates in Oregon but wasn't shy as a rule. Amelia collected herself and within minutes of introducing the children, Hosaih and Remata, the three were playing in the far corner of the room around a plastic box filled with toys and books.

"What's the baby's name?"

"Bayal…. He came early. Our midwife was afraid he wouldn't make it. She wanted us to go to the hospital, but we put our faith in his life force, and he elected to stay with us."

Amelia moved aside a bit of cloth so Tessa could see the sleeping child's face. "He's beautiful. I'm so happy for you all. Is your husband here? Sunny said he's a very nice man."

Amelia smiled. "He is. We're happy. I wanted Sunny to like it here, but I guess what's right for one person isn't necessarily good for another. She was bored and frustrated almost immediately."

"I'm trying to put together all the pieces of what happened while she was in Texas. She wasn't herself when she came back. Less open. Secretive."

"Sunny?" Amelia exclaimed. "You're kidding."

Her expression grew thoughtful then she motioned for Tessa to follow her into the adjoining kitchen. With a quick look at Joey, who was tentatively adding a block to the pile the other children were stacking, Tessa followed.

"Your son looks more like Sunny than you," Amelia said, putting a kettle of water on the stove.

"That's probably because he *is* Sunny's."

The kettle crashed on the burner. "He is? Sunny had a baby?"

Tessa watched Amelia do the math in her head. Her eyes opened wide. "She got pregnant while she was in Texas."

A statement, not a question.

"Who's the father?"

"That's partly why I'm here. Sunny wasn't happy in Oregon. At first, Mom and I thought she was suffering from postpartum depression, but the longer it went on, we finally figured out that she was pining for the man she loved back here. We tried to get her to talk about him, but she'd never tell us his name."

"Oh, dear."

Tessa sat down at the table. How much to confess?

Do I tell her I'm to blame for what happened?
"I…urged her to come back and confront Joey's father. I told her it wasn't fair to Joey to go through life not knowing."

Amelia filled a plate with cookies stacked on a cooling rack—the delicious scent Tessa had smelled but couldn't quite place. Amelia set them in front of her. "Of course you did. You're the only one who could really understand what that not knowing was like. I remember."

"I wasted so much time, so many daydreams creating my real father." *Someone who wasn't a dissipated, drug-addict musician.* "I couldn't stand the idea of Joey having to go through the same thing."

A hissing sound pulled Amelia back to the stove. Moments later she returned with two cups of hot water. Each contained an unbleached muslin bag filled with fragrant herbs. "So…you're wondering if I can shed any light on this mystery man."

Tessa nodded. "I have Sunny's diary, but it hasn't been a lot of help. You know how…convoluted she could make things."

Amelia chuckled softly. "Always. I once asked her why she didn't write things down in order as they happened, and she said, 'Where's the fun in that? If I ever look back at my life, I don't want it to read like some boring textbook.'"

Tessa had heard that before, too. A creative trait Sunny had inherited from her father, Zebulon Barnes. Poet, musician, troubadour, troubled human being. A sweet, ineffectual man who gave up on his dreams way too easily and took his family down with him.

"Do you have any idea what happened to Sunny after she left here?" she asked.

Amelia was silent a moment. "She went to San Antonio with Cole Lawry. He was the Realtor handling the purchase of a piece of land for us. He said he could get her a job answering phones at his office. He was a nice man. I didn't think he was trying to…I guess they say 'put the make' on Sunny, but you know how beautiful she is. Men can't help themselves."

Something in her tone made Tessa wonder if Amelia's husband had fallen for Sunny's charms. That could explain why Amelia hadn't known about Joey. Her sister might have been embarrassed to return any correspondence.

"I met Cole Lawry last night," she said. "He seemed genuinely upset about her accident. He admitted that he and Sunny were friends, but when I asked him to take the paternity test, he said he had to think about it."

"Cole? He was our go-to guy. Never pussyfooted around with our land deal. I wonder what happened to make him change?

The baby made a mewling sound and Amelia adjusted the tie to give him access to her breast. She smiled beatifically as the baby nursed. "I guess I shouldn't think too badly of him until we know the truth. He went out of his way to help the Spirit of Harmony families buy the adjoining farm. We never would've been able to do it without him."

"He said he's not a real estate agent anymore. I gather he's divorced."

"That's unfortunate. I hope Sunny didn't have anything to do with that. I mean…since I introduced them and all." Her hand popped up to cover her mouth and her cheeks turned apple red. "I shouldn't have said that. The poor girl is fighting for her life and I'm thinking the worst. Just because she wasn't happy here doesn't mean she wasn't a good person."

Their conversation ended when Amelia's husband returned, hungry and obviously not pleased that a hot lunch wasn't waiting for him on the table. Although Amelia invited her and Joey to join them, Tessa declined. "We need to get back to check on Mom and Sunny."

"This is one of those rare times when I hate not having a phone. Will you let me know what happens? I'd like to help any way I can. If you need someone to watch Joey for a few days, he'd be very welcome here."

Tessa was touched. "If the prognosis changes for the worst, I might take you up on that. Mom can't spend the whole day with Sunny then watch Joey while I take a shift. She's just too drained. Thanks for the offer."

She and Joey left a few minutes later, and as she drove back to the city, she thought about Cole. Who was he? Santa? Nice-guy Realtor? Good Samaritan? Or someone very skilled at playing whatever role was handed him?

He'd told her he wanted to see Sunny today. If he showed up, she might be able to draw a more reliable conclusion about the real Cole Lawry.

CHAPTER FIVE

TESSA WAS READING a book to Joey when the door to the motel suite opened. Her mother rushed inside, letting her bag fall to the floor. Her lovely silver hair, windblown and free of its usual braid, flew about her face as she hurried to the wing chair where Tessa and Joey were sitting.

"You're here. I was so worried."

"I called Sunny's room as soon as we got to town, but you didn't answer. Is everything okay?"

Autumn's eyes filled with tears, but she nodded. Dropping to her knees beside them, she held out her arms to Joey. "Hello, sweetheart, Grandma missed you something fierce. Do you have a hug for me?"

Joey threw himself into Autumn's arms and the two rocked back and forth. Joey wasn't nearly as demonstrative with Tessa as he was his mother and grandmother.

"Any change?"

Autumn looked over Joey's shoulder. "Not really. Another specialist came by this morning. They were worried about her kidneys. I guess they changed her medication and fixed whatever was causing the problem. My head felt like it was going to explo—" She stopped speaking and faked a smile for Joey's benefit. A moment later she added, "I went for a walk. I just couldn't breathe inside that building anymore."

Tessa reached out and touched her mother's shoulder. "It's not easy seeing someone you love in a hospital bed."

"Especially Sunny. This would make her crazy."

Autumn smoothed back her grandson's hair. "So, tell me all about your great adventure, Joey boy. Did you get to see Santa?"

"Sanna," Joey said, looking around excitedly.

Tessa picked up her purse and poked through it until she found her camera. "I think I got a couple of shots before…um… Joey had an upset stomach. As I said, we didn't stay long. They're not great, but one or two might be worth printing."

She turned on the power and tapped the control button back to the image she wanted. "See?"

Autumn held the display at arm's length. "I don't have my glasses, but…oh, yes, there you are, Joey. With Santa. Very nice." She handed the camera back to Tessa. "I'd like to look at them later. Do you have any of you-know-who?"

"No. The situation didn't exactly lend itself to that kind of thing. But he said he wanted to visit Sunny today, so you'll get to meet him."

"Are you serious? He's coming here?"

She'd known her mother wasn't going to be thrilled with this news. Tessa stood and walked into the kitchen area to put away the few groceries she and Joey had picked up on the way into town. "Cole said—and

Amelia confirmed—that he and Sunny were friends. He helped her get a job and find a place to live."

Her mother didn't reply, but a few seconds later Tessa heard the chatter of a children's video, and her mother joined her.

"I bought more water. Do you want one?" Tessa offered.

"Yes, thank you. I keep forgetting to drink."

"You've always been a stickler for staying hydrated."

"I think my brain is only working at half speed. Every time I step through the doors of that hospital, I feel like I'm going into a parallel universe."

Tessa cracked open a bottle, too. They moved to the small dinette table under the window. In the distance, she could see the lush green hills that had surprised her when she first saw them. Where was the flat, austere desert she'd expected? The terrain was so different from Oregon. Open and expansive with a sky that went on forever.

"Mom, I have a couple of things to tell you, and I think we should talk now, even though I can tell you're tired."

"Worn down is not the same as tired. I took a pill last night and slept very well, but I woke up feeling as though I'd hiked a dozen miles or more."

Tessa nodded.

"So, you might as well get it over with and tell me."

"I don't think Cole Lawry is Joey's father. He has blue eyes and light hair, but he just isn't Sunny's type."

"Did he deny the possibility that he *could* be Joey's father?"

"Not exactly. At first, he thought I was scamming him."

"Oh, for heaven's sake. As if you'd do something like that. If he's not the one, then who is?"

"I don't know. I thought I'd call the office where Sunny used to work and see if anyone remembers her. There are only two other names on the list. Maybe Mr. Big or the G-man is someone she worked with."

She took her phone from its slot in her purse and punched in the number she'd gotten from the Internet. A woman answered on the second ring. "BJM Realty. How may I direct your call?"

"My name is Tessa Jamison. My sister, Sunny Barnes, used to work for your company. Is there anyone I can talk to who knew her? I believe she was hired by Cole Lawry."

"Mr. Lawry no longer works here."

"Yes, I heard that. But maybe there's someone else who knew her. This was two years ago or so." Tessa gave the woman the address of the rental property Sunny had managed.

"Oh. Is your sister the pretty blonde from out West?"

"Yes. She's from Oregon. Did you know her?"

"No. Sorry. That was before I started here, but I saw a photograph of her at a staff party. She's really beautiful."

"Thank you. Yes. Um…she was in a car accident last week. She's in a coma, and I'm in town trying to piece together what happened. I thought she might have contacted some of the people she used to know. The only person I can remember her mentioning is Cole Lawry."

The line went silent a moment. "Oh, you poor thing.

This must be so tough on y'all. Most of this happened before I came to work here, but from what I've heard, Cole left not too long after your sister quit. He's very much a persona non grata around here, if you know what I mean. Messy divorce with the boss's daughter."

Tessa blinked. His ex-wife was his boss's daughter? "Oh? From what Sunny said, he seemed like such a nice man."

"Well, I guess that depends on who you're talking to. Big Jim—he's our head honcho—is probably the one to ask about your sister 'cause nothing happens in this company that he doesn't know about. But I'd leave Cole Lawry's name out of the conversation if I were you. This is Texas, and blood is a lot thicker than marriage vows, if you get my drift."

"Is…um…Big Jim there? Can I talk to him?"

"Sorry. He's in Dallas at the moment. Do you want me to take your number? He usually calls in for his messages."

Tessa thought a moment. "We're at the hospital a lot, so I'll try back. Thanks for your help."

"You're welcome, and I'll be saying a prayer for your sister, too. Bye, now."

Tessa closed the phone and gave her mother a condensed version of what the receptionist had told her. "Do you suppose Big Jim is Sunny's Mr. Big?"

"Sounds logical, but if he's old enough to have a married daughter, then he's way too old for Sunshine."

Tessa agreed, but she knew her sister had dated older men in the past. "I'll ask Cole about it this afternoon. If he shows up."

Her mother frowned. "Not all men are undepend-able, Tess."

Just the ones in my life.

COLE HATED hospitals. He could think of a thousand things he'd rather be doing than riding an elevator to the Intensive Care Unit. He'd never been to this particular hospital before, and even finding a parking spot in the huge, sprawling lot hadn't been easy. But here he was. With Tessa.

And strange as it sounded, he'd never been more glad to see anyone when she greeted him in the lobby of the hospital a few minutes earlier.

"How's she doing?"

"About the same. Mom had a scare this morning. Ap-parently, Sunny had some fluid buildup, which was stressing her kidneys. They got that taken care of. Now it's back to wait and pray."

His mother was big on the power of prayer. After his father died, overcome with grief and guilt, she'd turned to the church for solace, leaving her two children to take care of themselves. She'd provided a roof over their heads and food on the table, but that was about it.

Tessa pulled a lightweight shawl from her purse and wrapped it around her shoulders. "It's so cold in the hospital, then I walk outside and it's too warm. I keep thinking months have passed instead of days."

"Did it help getting out of the city for a few hours?"

She nodded. "The countryside is beautiful. There are so many trees—not tall, airy pines like in Oregon.

Dense and such a dark green. Kind of like a jungle, only not as humid."

"Wait till summer. It gets humid. Believe me."

"I guess I was expecting flat, sagebrush, oil wells."

"Just head west. You'll find that, too. Texas has some of everything. But having grown up in the hill country, I have to admit I'm partial to this landscape."

"Have you ever lived anyplace else?"

"Nope. San Antonio and River Bluff. That's it."

He could tell by her expression that she was puzzled by something. "What?"

"Well, I can see someone choosing to live in San Antonio—it's big and bustling. I spent some time on the Internet checking out business opportunities. If I were advising a client about opening a branch in this area, I'd definitely give San Antonio a serious look. But River Bluff…"

"Is the exact opposite?"

"It has a quaint charm…for retirees, but it doesn't seem to offer much in the way of earning potential."

"You got that right." Working for Makin' Hay Construction had been a huge step down from what he'd made as a Realtor in San Antonio.

"I hope you don't mind my asking, but why did you move back? You're a young man with a lot of working years ahead of you."

She wasn't the first to ask it. His sister. Brother-in-law. Friends. No one could believe he was happy working as a carpenter instead of working his ass off for big bucks like in the past.

What they didn't know was just how close his former career had come to killing him. The antidepressants and sleeping pills he'd been taking. The four-martini lunches. It would have been so damn easy to end it all.... And the temptation had been there.

"I like what I'm doing," he said as the elevator door opened. "Carpentry is a time-honored profession. All the way back to the Bible."

She didn't look as though his answer satisfied her, but she shrugged. "Right. Got it. None of my business. This way."

They signed in at the nurses' station. Seconds later, with his heart beating double time, he stood beside a bed underneath a bank of a high-tech life-support system.

Sunny. But not the Sunny he remembered—the vivacious blonde with the sweet smile. The person in the bed was a stranger. An uneven oval of hair had been shaved above her right temple. A scar was healing over the swollen area. The rest of her shoulder-length hair looked stringy and dull.

"My ex-father-in-law used to call her Goldilocks."

"Papa Bear was a real person?" Tessa asked.

"Huh?"

"In her journal. There was an entry called 'Goldilocks and Papa Bear—the *real* story.'" She looked at her sister and smiled. "Sunny was quite creative as a kid. She had about ten imaginary friends. I could never keep them straight, but she could tell me what they were wearing at any given moment and who wasn't talking to whom and why. They were always involved in ongoing dramas." In a soft voice she added barely loud enough for him to hear, "As if we didn't have enough of that in our lives."

"So, what was the *real* story?"

Tessa sighed. "I don't remember. I didn't realize this could be a clue. Maybe *he's* Joey's father."

"You think Big Jim McNally and Sunny had an affair?"

"I don't know. You worked for him. You tell me."

At the time, Crystal had been livid that Cole hired the attractive young woman with relatively no credentials or work record. "You picked her for her tits, didn't you? Just to tempt Daddy. As if Mama doesn't have enough to worry about without some slut flashing her boobs around the office."

Actually, Cole had been far more worried about Sunny giving in to temptation than Jim. Especially when the older man put on a full-court press that included a hundred-dollar bouquet delivered to her desk every Monday. Ostensibly the flowers were for the office, but everyone knew the truth.

"Sunny has always gravitated toward older men. Her father died when she was quite young."

"I know. She told me. It was something we had in common. My dad died when I was eleven."

"At least you knew your father," she said under her breath. She blushed, then quickly ducked her head and turned away. "If you'll excuse me a minute, I want to ask the nurse something. I'll be right back."

Alone with just the hum and clicking of the machines and Sunny's soft, steady breathing, Cole pulled up a chair and sat. He took her hand in his, a flurry of emotions racing through him. "Hey, kiddo, this isn't exactly how I pictured us meeting again. You know, it wasn't very polite to just take off. Actually, it wasn't like you. Nobody could understand what happened. I thought we were friends. You could have come to me."

He lowered his head. *But would I have been any help?* Around the time Sunny left, he'd hit the wall, professionally and personally. He'd barely even noticed she was gone, even though there'd been a lot of speculative chatter in the office. "I blew it, didn't I? You were pregnant and alone and I was so wrapped up in my life, I completely missed the signs that you needed help. I'm sorry, Sunny. You deserved better."

He squeezed her hand and started when her fingers returned the grasp. He looked up sharply, prepared to call for a nurse, but a hand on his shoulder stopped him. "They tell us that's her nervous system reacting to stimulation. Her eyes will track movement sometimes, too. It's freaky and confounding and I think it breaks my mother's heart a few pieces at a time."

He forced himself to take a calming breath then he let go of Sunny's hand. "This is just wrong. How do you take it?"

Tessa leaned over and kissed her sister's forehead. "I don't. This is about as long as I can stand to be here, and, believe me, I know how selfish and uncaring that sounds. I love my sister, but I'd rather switch places with her than sit here without being able to do anything. Mom understands. That's why I spend most of the day with Joey."

"He must be kinda bored being stuck at a motel....
I have a couple of hours before I have to get back to
play Santa. Would you like me to show you two around
San Antonio? We're not far from the River Walk and
the Alamo."

Tessa wasn't sure what to make of his offer. She
felt like a drifting, rudderless boat. She didn't know
this man. She still didn't have a clear idea of his relationship with her sister, although from what she'd
observed he seemed to be a friend and in genuine
pain.

He stood and faced her. "I can see you're still trying
to figure me out. Sunny and I were friends. If you'd have
asked me at the time, I would have said I was a big
brother to her, but..." He looked over his shoulder, his
forehead creasing in a frown.

"But..."

"I should have explained last night instead of putting
this off, but I'm not proud of what happened. I like to
think I'm not the kind of man who gets drunk and has
casual sex. But the timing of your nephew's birth has
made me question that. I'm afraid your sister's the only
one who knows the truth."

"If you take the DNA test, we can prove you're *not*
Joey's father. Actually, we could eliminate you simply
by blood type if you know—"

"Sunny and I are the same blood type. I remember
having that discussion with her one day at a citywide
blood drive. Everyone in the office participated."

"Oh."

He let out a sigh. "I'll give you my DNA, Tessa. My sister is opposed to the idea, but—"

Tessa took a small jar of balm from her purse and carefully applied some to Sunny's chapped lips. "Tell me something I don't know. She made that abundantly clear this morning."

"You saw Annie this morning?"

"She tracked me down at the motel. Since when do newspaper reporters ride bikes?"

He caught her purse before it slid to the floor, but the gallant gesture must have hurt because she saw him wince. "She's not a big advocate of oil companies."

"Another long story?" she asked, taking the bag from him. "Thanks."

"You're welcome. My dad's father was a wildcatter. Dad never had anything good to say about the oil barons who stepped on the little guy. Since Annie's older than me, she heard those stories longer than I did."

"How did he die?"

"Same way everybody does—he stopped breathing." Cole walked to the window. "I apologize if Annie acted somewhat overprotective. It's habit. She sort of had to take over being the mom for a while. After Dad was gone."

"Where was your mother?" she asked, picturing the friendly, kind soul who had rushed to help after Joey got sick.

"She had a sort of breakdown. She worked and paid the bills, but Annie did everything else."

Tessa knew how that felt. "Well, she was a bit pushy."

"I'll have a talk with her. She's supposed to be helping at one of the booths at the bazaar tonight. Speaking of which, I need to be back in River Bluff by six. If you'd like to see the Alamo, we'd better go now."

"Let me call Mom and see how Joey's feeling." But her gut reaction was yes. Even visiting the site of some historical battle that didn't interest her in the least was better than sitting around waiting for nothing to happen.

CHAPTER SIX

"THIS IS THE ALAMO? But it's so small."

The three of them stood in the open plaza in front of the historic fort, dwarfed by the buildings making up San Antonio's historic downtown. Joey, who was thrilled to be out of the motel and on an adventure of any kind, was practically hopping up and down with excitement. He let go of Tessa's hand, but before she could scold him, Cole bent over and scooped the little boy into his arms.

"Come on, kiddo, let's peek inside. It's bigger than it looks. And there's a great diorama that shows the actual battle."

"Wait. I'd better put some sunscreen on him. You were smart to wear a hat." She reached into her purse for the tube of SPF-30 she'd picked up a couple of days earlier.

"Good idea," he said, using his free hand to keep Joey's head still. "The sun can be intense around here— even in winter. Don't forget your own nose," he added, tapping it lightly with his finger.

The contact sent a shiver through her. That sounded flirty. Was he… No. It had to be a Texas guy thing.

She readjusted her sunglasses and looked around. "Where do we buy our tickets?"

"You don't. It's free."

"Seriously?"

"They accept donations, I think."

She grabbed her camera and started shooting as she followed the two into the thick-walled building. It was cooler inside. Voices took on a muted reverence, and Joey's eyes grew huge.

As Cole played tour guide, Tessa was conscious of the fact that the history of this site was tragic, to say the least. She stopped at each station to read the informational plaques.

Cole took Joey into the gift shop while she studied the scaled-down historical replication of what happened that day when Santa Ana's troops stormed the small sanctuary of El Pueblo de San Antonio.

"Tess. Tess. New hat."

She turned away from the miniature battle to see Joey waving what looked like a dead rodent's body up and down. Her expression must have read horror because Cole started laughing. He set Joey down in front of her and affixed a Davy Crocket coonskin cap on the child's head.

"Oh," she said, relieved. "Did Cole buy you a hat? Very…um…stylish. Did you say thank you?"

"Tan coo," Joey mumbled, biting down on the hat's tail at the same time.

She quickly took it out of his mouth and made him stand still while she removed the price tag. A rip-off, she decided, but since Joey was so happy, all she said to Cole was, "That was very nice of you. Thanks."

"You're welcome." He pushed back the cuff of his ecru-colored cotton shirt. "It's kinda early for supper, but there's a kid-friendly restaurant right down the street. Could I buy you two a hamburger?"

"Burga. Burga!" Joey shouted, drawing looks from the other tourists.

It hadn't been that long since she and her mother shared a microwave burrito, but it must have been long enough, because her stomach made a grouchy sound. Cole apparently heard since he grabbed her hand and Joey's and started leading them away from the Alamo.

As promised, they reached their destination just a few minutes later. The sound of monkeys screeching and elephants trumpeting warned her that this wasn't going to be a quiet, intimate lunch. Sure enough, a safari-dressed guide took them to a table beside a four-foot stuffed gorilla surrounded by jungle. A few feet away stood an elephant with a lifelike look in his eyes.

"I've heard of this chain," she told Cole, who was sitting across from her. "Aren't part of the profits donated to saving the rain forest?"

Joey, who was strapped into a booster seat in the chair adjacent to the jungle, pointed enthusiastically at the animals.

The server took their order then disappeared into the artificial rain forest.

"I don't know about that. And I have no idea how the food is. Even when I lived here, I didn't come down to this part of town too often. Mostly, when we had people visiting from out of the area. Everyone calls it the River Walk, but technically it's Paseo Del Rio."

"Did you ever come here with Sunny?"

He frowned and took a sip of his soda. "Once, actually. The company Christmas party. Big Jim rented Durty Nelly's, an Irish pub a few blocks from here. Dinner, drinks and a free boat ride." He looked thoughtful. "I think Sunny brought a date. Tall guy. Kinda thin. Good-looking." He paused. "Yeah. He was dressed in black. Reminded me of some country singer—except for the hair. He wore it pulled back in a ponytail. Raised a few eyebrows."

A singer? The fruit punch stuck in her throat. "Do you remember his name?" she asked after two tries at swallowing.

He shook his head. "No. I'm not even sure we were introduced. Crystal and I came together for appearances' sake, but I spent most of my time at the bar."

Joey was starting to fidget, so she pulled a small plastic bag with four fat crayons out of her purse and let him pick a color. "Is that purple? Like your book *Harold and the Purple Crayon?* Can you draw a picture to take to Grandma? She'd like that."

Joey nodded enthusiastically, the coonskin cap rocking back and forth on his head. The tip of his tongue stuck out between his lips the same way his mother stuck hers out when she was concentrating.

Tessa blinked twice and forced back her emotional response. But when she looked at Cole, she knew he'd seen her momentary lapse. "This area reminds me of Fisherman's Wharf," she said abruptly. "I lived in San Francisco right out of college, and whenever people came to visit, that's where they'd want me to take them. Pier Thirty-nine. Alcatraz. Ghirardelli Square. Tourist heaven."

"I've never been there. Where would you take someone who didn't want to do the tourist thing?"

"Nob Hill. Golden Gate Park. The Exploratorium. Grace Cathedral to walk the labyrinth. It's a great city if you can afford it."

"Is that why you moved? Too expensive?"

"More or less. I was recruited out of college with lots of promises for advancement, but within about six months of my moving there, the company was bought out. The management team they brought in had a completely different style. They alienated about half the team, and laid off six or seven of our best people. It was crazy. The entrepreneurial equivalent of the *Exxon Valdez*."

"You jumped ship."

"Darn right. But fortunately one of the people I worked with was also from Oregon. Marci. We'd spend our lunch breaks writing down all the things the new owners were doing wrong. Before long we realized we could help other companies avoid crashing and burning if we created a consulting company. That's what we did."

He set down his iced tea and sat forward. "Back in Oregon."

"Yes. In January, A.R.E. will be starting its fifth year."

"Nice."

He started to say something else, but suddenly the lights around the gorilla started to flash, and with a loud blast the gorilla came to life. Joey looked up, mouth dropping open.

In his eyes, Tessa could read the panic starting to build. When the gorilla beat its chest, Joey let out a shriek and tried to crawl out of the chair. She frantically unsnapped the safety belt and pulled him into her arms.

"Shh…shh…baby, it's okay. The big monkey's not real. Look. His fur is made out of the same material as your hat. It's pretend. Really. Look, Joey. It's okay."

Cole had left his seat at the first sign of Joey's distress and had squeezed into the space between her chair and Joey's to provide a buffer from the huffing and grunting primate.

"Oh, man, this was a mistake, wasn't it?" he asked.

Tessa felt almost as sorry for him as she did for Joey, who was finally starting to calm down. He still wouldn't look at the gorilla, but he'd released his death grip on her neck.

She took a deep breath just as their food arrived. Cole helped the waiter move them to a gorilla-free table, but Joey refused to leave her arms.

"We could get this in take-out boxes."

She sat down, Joey on one knee. "I don't think that's necessary. Do you, Joey? The gorilla isn't going anywhere and neither are we. We're not afraid of any silly gorillas, are we?"

He shook his head but wouldn't budge from her lap. By leaning sideways, she managed to eat the rather tasty chopped salad she'd ordered, while Cole and Joey both inhaled their burgers. Afterward, Cole tried to interest Joey in a visit to the gift shop but he refused. "Go," he said, casting a nervous glance behind them.

They left the building and strolled a short distance down the walking path that bordered the famous winding river through the heart of the town. She took it all in. The tiny lights in the trees. Motorized passenger boats. People strolling, stopping to inspect the sidewalk vendors' displays or read menus while hawkers extolled the virtues of a certain restaurant's cuisine. The atmosphere reminded her of New Orleans.

"We'll come back when your mommy is feeling better," she said, taking Joey's hand as they climbed the stairs to street level.

"Have the doctors given you any kind of prognosis?" Cole asked.

"Nothing solid. They're annoyingly ambiguous, but one of the nurses mentioned moving Sunny to a kind of nursing home if she doesn't regain consciousness soon. Apparently even the best medical insurance plan has a spending cap."

When the light turned green, they started walking. Cole picked up Joey to make sure they made it across the street in time. "Where was Sunny working that gave her such good coverage?"

"Well, um, theoretically, she's my assistant. Putting her on the payroll was the only practical way to get her insured. Marci has a family member who works for us, too. He's our tech guy."

"Wow. That's generous. When I asked Ron, the guy I work for, about group coverage, he laughed at me. I guess construction is different, but it's kinda sad considering some of the guys on his crew have families and they've worked for him for years."

Tessa shivered, recalling a time when her mother had had to choose between buying food for her daughters or paying for a prescription for her husband with a raging fever. Health care insurance wasn't an option in her book.

It was on the tip of her tongue to ask him why he worked for a guy like that, when he said, "If you have to move her to a skilled nursing center, would they let you take her back to Oregon?"

"I don't know. I haven't looked into it. We're just taking this one day at a time."

"I understand. And I'm sorry I brought it up. Maybe after the toy drive is over, I could come and relieve you and your mother some evening."

"Thanks. That's nice of you to offer. I don't know if we could pry Mom this far away from Sunny's bedside or not, but I have to say, getting away from the hospital for a few hours has been good for Joey and me."

"Even though I chose a restaurant that scared the bejesus out of him?"

She laughed. "He loved the Alamo. He'll probably want to sleep in his coonskin cap."

They were just about at the parking lot where they'd left his truck when he said, "Would you and Joey like to come to my house tomorrow? We're having a small work party. My boss is delivering a table in the morning, and I invited a couple of my poker buddies to drop by and pound a few nails in return for chili rellenos—my mom's specialty. Mom and Annie will be there, too."

Tessa thought a moment. Her mother wouldn't approve. Another day away from the hospital. This time she couldn't even use the excuse of looking for Cole. She'd found him.

"I don't think—"

"I have a dog," he added.

"Dog?" Joey asked, his head swiveling so fast the tail on his cap whipped past her nose.

"His name is Pooch. He's my very sad excuse for a watchdog."

Before she left for Texas, Sunny had told Joey she was going to buy him a puppy for Christmas. Sunny and Tessa had argued about it on the way to the airport.

"You're living with your mother in a two-bedroom cabin on an organic farm. The last thing either of you needs is a dog."

Sunny had held firm to her conviction that every boy needed a puppy. "If we adopt from the humane society, we'll be making two souls happy this Christmas," she'd insisted, making Tessa feel like the grinch for suggesting it might be smarter to wait until Joey was older and could help with the animal's care.

"There's lots of open space for Joey to run around."

She looked at her nephew. The poor kid was used to being in the country. "We'll try. It depends on Mom. And how Sunny is doing, of course."

"I'll give you directions before I leave. I'll understand if you can't make it, but one thing you might want to consider…Annie is a good reporter. She can dig out information nobody else can. If you let her look at Sunny's journal, she might see something you missed."

Tessa frowned. *Give Sunny's diary to the woman on the bike?*

Cole had no trouble reading her expression. Kind of like the look on her nephew's face when the gorilla started grunting.

They'd reached his Forerunner. He started to open the rear passenger door first, but Tessa said, "I'd like to change him before we start driving, if you don't mind. He might fall asleep on the way back to the motel, and he's probably wet."

"Sure. No problem," he said, hurrying to the rear of the truck. He had to push aside his tool belt and the shiny black Santa boots his mother had given him when he dropped by her place on his way out of town. The beard was still drying, but she expected to have it ready by the time he got back.

"Just a sec." He spotted his grubby Makin' Hay Construction sweatshirt in the far corner and quickly covered the boots. "There. Plenty of room. Sorry it's kinda dusty."

"It's fine. I carry a changing pad."

"In your Coach diaper bag."

She set Joey down while she dug out what she needed. "You recognized the label on my purse?"

"My ex was a big shopper. She and her mother went to New York three times a year to buy clothes."

"Lucky girl."

"Spoiled girl."

She didn't say anything, but Cole had a feeling she didn't approve of his opinion. He moved to the side of the SUV to give Joey some privacy, but he was close enough to carry on the conversation. "When I was making a lot of money, I didn't stress over how Crystal spent it. She earned her share by entertaining clients and coming up with hot leads. She's a smart, clever woman who has been around the industry since she was Joey's age. But…"

"But…?"

"I made a bad investment. One of those sure things…that turned out to be a disaster. We probably could have weathered the loss if Crystal had been able to suck it up and live within a budget for a few years, but she decided her Manolos were more important to her than our marriage. She moved home to Mama and Daddy."

"And you moved home, too?"

He smiled. She was direct. He liked that.

"Yep. Although Crystal's parents were living in a million-dollar McMansion at the time and my house didn't have running water. But I still think I got the better deal. At least now I don't have to pop a Valium before opening my credit card bill."

Or double up on the sleeping pills just to get through the night. Or reach for the bottle of Gray Goose in his office drawer at eleven—a hit of courage before his liquid lunch.

Hitting rock bottom had probably saved his life, but

he had a feeling that was something Tessa couldn't understand. From what he remembered of Sunny's description of growing up in Oregon, the two sisters had had an idyllic childhood. Her musician father. Wife and daughters traveling with him in the summers. Cole recalled thinking the whole thing sounded kind of new age, but Sunny had glowed whenever she spoke of her family.

Nope. He and Tessa had nothing in common.

"WE'RE NOT on vacation, Tessa."

Joey, exhausted from their outing, was asleep on the bed. Cole had insisted on carrying the sleeping child to the second-floor room, despite the noticeable catch in his gait by the time she opened the motel-room door for him.

Autumn had returned from the hospital about an hour later. Tessa had never seen her look as exhausted and defeated—except possibly when Zeb died.

"I know that, Mother. This sounded like a way to keep Joey busy and give him some fresh air and exercise." She hadn't planned to mention Cole's party the next day, but her mom kept digging for information, and his suggestion that Tessa let his sister look at Sunny's journal had popped out—along with the invitation to his house.

"You're trying to avoid spending time with your sister, aren't you? Seeing her lying on that bed makes you feel guilty. I understand but—"

"I'm sorry I encouraged Sunny to come to Texas, but why should I feel guilty about an accident? I love my sister, and I hate it that something bad happened, but I wasn't driving the car."

"You bullied her into coming here."

There. The truth.

"When I said this was my fault, you told me not to blame myself, so which is it, Mom? Guilt or no guilt?"

Autumn, who was sitting with her legs tucked under her on the wing-back chair, dropped her head into her hands. "I don't know. Zeb would have said this was her karma. I don't know why. How could someone as sweet as Sunny deserve to have something this awful happen to her?"

"It was an accident, Mom. She's not a very good driver. You've ridden with her. You know what I mean. Besides, Libras are the most accident-prone of all the astrological signs."

Autumn appeared to consider the idea. "Maybe. But do you think it's a good idea to drive the same road going to that man's house? You're tempting fate."

Reclining on the bed a few feet away, Tessa stretched out her feet and leaned against the headboard. "I'm a good driver, Mom. I've never had an accident, and I'm extra careful when I have Joey in the car. I figured I'd go to the hospital in the morning so you and Joey could spend some time together, then after lunch I'd take him to Cole's. He can play outdoors with Cole's dog. Look at how well he's sleeping after his action-packed afternoon."

Joey was curled up in a ball on the other bed. Her mother's expression softened as she watched her grandson sleep. "What about the paternity test?"

"Cole said he'd take it. His sister is against the idea, but she'll be at his house tomorrow, too. Maybe I should let her look at Sunny's diary. A fresh set of eyes might help."

"You like him, don't you?"

Tessa knew that tone of voice. "He's a nice guy, but he's got no ambition. You know how I feel about that."

Her mother frowned. "Your stepfather had tons of ambition when I first met him. He was so talented. Oh my goodness, he could play that guitar and fiddle. He was brilliant. A lot of people said so, not just me."

"I know, Mom. But just because you have a couple of bad breaks doesn't mean you stop trying. Cole was, like, the top salesman in the local real estate market one year. Then something happened. An investment gone bad, he said. I'm not exactly clear what that means, but I gather he lost his shirt." A designer label, no doubt. "And instead of getting back in the game, he quit. Now he's working as a carpenter."

"At least he's working."

Tessa got up and gave her mother a hug. When Zeb gave up on his dream of making it big in the music industry, he also quit everything. Except drugs.

"That's true. And it's none of my business what he does with his life unless he's Joey's father. Which I don't think is the case. Which means I need to figure out who else it could be."

Her mother's slim shoulders rose and fell with a weighty sigh. "I know you think you're doing the right thing, Tessa, but you need to be careful that the can of worms you're opening doesn't turn out to be filled with snakes."

Tessa shuddered. "Thanks. There's an image I could have gone all night without picturing."

"Well, this is Texas. They've got a snake called the sidewinder. You don't even see it coming until it's bitten you."

"Stop. I'm going to have nightmares. Joey will be wrestling with gorillas and I'll be chased by snakes. Do we have any sleeping pills?"

Her mother went into the bathroom and returned with a bottle, but Tessa had changed her mind. She didn't like the way they left her feeling groggy in the morning.

Besides, the night before she'd had an interesting dream. She'd been making out with a man with a white beard. It might have been creepy if he hadn't had blue eyes and warm, soft lips.

CHAPTER SEVEN

"CAREFUL. CAREFUL. We gotta turn it sideways. Trust me. It won't fit head-on."

"We know, Ron. That's why I suggested taking it through the patio door," Brady said.

"This door's wider. I built the place. I should know," Ron argued.

Brady, who was on the same end of the table as Cole, smirked. Cole knew Ron wasn't one of his friend's favorite alternate poker players, but Brady Carrick wasn't the type to make a scene. He got things done his way and didn't make a big deal about it. Unlike Ron, who went out of his way to call the shots. But since he was holding up one corner of the beastly heavy table that he'd donated so Cole could host the upcoming poker game, Cole kept his criticism to himself.

"Holy sh—" Luke complained, glancing at Annie. "This thing weighs a ton. What's it made of, brick?"

"If it was brick it wouldn't scratch," Annie said.

"You're a big help, Annie," Cole said, using his shoulder to brace the table. His ankle was already starting to throb and he was only carrying one-fifth of the weight. "Could you at least keep the door open?"

He'd recruited Brady, his other poker pal, Luke Chisum, and Blake to help move the table after Ron had called at six to say the helpers he'd lined up had bailed on him. It was now eleven and Cole's frustration at losing a whole morning of work on his house was magnified by the frustration of not knowing whether or not Tessa would show up.

It didn't help that his mother and sister had arrived right behind the truck carrying the table and chairs. He'd hoped to have a couple of minutes alone with them so he could forewarn them about Tessa's possible arrival. He'd intended to tell them both at the bazaar last night, but from the moment he stepped into costume until the minute the North Pole closed, he'd been swamped with kids.

He hadn't even seen Annie, who was running the hot-chocolate booth just a few yards away. That, he figured, was because she was avoiding him.

He wanted to explain what was going on to his mother and he planned to order Annie to back off Tessa. His sister could keep her suspicions to herself. His mother could pray from afar. Period.

But now he had to figure out a way to explain without his friends overhearing. They'd ask questions Cole wasn't ready to answer. Fortunately, it seemed his brother-in-law had been true to his word and hadn't mentioned the paternity question to the other poker players.

Of course, that may have stemmed from the fact that

while Blake was a regular player in the Wild Bunch, he hadn't grown up with Cole and his friends. Cole had introduced him to the group shortly after Annie and Blake got married—the first time. He'd seemed to fit right in, and was a natural-born card player. The entire group had mourned when they learned Blake had been abducted by terrorists while on a business trip to the Middle East. He'd been held captive for four long, grueling years— and the whole time his family and friends back home believed he'd been killed.

Now that he was home again and he and Annie had reconnected, Blake was back with the group, as well. And Cole couldn't be happier. Blake truly was the brother he'd never had.

"Cole, where do you want this damn thing?" Blake asked, his voice gruff with exertion. "You know I *pay* people to do this kind of stuff, don't you?"

"Suck it up, man. Those biceps are going to waste away from counting beans all day," Brady challenged.

"A lot of beans," Luke added. "Did you see the car he's driving?"

"That's Annie's car," Blake countered.

"Which she refuses to drive because it isn't a biodiesel," Annie said from beside the door she was holding open. "I told him, 'Global warming,' and he said, 'Heated seats.' The conversation went downhill from there."

Cole snickered. His sister was too much at times, but he loved it that she stuck by her principles.

"I said, 'Side air bags and highest safety rating of all

SUVs in its class,'" Blake countered. "It's a whole heck of a lot safer than a bike seat and a helmet."

"I've heard you can buy those pull-along baby carriers with titanium roll bars," Luke said.

"Really?" Annie asked.

Blake groaned. "Don't encourage her. She needs to start driving a car. This car."

Cole spotted the look on Annie's face and quickly diverted the conversation. "Annie, turn on the overhead light in the dining room. Please."

She dashed around him, still agile despite her thickening waistline.

The dining room overlooked the front of the house and was separated from the living area by a two-way fireplace. Although Cole didn't have much furniture, he could picture big, comfy leather couches facing the bank of windows that afforded a spectacular view of the oak-covered hills and Medina River valley.

Presently, his only furnishings consisted of a pair of recliners and an entertainment center with a fifty-eight-inch plasma TV that he'd had to fight to keep in the divorce.

"Great job on the ceiling, Cole. Did you stain it or what?" Luke asked.

"Whitewash. Seals the wood and lightens it up."

"Nice," Brady said, stumbling as he tried to walk and look up. He'd been one of the best wide receivers in football until a career-ending knee injury. Now, he and Cole joked about hobbling around together with high-tech canes in their waning years.

"We offer that choice to our clients, too," Ron said, his voice coming in short puffs. Supervising didn't afford him the daily physical exercise Cole got. "Most women prefer the lighter color, while their husbands go for clear cedar. It's got more of a hunting-lodge look, I guess."

Annie, who had dashed around them once they cleared the front door, appeared at Cole's side. "Anything else I can do?"

"Help Mom with lunch, I guess. I didn't have a chance to call her this morning to tell her I invited a couple more people."

Annie shimmied sideways. "Who? These are your only friends. Except for Jake, but he's still hiding out at the Card."

"I have tons of friends. They just don't live around here."

"The people you're referring to in San Antonio aren't your friends, Cole. They were work associates, and most of them erased your name from their Palm Pilots the minute you and the devil woman divorced."

She was right, which pissed him off.

"Not a big loss, though," she went on. "Crystal and her friends are social parasites. These guys might be losers, but at least they're real."

"Losers?" Brady sputtered. "I played for the Cowboys."

"I have a Purple Heart," Luke called out.

"Jake's a millionaire," Blake added.

Annie put her hands on her hips. "I meant that in a tough-love, big-sister-to-you-all kind of way. You're not *loser* losers, but you are in your thirties and living back at home and none of you are married or have any children."

"Mine is on the way, and Cole might already be a daddy," Blake said as they carefully muscled the table into an upright position and lowered it.

Every person in the room looked at Blake, who shook his head and swore. "I can't believe I said that. Annie, this is your fault. You know how much I like to win an argument. Sorry, Cole."

The place erupted, with everyone speaking at once.

Cole blew out a sigh. He'd known the saga would come out eventually, but he'd hoped to discuss the matter without Ron present. "Okay. Okay. The night before last, I met a woman at the North Pole who had her two-year-old nephew with her. Turns out her sister, the kid's mom, was—is—a woman I used to work with. She was in an accident a week ago and is in the hospital in a coma. Her sister is trying to find Joey's father."

"And, naturally, she came to Cole first, because…" his sister said, her tone heavy with sarcasm. "Oh, right, because he's such a player."

His friends, including Ron, exchanged expressions of bafflement and disbelief.

"Well, it's not as if Tessa knew that," Cole said in her defense.

"How'd your name come up in the first place?" Ron asked.

Cole pulled on the neckline of his shirt, which suddenly felt too small. "Apparently, Sunny—her sister—wrote about me in her diary. We were friends."

"You must have been awful good friends for her sister to think you slept with her. Is she hot?"

Cole looked at his boss and frowned. "Sunny was—is—beautiful. Every guy in the office tried to hit on her. Even Big Jim had a thing for her. As far as I know, she turned them all down."

"Did she turn you down?" Brady asked. He'd turned sideways to rest one hip on the table. The others remained where they were, like members of a dinner party without any chairs. "No, wait. You didn't even ask, right? The rest of us…yeah…I could see any one of us making a play for her, but not you."

"I don't know whether that's supposed to be a compliment or an insult, but I honestly can't say for sure. I got hammered one night and wound up sleeping at her place."

"But you're not the type to screw 'em while you're passed out," Luke said, nudging his Stetson back with his knuckle. "We expect that kind of behavior from pro ball players, but not you."

Brady flipped him off. "I see my reputation as a lover has gotten around. But even at the peak of my career I was conscious when I was with a woman."

Ron folded his arms and tried to look serious. "As your boss, I'd advise you to fight this, Cole. If you wind up paying child support, don't let the D.A. attach your wages. The paperwork is a pain in the butt, and my wife, who writes out your check each week, hates doing it. I've never actually let someone go because of that, but…"

Was he implying that Cole would be out of a job if

it turned out he had a kid? Cole ground his teeth together to keep from telling his friends to load the table back up.

Annie stepped beside him and tapped the fingers of her left hand against the fist he held clenched by his side. "Hey, Ron," she said. "Didn't you say your wife was waiting for you? Little League or something? We'd better get those chairs out of your truck before she starts calling."

"Football," Ron corrected. "Ronnie plays center. Little League doesn't start until spring. And, by the way, he's the oldest of my three. You forgot that when you said none of us had families."

Annie kept her expression neutral. "Three. Wow. You must be proud."

"Just make sure you're more accurate in the news-paper."

"I will. Thanks for reminding me."

"Annie, will you go to the kitchen and tell Mom we're almost ready for lunch?" he asked, hurrying his boss out the door before the man could dig his grave any deeper.

"It's a shame you can't stick around to eat, Ron." He motioned for his friends to follow and help with the chairs. "You know Mom's chili relleno casserole is the best."

His mother's spicy cheese and pepper dish was renowned in this part of the country. He'd had just enough time after dropping off Tessa and Joey the day before to stop at an H-E-B and pick up the ingredients for his mother.

As his friends piled outside, Cole heard a faint bark. Pooch wasn't anywhere to be seen. Cole reversed directions and walked to the end of the porch, which afforded a view of the gravel road leading to his driveway. A cloud of dust drew his gaze to a familiar white Camry tentatively inching toward his turnoff.

After a slight pause, it turned onto his rutted lane.

"Tessa," he exclaimed, hurrying down the steps past Brady, who was carrying two oak ladder-back chairs. "Good job, man. Thanks."

The tires against the limestone road base made a loud crunch that drew everyone's attention. There wasn't any grass or landscaping to muffle the sound. The glare of the sun overhead and tinted windows kept him from seeing into the backseat, but he assumed Joey was there, too.

He walked to the driver's side after she parked and waited while she rolled down the window. "Hi," he said. "I was hoping you'd come."

"I probably shouldn't have," she murmured. "You have a lot of company. I guess I thought… I don't know what I was thinking. You did say it was a work party." And she'd dressed for the occasion, although he'd have bet money her jeans were Hilfiger and her sneakers Sketchers. Her T-shirt was the one she'd bought at the Alamo. It bore the five-point Texas star against a red-and-blue background.

"Not everybody is staying. My boss is just about to leave, and I don't expect Brady or Luke to stick around long, although there have been a few hints about a game. I think we might as well scratch the work element."

"You're sure we won't be in the way?"

"Absolutely not. Come in. I promise they won't bite."

After a glance over her shoulder, she said, "Joey's asleep. I hate to wake him."

"Pull over by that big SUV. It's shadier and close enough to the house that we can hear him if you leave the windows open."

As he followed the car to an open spot near his brother-in-law's new vehicle, he noticed his mother step out of the kitchen. She waved and headed his way.

Tessa lowered the power windows but didn't get out. "I should probably wait here until he wakes up."

"Let me," his mother said, coming up behind Cole. She gave him a light, one-armed hug as she shook Tessa's hand through the window. "Hello, again. It's Tessa, isn't it? I've been thinking about you so much since that night at the bazaar. How's your sister? I've added her to my church's prayer list. I hope you don't mind."

"Not at all. Sunny would like that. We'll take all the prayers and good wishes we can get, Mrs. Lawry." Tessa opened the door and got out.

"Please call me June."

Tessa brushed past Cole, who held the door for his mom. The unexpected sensation he got from touching Tessa's bare skin made him step back. His foot landed awkwardly on a small rock, twisting his ankle sideways. An involuntary grunt of pain made his mother say, "Careful, Coley. Remember what the orthopedist said."

Coley. He needed to break his mother and sister of that nickname. "I know, Mom. I should have worn my work boots. I'm fine."

He turned to ask Tessa if she was okay with leaving her nephew while he introduced her to his friends, when they heard a horn blast. He bent over to look in the back seat. The child moved but didn't open his eyes.

"Damn it, Ron," he muttered, starting toward his boss's truck. "Hold on a second." He made a staying motion toward Tessa. "Excuse me. I'll be right back."

"Isn't Ron staying for lunch?" his mother asked.

Cole shrugged. "He said he had to go. Is everything ready?"

"All but the salad. Annie's making the dressing. We could send a plate along with him."

"I'll ask. Thanks."

"Tessa," she said, "go with Cole and meet the others. Joey will be fine. I promise."

She shooed the younger woman along. "I already told Annie not to wait dinner on me. I have a separate bake dish set aside. I don't like mine as spicy as y'all." She waved her hand in front of her mouth as if fanning a flame. "Been in Texas too many years to count, but I was born in Vermont. My taste buds never quite acclimated."

Tessa smiled. "Are you sure you don't mind? He can be a handful if he wakes up on the wrong side of the car seat."

June sat behind the wheel and let out a sigh. "I haven't had a moment to myself since the holiday bazaar started. This will be lovely. Run along. I'll call if he needs you."

Impulsively, Cole took her hand. "Quick. Before Ron lays on the horn again."

"Wait," she said after two steps. "My purse." She pulled her hand free. "I might need my camera."

When she returned to his side a moment later, she kept an obvious distance between them.

"How's Joey doing? Any nightmares from our lunch yesterday?"

"Not a one. He told Mom all about the big gorilla with such passion you'd have thought he loved every second."

"Maybe he did. Little boys like scary things, even though they don't like to be scared."

"I don't think the thrill is limited to boys. Sunny adored roller coasters, the bigger and twistier the better. She'd scream her head off, then line up to go again."

"Not you?"

"I prefer to stay on the ground taking photos. I was always quite happy to pee my pants vicariously."

He was still chuckling when they reached Ron's three-quarter-ton Dodge pickup. The Cummins diesel clattered loudly.

Ron was already behind the wheel. Recalling his boss's comment about child support, he kept the introductions short and sweet.

"Welcome to River Bluff," Ron said. "Sorry to hear about your sister, but I gotta say you're barking up the wrong tree where this guy's concerned. He's no love-'em-and-leave-'em Lothario." He drew out the word with a southern twang.

Tessa looked at Cole, her expression unreadable, but he sensed she wasn't pleased to have been the topic of discussion among Cole and his friends.

"He's—"

Cole cut him off. "Thanks, Ron, but we don't want to make you late for your son's game. Tell your wife the table looks great. You're sure we can't send a plate with you?"

Ron shook his head. "Naw. We've got some kind of tailgate thing going. Just save me a place at the game on Wednesday. See y'all later." He nodded at Tessa then drove away.

Cole watched him leave. "He's a good guy, but opinionated."

"Unlike your sister."

He groaned. "Right. I forgot about Annie."

As they walked to the house, he said, "I was hoping to get a chance to talk to her, but we haven't had a minute alone. Like I probably told you, she tends to be protective of me."

They paused at the bottom step. "I get paid to deal with people, including those who consider me a threat because I might point out to their employer that their job is superfluous. I can handle your sister. She just caught me off guard the other morning."

"Like Joey and the gorilla."

"Exactly."

"Ahem." They heard a staged female cough.

"Speaking of Annie…" Cole ushered Tessa the rest of the way onto the deck. "I don't think you two were formally introduced. Tessa Jamison, meet Annie Smith. The one-hundred-ten-pound gorilla in the family."

Annie gave him a dark look. "Why are you telling

people my weight? I'm pregnant. I'm pregnant, not fat." She put her hand on her stomach protectively. "And I don't know what that gorilla crack is about, but I *have* been craving bananas lately. Mom says my body needs the potassium."

"Sunny craved bananas, too, when she was pregnant. Only she wanted hers in a sundae with pistachio ice cream and chocolate sauce," Tessa said.

Annie let out a whoop, her face opening up into a big grin. "My kind of girl. I hope I get to meet her someday." She reached out imploringly but didn't touch Tessa. "I mean that. Cole said her condition is serious, and I'm sorry if I added to your stress."

Tessa could tell Cole's sister was sincere. There were even sparkling tears in her lovely blue eyes, a softer shade of blue than Cole's.

"Thanks. We were hopeful this morning. She seemed to respond differently when my mother entered the room. The doctors are still evaluating her, but Mom was so happy she actually encouraged me to come today and bring Joey here for fresh air and exercise. He's wild about dogs."

"Too bad Pooch is so skittish. He adores Cole but seems to disappear when other people are around. Do you know how he'll react to kids, Coley?"

"Will you please stop with the Coley? Remember what I did to you when you were fifteen and called me that in front of your girlfriends?"

Annie stuck out her tongue. "Try that again and my husband will hurt you."

Cole shook his head. "Mom said you were making the salad."

"All done. I figured we'd serve our plates at the counter—the plywood counter that I covered with one of Mom's tablecloths," she added pointedly. "When are you going to install a decent countertop?"

"When I can afford it."

She sighed. "Well, at least we can eat at the new table. It's huge. Are you sure it'll work for poker? You'll have to use one of those croupier thingies to collect the bets."

"It'll have to do unless someone can talk Jake into fixing up the Wild Card."

Tessa listened to the pair as she followed them into the house. There were voices off to the right. She inhaled the smell of fresh paint, new wood and something spicy. She immediately liked the part of the house she could see. A vaulted, natural-wood ceiling and abundance of large windows made it open and airy. The absence of furniture may have accounted for the spaciousness, but since she was a minimalist herself, she found it appealing.

"Nice place."

"Thanks."

"Yo, tall men gossiping," Annie called out. "Get your butts in here." To Tessa she said, "I swear, there are times when I think they're all twelve and holding."

They sure don't look twelve, Tessa thought as the three men who'd been standing together near the giant table in the dining room walked toward her. Real Texan men.

Two wore cowboy boots, western-style jeans and

belts with shiny buckles, although one topped those items with a snug black T-shirt and the other a crisply ironed, long-sleeve white shirt. T-shirt guy, the tallest of the three, moved with an athlete's grace. He was the first to approach. White shirt had a military set to his broad shoulders and an unreadable look in his eyes. The last to approach was more casually dressed in black slacks and a bulky fisherman-knit cotton sweater, but his boat shoes, worn without socks, appeared to be Italian leather, and the sweater shouted "handmade in Ireland."

All three stared at her intently, and despite her initial instinct to run, her professionalism as a businesswoman kicked in. She cleared her throat and straightened her shoulders. "Hello."

Cole made the introductions. "Tessa, this is Brady Carrick, former football star turned horse trainer. Luke Chisum, who was piloting a helicopter in Iraq a year ago but is now helping out at his family's ranch. You drove past twenty or so miles of Circle C fence line on your way here. And this is Blake Smith, my brother-in-law."

Tessa shook hands with each of them. Prior to her marriage, Marci would have been drooling. Tessa found them intimidating. Especially when they clearly regarded her as a threat to their friend. "Nice to meet you. Sorry if I'm intruding."

Cole started to say something, but Tessa stepped around him and said, "I understand you're all poker players, so I'd like to put my cards on the table. You've obviously heard why I came here. It wasn't to pin a paternity rap on your friend."

She looked at Cole, who appeared surprised by her initiative. She went on. "My sister was headed in this direction when her car rolled over. She'd told us she planned to confront the man she loved and tell him about his son. She didn't reveal his identity before she left, so I was merely trying to carry out what she started."

The tall one, Brady, spoke first. "Cole would make a great daddy, but he would know if he's got a child."

She'd already come to that conclusion herself, but before she could say so, the military guy—Luke—added, "He's got a big heart, and we just don't want to see it get tromped on…again."

His brother-in-law started to add something, but Cole let loose an earsplitting whistle. "Hey, I'm right here. Enough already. Guys, play nice. Tessa doesn't need any cr—hassle from you."

"Yeah," Blake said. "My wife already took care of that."

Annie stomped her foot. "Everybody quit talking and come dish up your plates. Tessa, you're Cole's guest. You go first."

Tessa would have preferred to go last, but the delicious aroma—and the fact she'd been so wrapped up in Sunny's condition that morning that she'd skipped breakfast—sealed the decision. "Thank you," she said, taking the thick paper plate. "It smells wonderful. Is it spicy?"

"The cheese helps tone down the bite of the chilies, but you can top it with sour cream, if it's too much for you."

Tessa's mouth was watering. "No. I'm sure it will be wonderful. I love spicy food."

"Really," Brady said. "I used to play ball with a guy from Oregon, and he lived on granola and yogurt. I figured that was the state dish."

She grabbed a napkin from the pile. "It is. But I like mine with Tabasco sauce and jalapeños."

The rich masculine laughter that followed chased away the last of the tension in the air.

"Nice," Luke said. "Reminds me of the Dallas-Eagles game where the defensive linesman clipped you right at the knees just as you were about to nail that winning catch."

Chuckling, Blake added, "Or that time when you were playing New Orleans and—"

"All right. I get it. Don't pick on the new girl." To Tessa, he bowed over her plate and said formally, "With sincere apologies, I would like to welcome you to the group."

She smiled. "Thank you…I think."

Cole cuffed his friend lightly on the shoulder. "They're not that bad, Tessa."

"Actually, we're very good," Luke said. "As poker players. It's the touchy-feely stuff where we sorta lose it."

"Speak for yourself," Blake returned huffily. "I touch and feel quite well. Tell 'em, Annie."

Cole's sister just laughed and shook her head. "Don't look at me. I know everybody's secrets and none of them make for good lunch talk."

Cole smiled at Tessa reassuringly. "Want to sit down?"

Gradually everyone filled their plates and joined them. Tessa glanced out the window behind her to see if Joey was still sleeping, but the angle of the other car made it impossible to tell.

"He's fine," Cole said in a low voice. "Mom's been practicing to be a grandmother on all the toddlers at her church for years. She runs the Sunday-morning day-care program."

She placed her paper napkin on her lap. "It's just that Joey's not used to being around strangers."

"We're close enough that you can be out there in a second if he cries. Okay?"

She let go of her nervousness enough to take a bite. The warm, spicy mixture of cheese and peppers melted in her mouth. She closed her eyes to savor the taste. "Mmm. This is wonderful."

"June's chili rellenos are the best," Blake said.

"To die for," Brady agreed.

Luke chewed and swallowed before adding, "I used to dream about these when I was in Iraq."

Tessa smiled as the conversation swelled around her. Despite a rocky beginning, she felt comfortable in this close-knit group. That surprised her. Outside of her relationship with Marci, Mom and Sunny, she was a loner. And she liked it that way. Or so she thought.

They were about half done with the meal when Cole's brother-in-law—after a brief, murmured conversation with his wife—said, "Our regular poker night is Wednesday, but Brady and Luke and I were just talking about christening the table with a quick game before Santa here has to head off to the North Pole. Would you care to join us, Tessa?"

"Um…thanks, but I don't know how. And I promised Joey we'd play outside this afternoon. But, please, go ahead."

"Mom and I could take him for a walk down by the pond," Annie volunteered. "There were ducks the last time we were here. Right, Cole?"

He nodded. "A pair of mallards."

"How long does a game last?" Tessa asked, wishing she could enjoy their camaraderie longer.

"Depends on how many are playing."

"And who's winning," Luke added. "I've been known to clear a table in a few hours."

Brady laughed. "On the nights somebody serves beans."

Annie groaned. "See? What did I tell you? Twelve and holding. How long do think your nephew will nap?"

"Hard to say. His mother was never big on schedules, so I try to go with his flow. Mom says I spoil him, but I figure he's picking up on all the emotions around him and trying to deal with not having his mother, so why stress about the small stuff?"

"Sounds smart to me. I've read at least ten books on parenting and none of them agree on anything. Well, consistency and routine, but how consistent can you be when you're living out of a suitcase, right? Are you done? I brought a cheesecake for dessert. Do you want to help me serve it?"

Tessa got up. She was moved by the other woman's compassion—and more than a little surprised by her apparent about-face. She paused to look toward her car then hurried after Annie. Once in the kitchen, she asked, "What do you need me to do?"

"Nothing. I was just rescuing you from the blast of testosterone. They can't help it. Brady was a pro-ball player for the Cowboys. Luke was a Special Ops helicopter pilot in the war. And my hubby is an expectant father. They're not sure how to deal with you."

"Because I'm a threat to one of their own?"

"Bingo."

"Annie, I meant what I said. I'm not trying to pin Joey's paternity on your brother. I just don't want my nephew to grow up without a father."

Annie put down the carafe she'd been holding and closed the distance between them. "I jumped to Cole's defense because he's been through such a rough time the past couple of years. I didn't even stop to consider your side of the story. What kind of journalist does that make me?"

Tessa looked over her shoulder. Cole was still sitting at the table joking with his friends. "I talked to a woman at the real estate office where Cole worked. She implied that he left on bad terms. Did he get fired?"

Annie pounded her fist twice on the counter. "He got the shaft, thanks to that spoiled-brat ex-wife of his. Jim McNally was Cole's boss, but he was more than that, really. He was like a substitute father, and when Crystal ran home to Daddy, Big Jim closed ranks and bought his daughter the most cutthroat divorce lawyer in town."

Tessa didn't know what to say so she changed the subject. "Cole suggested I show you Sunny's diary.

Maybe another pair of eyes might see something I missed. Are you interested?"

"Sure. I love a good mystery."

Tessa pulled the plastic bag with the journal in it out of her purse just as the kitchen door opened and June and Joey walked in, holding hands.

Joey looked sleepy and not quite sure what was going on while June appeared so happy you could have sunbathed in her smile. "This boy is hungry," she said.

Although her instinct was to pick up her nephew, she knew how grouchy he could be when he first woke up. She usually handled him with kid gloves. Not June. She whisked him up and carried him to the table, shouting orders to Annie. "Bring us the small pan in the oven and the sour cream. Does Joey eat salad?" she asked Tessa.

"Um…sometimes."

"Well, bring that along, too. We'll be just fine."

She reached for the large wooden salad bowl, but Cole beat her to it. He winked. "Mom was a drill sergeant in another life." Then he hurried out of the room, Annie right behind him.

Tessa stood rooted to the spot. She was used to being the person in charge. The one giving orders. The one planning what came next. Suddenly, she had nothing to do.

The concept was both scary and exhilarating.

Although there was one thing she could do—figure out why she was attracted to Cole. Why did his accidental touch—just the back of his hand against her arm—send an electrical charge through her body? How could his playful wink make her feel so thrilled to be included? She'd never been "one of the gang," so why did earning the approval of these strangers seem so important? What was it about his friends that tempted her to try playing a game she was sure to lose?

In the big scheme of things, it didn't matter whether or not his friends liked her. She was only in Texas long enough to help her sister. Hopefully, the doctors would give them permission to move Sunny home in the very near future. Nothing about this whole agonizing mess had been cheap. Money was flying out the window and Tessa wasn't bringing any in. Only a fool would risk hard-earned cash—even the smallest of stakes— playing cards with a group of seasoned gamblers.

She didn't gamble. And she didn't fall for men who were all wrong for her. Period.

CHAPTER EIGHT

"YOU ARE IN the midst of greatness when it comes to this fine game," Brady said.

Tessa wasn't sure if he was boasting or joking. "I am?"

"We're all outstanding players. Well, most of us. Cole here doesn't have the ruthlessness necessary to go for the kill, and his bluffing skills are next to none, but several of us are legendary."

"Some of them have legendary egos is what he meant to say," Annie corrected. "Don't listen to a word any of them has to say, and whatever you do, don't risk any money on the game. My husband is the only one I know who wins consistently, but that's because he plays with his head, not his heart."

A loud roar went up as the men laughed. "Oh, Annie, you call yourself a reporter? That's completely not true. Blake wins when I let him," Brady said. "You know gambling was my second career for a while."

"*Was* being the operative word," Luke put in. "Till I got home and taught him a thing or two." He was juggling a pair of dog tags.

Tessa watched the verbal volley that followed like a spectator at a tennis match. She never did see a clear winner, but all of the participants seemed to enjoy them-selves. The debate ended when Joey and June rejoined them. Joey looked full and satisfied, but he had that anxious expression on his face that told her he was missing his mother or grandmother. It broke her heart.

She crossed the room to pick him up. "Hey, sweets, did you like your lunch?"

He nodded.

"Did you tell Mrs. Lawry thank you?"

He looked at Cole's mother and murmured, "Tank you."

"He ate like a trooper," she said. "And I asked him to call me Nanna June. That's what the children in the church nursery school call me."

He was staring at the men and Tessa could tell he would have liked to get his hands on a few of the colorful chips or the deck of cards that Cole's brother-in-law was shuffling. "The men are playing a game," she told him. "Do you want to watch?"

He nodded. She started to pull out a chair at the far end of the rectangular table—well away from the action—but Cole hopped up from where he'd been sitting. "Sit here. You and Joey can play my hand. I'll coach you."

She shook her head. "Joey doesn't have much of an attention span and I don't want to disrupt your game."

The other men assured her that this was just a friendly practice run to see how well the table worked, so she sat down, Joey perched on her lap. To her surprise, he seemed content to rearrange the chips that

Cole had sitting in front of his place. Next to the stack of chips was a beautifully tooled silver and turquoise money clip.

When Joey went to pick it up, she nudged it away.

"He can play with it," Cole said. "If it was full of money maybe not, but these guys are trying to take my last dollar."

She didn't know if he was serious about hurting for money or just blowing smoke for his friends' benefit. She'd read up on poker online last night after her mother and Joey were asleep. One thing she remembered was the term "gamesmanship." Apparently that applied to things like bluffing, props, the clothes you wore, which might include dark glasses, and pregame banter.

"Is it your good-luck charm?" she asked, examining the money clip before handing it to Joey.

"It belonged to my dad," Cole said. "Didn't bring him much luck, but I've had it in my pocket for so long, I feel naked without it." He pronounced the word "nekked" and sort of nodded to his sister when he said it. She wondered how his father died.

Joey held the clip respectfully, running his fingertips over the polished stone. "Mine?" he asked hopefully.

She smiled. "Cole's. He needs it to place on top of his cards, I think."

Cole pulled up a chair beside her and Joey. "I thought you didn't play."

"I Googled some online, learn-to-play sites last night."

She watched with interest as Blake dealt two cards facedown to each player. He tried to explain. "There are two blinds, the big and the little. Luke is the big blind this time. The person to the left of the big blind—Brady, in this case—bets first.

Tessa tried to follow, but her main concern was keeping Joey from exposing Cole's hole cards.

Cole leaned close and picked up his cards. He showed them—the four of diamonds and two of clubs—to Joey and Tessa by cupping his hand to make sure no one else could see. "What do you think, pal? Should we stay for the flop?"

"Plop!" Joey shouted. Cole showed Joey how to toss two chips into the pot in the center.

"Okay. Here's the plop," Blake said, turning over three cards, one at a time. "Too bad we aren't playing low ball."

He revealed the five of spades, two of diamonds and eight of diamonds.

Cole leaned over and whispered something in Joey's ear. The boy nodded then placed Cole's money clip on top of his cards. A bet was made. Cole matched it. "Now for the turn."

The ace of diamonds took its place in line.

"There's a sweet rock," Brady exclaimed. "Looks about the size of the one Blake gave Annie."

Annie, who was standing beside her husband, groaned. "I'm going to make coffee. Cole, please tell me you have something besides that usual swill you drink."

"Fair-trade organic. In the freezer. I bought it at the H.E.B. after you gave me a lecture the last time you were here." He looked at his brother-in-law. "Is she this bad at home?"

"Absolutely," Blake said, studying the table.

A collective inhale from his friends made him look up.

"Absolutely not, I meant to say. My wife makes the best coffee in town and that's all I'm going to say on the matter."

"Smart man," Luke said.

"Moving on…" Brady said.

"Here's the river," Blake said. "Read 'em and weep."

The three of hearts. Cole had a pair of twos. That didn't seem like a very good hand, but he and Joey, after a brief consultation, decided to go all in.

Tessa's heart rate went up. She had no idea how much money the chips represented, but to take that kind of risk on the first hand seemed foolish. She swallowed and watched as the rest of the players called or got out of the game.

"You dog," Brady said. "I take it back about you not being able to bluff. This is not your usual playing pattern."

"Are you going to call me or not?"

"Call."

The man pushed his stack of chips into the pile, then both men showed their hole cards. "Joey and I have a straight," Cole said, lifting Joey's hand so they could share a high five. "Ace, two, three, four and five."

"Nice. Unfortunately, I have a flush," he said, turning over a queen and six of diamonds. He apparently didn't use a card holder.

Cole groaned. "Well, Joey, we tried, didn't we?"

Brady raked in his winnings. "I think this is a new record. Cole's out of the game in one hand."

"Give the guy a break," Luke said. "He's preoccupied."

"Could be the table is jinxed," Blake said. "From all those undoubtedly happy meals at your boss's house."

Cole looked at Tessa and smiled. "The guys don't like Ron because he beats them at their own game."

There was some dispute about whether or not that was true, but Tessa didn't have time to follow any of it because Cole stood and said, "Just as well. Now I can introduce Joey to Pooch."

"Are you out already?" Annie asked, meeting them in the doorway, a cup of aromatic coffee in hand.

"I went down in a blaze of glory—kinda like Luke in his helicopter. Luckily, we're both still kicking. I'm going to show my guests around the place. You can take my chair, if you want."

That suggestion sent up another heated debate. Tessa gathered it had to do with the pros and cons of having a husband and wife playing at the same table, but soon the voices became a low murmur as they left the house. "Should I help your mother clean up?"

"Oh, no. Why do you think Annie is at the table? Mom has her own way of doing things. I think it was her way of escaping when Annie and I were younger. As soon as she's done, she'll probably hide out in my room and read. She always has her nose in a book."

"What kind of books does she like?"

"Historical romances."

"My mom, too, although she says she can't even

stay focused long enough to read at the moment. I wish she could. It might help pass the time at the hospital."

Cole started to say something but Joey interrupted, tugging on Tessa's hand. "M'hat."

"Did your coonskin hat come off while you were sleeping, Mr. Crockett? Yes, of course, let's get your most favorite possession in the whole world."

He gave her a confused look, which she turned into a smile by tickling him under the arms. Hand in hand, they walked toward the Camry. Sure enough, the scrap of fake fur was on the floor of the backseat. Once it was affixed jauntily on Joey's head, they turned to face Cole. "Now we're ready to see your property."

Cole seemed pleased that his gift was so valued. He gave a short whistle and called, "Pooch. Come meet our new friends, boy." A shaggy, mostly brown dog shot around the side of the building, drawing up short when he realized his master was standing with two other people. Strangers. His hackles went up and he turned to slink away.

"Pooch," Cole called. "Come here, boy. It's okay. Joey is a great kid. Very gentle. You'll like him."

The dog walked with obvious reluctance to his master's outstretched hands. Cole motioned for Joey to join him. With great patience, he introduced the two.

Tessa watched, poised to sweep in and rescue her nephew if the dog suddenly turned vicious, but she relaxed after a minute. The animal was shy, not mean. "How come he doesn't like people? Was he abused as a pup?"

"Could have been. I don't know. He was full grown

when I found him. Or, rather, he found me. Showed up on the back porch about a week after I moved in. I tried my best to find his owner. Put up flyers with his photo on it, but nobody ever called me back. He's a sweetheart—just timid."

Tessa understood completely. She felt the same way about social encounters. On the job, she was fearless, but put her in a room full of strangers—without an agenda—and she ducked behind her camera. Speaking of which… "Just a minute. I left my camera in the house. Joey, will you wait here?"

He seemed engrossed petting the dog, which had rolled onto its back to have its tummy rubbed. "Joey?"

He nodded but didn't look up.

"Just like his mother," she said. "She only listened to me when she chose to…. I wish she hadn't listened to me about coming back to Texas."

She left before Cole could say anything. She dashed to the house and slipped inside as quietly as possible so as not to draw attention from the card players. Her purse was sitting on the floor by the hall leading to the kitchen. She'd just picked it up when she heard someone hiss her name.

"Tessa," came the loud whisper.

She looked around. June Lawry was standing at the end of the hallway, motioning Tessa to join her.

"Yes?" Tessa said, heading that way reluctantly. "Um…Cole and Joey are waiting for me outside."

When she joined the woman at the entrance of what she assumed was the master bedroom, June took her hand. "Come. This will only take a minute. I have something for you to take back to your mother and sister. Annie told me you didn't want any help, but when I mentioned your situation to a couple of my friends…well, we couldn't help ourselves."

June pointed to three paper grocery sacks filled with what looked like wrapped gifts, food items and a huge bouquet of flowers. "And a lot of people have asked about where to send donations."

Old, ugly, painful memories bombarded her— images of soliciting handouts from people who treated her like dirt—or worse. She'd vowed never to let herself sink that low again. Never be in a place where she had to ask for help. "I…can't. Thank you, but…no."

She turned away, tears blurring her vision, and staggered blindly into a pair of warm, strong arms. "Tessa?"

She broke free and stumbled outside. She couldn't take comfort in Cole's arms. Another lesson from long ago. Even comfort wasn't free.

TOUCHING HER was not a good idea, Cole decided— after the fact. Fortunately, she didn't let him hold her for long. Two, three seconds tops, then she ran out the door.

He looked at his mother, who appeared ready to cry herself. "What happened?"

"I offered her these bags of goodies. Toys for Joey. Books and magazines for her mother. Some homemade cookies. Do you suppose she was offended? Some people aren't comfortable with charity."

He patted her shoulder. "I don't know. I can't get a

clear read on her. I used to be good with people. Now I only know two-by-fours."

Mom smiled indulgently. "Where's Joey?"

"Out front with Annie and Pooch. I came in for a hat. Apparently, my sister has turned paranoid about skin cancer."

"Oh, yes, she was telling me about the interview she had with a young man your age dying of the disease. He leaves behind a wife and three young boys."

"That explains it." He grabbed a blue and silver Dallas Cowboys ball cap from a hook inside his closet then headed in the direction Tessa had taken. "I'll find her. Don't worry. She's probably just overwhelmed." He paused. "Thanks for trying, Mom. You're the best. Would you do me a favor? Tell Annie to bring Joey to the riverbed in a few minutes. I want to talk to Tessa alone first."

SHE HADN'T GONE far—just to the end of the deck, which offered the prettiest view of his place. He doubted if she even noticed. She was sitting on the bentwood glider his mother had given him as a house-warming present, a tissue in her hand.

"I'm so embarrassed. I need to go apologize to your mother." She started to stand, but Cole stopped her. He gently eased her back down then joined her on the bench.

"She's only upset because you're upset. She didn't mean to insult you or hurt your feelings."

She took a deep breath. "I don't usually talk about this. I'm not looking for sympathy…. We were poor when I was a kid. My stepdad was a drug addict and he was HIV-positive at the end. I did my share of Dumpster-diving, and there came a point when I told myself I'd never take charity from anyone. But that's my problem, not your mother's."

He didn't know what he was expecting, but that blunt and candid confession wasn't it.

"After our dad died, Annie and I probably would have starved if not for the neighbors and our friends. I guess we were lucky to be part of a community that gives before you have to ask."

She looked away. "Yeah. Holding out your hand is no fun." She sat up straighter and shrugged. "Although I remember once before Zeb got sick, he was playing for money near the Amtrak station. He'd taken me with him that day, and he made a game of it—like musical chairs. I'd try to pick up the coins that bounced out of his guitar case before the music stopped. It didn't feel so much like begging then."

Cole had no words. He couldn't imagine a childhood with that kind of fear and deprivation. The image didn't jibe at all with the version of her childhood Sunny had told him. "Your sister never mentioned any of that."

"I'm not surprised. She worshiped her father. I did, too, until I was old enough to understand that most people didn't live like us."

"Where was your mom?"

"Taking care of him. She worked as a waitress, did some part-time things. It's hard to keep a steady job when you're married to a guy in a band. We traveled around a lot."

"And school?"

"Mostly homeschooled. I was an avid reader. I took the GED when I was sixteen. Went to college on a scholarship. Plus, worked three jobs to help Mom and Sunny."

"No wonder they depend on you."

She made a careless gesture of dismissal. "Mom's doing the hard work right now. The only thing they're counting on me for is not to lose my nephew. Do you know where he is?"

"Annie and Mom took him to the creek. I told them we'd meet there." He stood and led the way down the steps. He was glad to know about her past, but he felt uneasy, too. Awkward. "Annie can use the kid-time. It's good practice."

"Does she know if she's having a boy or a girl?"

He started toward the cleared path leading into the underbrush. "No. It's a running argument between Annie and Blake. He wants to know. She wants to be surprised. They don't often agree on anything, but they love each other to pieces."

"Did you and your sister grow up around here?"

He pushed aside a low-hanging branch to let her pass.

"Yeah. Our folks moved to River Bluff after Dad was discharged from the air force. He got a job working on the Medina dam."

"And the other guys? They're native Texans, too?"

"Even more so. The Carricks have been in this county

since shortly after the Alamo fell, I think. Luke's family settled here a generation later, but they proceeded to buy up every acre of land that wasn't deeded to God."

She smiled. "I take it that makes you a newcomer?"

"You got it. My dad was an air force brat who didn't call anyplace home. He was stationed at Randolph Air Force Base when he and a bunch of friends took a road trip to New Mexico. They broke down the other side of Abilene. That's where he met my mother. She was a waitress in a diner."

"And your mother never remarried after your father passed away? Mine, either."

"I don't think Mom ever forgave herself for not being there when Dad died."

She nodded. "I watched my stepfather waste away for four years. In the end, he passed away in his sleep. Mom was sitting in the chair right next to him and didn't know it."

He started to tell her the rest of his story, but Pooch's half-strangled bark interrupted him. Joey let out a cry when he spotted his aunt and immediately bolted toward the dry creek bed that separated them.

Annie lunged to grab the back of his shirt but missed. June hurried after him, nearly losing her balance. Cole sprang forward, sliding precariously on a spot of loose shale. His ankle protested, but he managed to catch Joey before he tripped.

"That child is all daredevil," Annie called, holding her side as if she had a stitch. "Is it too late to start praying for a girl?"

June, who was breathing hard, as well, laughed. "He's just like Cole was, part monkey and completely fearless."

Tessa, who'd rushed to his side and taken Joey from him, visibly stiffened. Cole understood why, but he also knew his mother didn't mean anything by the comparison. At least not what Tessa probably assumed she meant.

"Are you referring to the time I fell out of a tree and broke both my arms?"

His mother looked at Tessa. "I think he means the time he fell off the roof of the Wild Card Saloon."

Cole's jaw dropped. "You knew about that? How? Jake said his mother didn't have insurance and she'd lose the place if we told the truth, so we made up the story about the tree."

Mom nodded. "Lola figured that's what happened. Her insurance had lapsed, but she wanted me to know the truth even if I decided to sue. Over what? I asked her. Bad luck? Wild boys are wild boys. It could have happened anywhere. To any of you."

Annie looked from Cole to Mom and back, her mouth slightly gaped in shock. "You knew he was lying and you let him get away with it? That was the year I wanted to take ballet lessons, and we couldn't afford it because of Cole's doctor bills." She turned his way, furious. "You owe me."

He started to laugh. "Okay. Do they make maternity tutus?"

"Oh, shut up."

She turned on her heel and marched away. June

followed a few seconds later, calling, "Annie, slow down. Think about the baby."

When he turned to look at Tessa, she was grinning. "Sunny excelled at marching off in a huff. Had it down to an art."

Her smile faded. Neither of them said anything until Joey squirmed to get down. "Ball?"

Pooch, who had been resting in the shade nearby, jumped up and poked around in the brush until he came up with a slimy-looking tennis ball.

Cole groaned. "Pooch isn't much of a watchdog, but he came with a built-in fetching program. He's inexhaustible. If I throw it around here, he comes back covered in burrs and stickers. Let's head back to the house."

Cole got a nod from Tessa then whistled for Pooch. He took Joey's hand and started off. She fell in step behind them, but when they reached his driveway, she said, "Would you mind if I go find your mother? I'd like to talk to her about, well, you know."

"Sure. It looks as if the others have left, but Blake's car is still here, so she and Annie are probably packing up the rest of the food. I'd try the kitchen first. But, Tessa, it's not necessary."

"No. It is. I'll be right back, and then Joey and I need to leave, too. Thanks for keeping him occupied."

"My pleasure. Believe me. Mine and Pooch's."

CHAPTER NINE

"MOM'S IN THE BEDROOM reading. We're just waiting for Blake to finish a call. Work," Annie added with a sigh. "Have a seat. We need to talk."

Tessa looked at the woman sitting on the second step of the porch, elbows propped behind her, her legs out in front of her. Her rounded belly was a lot more obvious than her cotton blouse had made it look earlier.

"Has anyone ever commented on your tendency to boss people around?" Tessa asked, choosing a spot a few feet away. Fortunately, the hand railing made a comfortable backrest.

"Can't help it. It's my nature. First-born, like you, right?"

"Yes. Although my business partner, Marci, is the youngest of five and she's the same way, so I'm not sure birth order is a valid excuse."

Annie smiled. "Touché. So you're self-employed, huh? What do you do?"

"Marci and I own a consulting firm. We work with small companies that have peaked at a certain level and need help to break through their self-imposed glass ceiling."

"Interesting. I can think of several of my friends who could use your help."

"Thanks. I'm always happy to get referrals."

Annie let her head fall back against the dusty steps. "So, you don't work exclusively in Oregon?"

"Last year, I was in Seattle, Denver, D.C., Birmingham and Atlanta."

"Yikes." She suddenly sat up straight and rocked forward, wrapping her arms around her knees. "That's a lot of travel. Is that why you're not married?"

Tessa pressed the heel of her hand to her forehead. "Talk about a non sequitur. Do they teach you that in journalism school?"

"Just curious. I think my brother likes you."

Oh dear. "Listen, Annie, unless Cole is Joey's dad, I'm just passing through. And to answer your question, being on the road a lot isn't the only reason I'm not married. Most men aren't comfortable with their wife earning more money than them—especially if that means she has to give up cooking three squares a day to devote her attention to her job."

Annie looked at her curiously. "You actually believe that?"

"Yes." Tessa stood up—she still wanted to apologize to Cole's mother.

"Is your partner married?"

"Last summer. Her husband is our tax accountant."

"And he doesn't mind her working long hours and traveling all around the country?"

"Not so far. Plus, he went into this knowing what

she's like and how important our work is to her—he's done our taxes since we started."

"Hmm. But marriage is a whole 'nother game."

The comment reminded her that she hadn't received a reply to her last e-mail. Marci was usually ultraconscientious about answering. "Well, we've worked with a lot of partnerships and we always tell people the key to success is communication and planning. If Marci wants to take fewer out-of-town jobs next year, we'll budget for it."

"How does your sister's situation factor into the equation?"

Questions. Questions. Questions Tessa had been avoiding asking. She brushed off the seat of her pants and climbed the rest of the steps. "I'd better go find your mother and tell her goodbye. Joey and I should be heading back soon."

Annie didn't take the hint. She got up, too. "Listen. I admit I was wrong about you. You're obviously not an opportunist trying to take advantage of my brother. But I meant it when I said the people of River Bluff would fall over themselves to help you and your family if they knew about your situation."

Tessa's shoulders stiffened. "I appreciate the offer, but—"

"You're proud. And private. I get that. But it's Christmas. The time of year when we spend too much time and money on mass consumption and welcome any chance to do something that makes us feel less greedy and self-absorbed."

Tessa had her hand on the doorknob but didn't turn it. "That's a rather stark way of looking at things." *Reminds me of me.*

"Unsentimental. There's a difference. Cole and I learned at a young age that the holidays can suck bigtime if you let them. He has his way of dealing with the memories. I have mine."

Tessa wasn't sure what Cole's way amounted to—maybe dressing up as Santa at the church bazaar—but she realized trying to prevent Annie from doing anything she had her mind set on would be futile. Besides, this wasn't her call alone. Her mother had a say in the matter.

"I suppose we could use a few kid-friendly gifts, some books or DVDs, but I don't want to become a tragic poster family."

"Tragedy with hope," Annie said, using her hands to give the impression of a headline.

Tessa groaned. Before she could reply, Annie nudged Tessa away from the door. "Pregnant woman coming through. Gotta pee."

She left the door open, but Tessa was reluctant to step across the threshold. Had she made a mistake giving Annie permission to write about their situation?

Annie stopped about ten feet into the open living room and turned, fidgeting with obvious impatience. "I almost forgot. I read Sunny's diary. Mr. Big is definitely Big Jim McNally. Kills me to admit that. Believe me, I'm praying the DNA proves it's the other guy— the G-Man. No idea who that is, but…" She gave a delicate wince. "Oh dear, I have to remember to buy some panty liners."

She disappeared down the hall and into the bathroom.

Cole, with Joey on his shoulders, joined her a moment later. She'd been so focused on Annie's comment she hadn't even heard them approach.

"You're frowning. Is something wrong?"

"Your sister thinks your ex-father-in-law is Mr. Big."

He didn't react outwardly, but she sensed that this upset him. What kind of man was this Jim McNally?

"Joey's thirsty," he said, lowering the child to the terrazzo tile of the entry. "Didn't I see a kid's cup of some kind around here?"

She hurried toward the kitchen where she'd left her purse, which doubled as a diaper bag. The Blue's Clues sippy cup was right where she'd left it. "Here, honey. I found your juice."

She lifted Joey to the counter since there weren't any stools. He drank greedily. A real mother would have known better than to let him get this dehydrated, she thought.

Cole filled a glass from the faucet and drank, too. Maybe they'd both just worked up a thirst playing ball.

As Tessa waited for Joey to finish, she heard voices coming from the hallway. Annie, June and Blake walked in.

"Who won?" Cole asked.

"Me. Of course," Blake boasted, but he said it with a smile. "Actually, we had to break up early. Brady got a call about one of their racehorses. The vet was on his way, but Brady needed to be there. Since Luke was driving, he had to go, too."

"Is the table going to work out?"

Blake shrugged. "It's not ideal, but it'll do until we can get Jake to change his mind about selling the Card. Are you two ready?" he asked his wife and mother-in-law.

"I am. Cole, would you and Blake bring me those sacks in the bedroom?"

Tessa knew which bags she meant and felt her cheeks heat up. She wanted to draw Cole's mother aside to apologize in private, but she couldn't step away from Joey. Annie solved the problem by snatching a bag of store-bought cookies from the counter near the coffee-maker. "Can Joey have a treat for the road home?"

"Sure. Thank you."

The two women changed places. Joey, happily occupied with his Oreo, didn't seem to notice when Tessa walked to where June was standing. "I owe you an apology, Mrs. Lawry. You were only trying to be kind, and I overreacted—badly."

June smiled and laid her hand on Tessa's forearm. "It's okay, Tessa. I overstepped. Shall we put this behind us and start over?"

"Yes, thank you. And I'd very much like to take those bags you offered back to Mom and let her go through them. I'm sure if we can't use all the items there are others around the hospital who can."

"Wonderful. That does my heart good."

Tessa felt as though a weight had been lifted from her shoulders. Then June asked, "What's your next step?"

"Well, given your daughter's interpretation of Sunny's diary, I guess I'll go see Mr. Big, her ex-boss, on Monday."

Cole, who was close enough to hear her comment, stopped so abruptly his brother-in-law, who was carrying two of the brown paper sacks, bumped into him. "Dammit, Cole. Signal next time."

"Sorry."

He exchanged a look with his mother and sister that made Tessa's shoulders tense. "What? You don't think that's a good idea?"

June took the bag Cole had been carrying. "We'll load these into your car. Take care, Tessa. You'll be in our prayers."

"And I'd like to try putting Joey in his car seat, if you don't mind," Annie said. "I've heard some brands take a rocket scientist to figure it out. Come on, Blake, you need the practice too."

"I'm expecting another call," he warned, following after them.

Cole waited until everyone had left before he answered her.

"Jim's an astute businessman. He taught me a lot when I was working for him. I don't blame him for what happened to me—he advised me not to get involved with the people who eventually screwed me over, but there's one thing you should know about Big Jim. He protects his own. If there's any chance Joey is his child…well, he's got a lot of money and he knows a lot of people. Powerful people, if you get my drift."

Tessa's stomach felt as if someone was using it for a bowling alley. "I can't believe Sunny would sleep with a man like that."

"I'm not saying she did, but he's a salesman. A very persuasive salesman. Plus, he's not bad-looking for his age. Drinks too much, but he works out with a private trainer. At least he did when I knew him."

Tessa weighed her options. "I suppose I don't have any choice. This is about Joey's future. He deserves to know who his father is."

Cole didn't reply, but he didn't seem happy. She picked up her purse, and she and Cole walked outside.

His sister was standing beside Joey's door, consternation on her face. "I give up," she said, hands in the air. "The darn thing beat me. Blake's hiding behind his phone. He wouldn't even try."

Tessa could see him at the wheel of the couple's SUV. June waved from the backseat.

Hurrying around the car, she quickly demonstrated the complicated procedure then gave Joey a kiss on the nose and closed the door. "It took me a few tries, too," she mumbled, searching to the bottom of her purse for her keys.

When she looked up, she noticed the tension emanating between brother and sister. "You have to go with her," Annie whispered fiercely.

"My being there would only make things worse."

"Coward."

"I am not."

Tessa cleared her throat. "Is there a problem?"

Annie spoke first. "If you're determined to meet with Big Jim, you need to take Cole with you. For one thing, Jim and Botox-woman live in a gated community and Cole knows the code."

"Botox-woman?"

"My ex-mother-in-law," he supplied, obviously trying not to smile. "And I'm sure the code has changed in two years. Hell, Jim and Loretta might not even live in the same subdivision. He trades in houses like some people do cars."

"Still. You know people. You could find out where he lives, and you could get her in. If Tessa has to go through the office, she'll have to deal with Crystal. She's still Jim's personal assistant, right? And do you think for one minute the ice princess is going to let some new kid have a shot at her inheritance?"

Cole frowned.

Annie had her hand on his arm. "If you go tomorrow after church, Mom could babysit while Tessa's mother is at the hospital."

Tessa wasn't used to letting others plan her actions, but before she could voice her objection, Cole looked at her and said, "What time do you want me to pick you up?"

COLE PULLED his truck to a stop in front of a house he didn't recognize. Two stories. Native rock and brick facade with a turret that looked out of place in Cole's opinion. He'd never liked designs that didn't blend with the surroundings. Too ostentatious. Every inch of this four-thousand-square-foot home cried, *Look at me. I'm richer than you are.*

Jim and Loretta had probably moved at least twice since the last time Cole had been welcomed into their home. Building and selling on spec was another way Jim cashed in on San Antonio's ever-growing housing market.

Their closest neighbor was a football-field length away. At least Cole gave the designer of this gated community credit for not squeezing uber-mansions onto tiny lots. Instead of trying to bluff his way in, he'd called Jim's private line that morning.

"I have someone who needs to talk to you. It has nothing to do with work and practically nothing to do with me. I'm just the middleman," he'd explained on the phone.

Hearing his ex-father-in-law's voice for the first time in nearly two years had been rough. Although he didn't want to admit it, Jim's defection had hurt…maybe even more than Crystal's abandonment. Deep down, a part of him—the kid who grew up without a father—wondered if Jim had ever cared for him.

"I could have done this myself," his passenger said, jerking him back to the present. "In fact, why don't you wait in the truck. You probably have a lot of hard feelings where your ex-in-laws are concerned. I'll just lay out my case and see what happens."

He looked at her—big-city stylish in black slacks, dove-gray turtleneck and boots with skinny heels. The outside temperature was already too warm for the leather jacket resting between them. He'd pulled on Dockers and a white shirt for the meeting. The best he could do since he'd given away all of his suits when he moved back to River Bluff.

"Jim's expecting me. Don't worry. We're grown-ups. I won't let my issues get in the way of yours."

"That isn't what I meant. I just—"

He opened the door and got out. "Whatever my sister told you about me being broken up over my divorce is crap. She saw one version. I lived another. If Crystal were here today, which God willing she isn't—for your sake, not mine—I'd thank her. I'm a lot better off now than I was two years ago."

He could tell she didn't believe him.

He walked around the truck to help her out. The S-shaped path from the street to the door was made of stamped concrete designed to resemble cobblestones. A border of rose-colored pebbles complemented the pinkish trim on the house and matched the evenly spaced flowering shrubs. To his practiced eye, he'd say the landscaping added twenty thousand dollars' worth of curb appeal. Maybe more.

She adjusted her bag over the shoulder of the black leather jacket she'd pulled on. "If you're sure…"

"I am."

They walked slowly since the decorative walkway was a bit treacherous in high heels. "I hate to admit it, but I'm more nervous now than I was the night I took Joey to meet you."

"Didn't show then. Doesn't show now." He kept his reply short because he didn't want his voice to give away his own uneasiness.

"A credit to my many years of practice, I guess," she said softly.

He wondered if she meant in her line of business or in her personal life.

He stopped, his finger an inch from the doorbell. "We could wait until the results of my DNA test come back. This might not be necessary."

She gave him a look that said she already knew the results would be negative. She pressed the button.

Moments later, a petite, svelte blonde was standing before them. She looked exactly the same as the last time he saw her. "Hello, Loretta."

"Cole." Crystal had once commented that her mother spent more on her personal trainers and cosmetic surgery than most people made in a year. "Big Jim said you were coming, but I didn't believe him. How long has it been? You're living in River Bluff, aren't you?"

"Yes, ma'am. Just about done with the house. It's come a long way since the last time you were there. We barely even had the walls up."

He could tell she didn't remember. Crystal had catered a rafter-raising party that her father and mother had attended. The guest list had also included two of the investors who'd been poised to take Cole to the cleaners. Not that he'd known that at the time.

"Oh, yes, of course. Hello," she said, noticing Tessa. "And you are…?"

He quickly made the introductions. "Tessa needs to talk to Jim. Old business. Sorry to intrude on a Sunday."

Retta pursed her lips. Cole knew she didn't like being left out of any loop— especially one that included a beautiful young woman. "He's upstairs, but I'm sure he heard the bell and will be down in a minute. Come in."

They stepped into the impressive foyer—two stories, plus the turret, which offered natural light bouncing off prisms in the curved glass. "Beautiful place, Retta."

"Why, thank you, Cole. We like it, although we're looking at a lot in Garden Ridge. To be closer to Crystal. Did you know she bought a home in Cibolo? It's just lovely. Nearly as big as this one." She looked at him shrewdly. "You heard about her engagement, right? To Bill Yardley? They're planning a December wedding *next* year. Goodness, it's going to take us at least that long to plan it. She wants to do things right this time."

A reference to the fact that she and Cole had eloped to Vegas. "Bill Yardley. The name's familiar but I can't place him."

"He took over your job after you left."

"In more ways than one," he murmured to Tessa.

The news of his ex-wife's engagement didn't surprise him, nor did the sight of his ex-mother-in-law swaying in her Jimmy Choos, tipsy even though it was only midday. Loretta had always been a drinker.

"Well, congratulations. I wish them both all the best." He looked at his watch pointedly. "I hate to be rude, but we're in a bit of a hurry."

She walked with exaggerated care to the gleaming

natural-oak banister and called, "Big Jim. You have company."

He could tell she was peeved at being left out of the discussion. "I'll just leave you to your important talk then. Goodbye." She slurred the last word slightly.

Tessa looked at him, but he waited until his ex-mother-in-law was out of earshot. He leaned closer and said softly, "They must have been serving mimosas at the country club this morning."

Her lips formed a pretty *O*. Her perfume was a refreshing antidote to the heavy-handed application of Youth Dew Loretta tended to bathe in. He leaned closer and inhaled deeply.

She cocked her left brow suspiciously and stepped away as the sound of a door slamming on the second floor echoed above them. He saw her fix her shoulders as if preparing to take on the enemy.

"Cole," Big Jim's deep voice bellowed. "Sorry about that. I was on the phone and didn't hear the bell."

Liar. Big Jim always kept people waiting. It was part of his power play.

His ex-father-in-law sauntered down the steps. Jim rarely rushed anywhere. He looked ready for a game of tennis in pristine sneakers, white shorts that stopped just above his knees and a navy-blue polo shirt with the logo of an exclusive golf club Cole had played at a couple of times when Jim had invited him.

"Hello, Jim. Thanks for seeing us." The two shook hands. "This is Tessa Jamison. She's Sunny Barnes's sister."

"Poor Sunny," Jim said, taking both of Tessa's hands in his. "My receptionist told me you called the other day when I was out of town. Something about a car wreck. I'm so sorry. How's she doing?"

"Still in a coma."

"Gawd damn, that's bad news," he exclaimed, his Texas accent kicking in. "Come on in, you two. Let's sit down. Tell me what you need from me."

He led the way into a white-carpeted parlor furnished in yellow and pink chintz. The sofa had so many throw pillows on it, he and Tessa wound up sitting close enough that their thighs almost touched. Cole looked around but he didn't see any photos or knickknacks that he remembered.

"I'm trying to put together the pieces of Sunny's life when she lived in San Antonio," Tessa said. "Most of that time she was working for you."

Jim, who was seated opposite them in an overstuffed armchair upholstered in cream and gold-striped silk, relaxed with one ankle resting on the other knee. "I doubt if I'll be much help. I have approximately fifty people on my payroll at any given time. Don't I, Cole?"

"Probably. I don't remember. But I do recall quite clearly the impact Sunny had on the office. And you."

Jim's demeanor changed subtly. "What exactly is it you want, Miss Jamison?"

"As her employer—an employer who reputedly bought her flowers every week—I was hoping you could tell me about her personal life. Was she seeing anyone? More specifically, was she seeing you outside the office?"

Cole was impressed by how cool Tessa was playing this. Jim, on the other hand, no longer looked relaxed. He'd uncrossed his legs and sat up straight. "She was a beautiful girl. I bought her flowers because it made her happy, and brightened the office."

"Understandable. A legitimate business expense. And did Sunny appreciate your gift for what it was or could she have read more into it? She was young and not particularly worldly."

Jim made a scoffing sound. "No matter what you think, your sister wasn't dumb or naive. Young, yes. Beautiful, yes. But she could flirt with the best of 'em then shut a man down just like that." He snapped his fingers for emphasis. "As for her personal life, I'm afraid I can't tell you much. She acted coy—evasive— when I asked."

"You did ask?"

"Only to make sure she wasn't hanging out with the wrong crowd. She's younger than my daughter. I didn't want anything bad to happen to her."

"You took a fatherly interest in her?"

Jim's ruddy complexion darkened. Cole wasn't sure he'd ever seen his ex-father-in-law as disconcerted. "I liked her. I'll even go so far as to say I was attracted to her, but the one time I dropped by her apartment, she made it clear she had another fish on the line. A singer or musician of some kind. Tall guy with long hair."

Tessa let out a small gasp. Her face seemed several shades lighter, and he wondered if she was going to faint. "A musician?" she asked softly. "You're sure?"

Jim shrugged. "He had a guitar in his hand when I showed up. I didn't think he planned to whack me over the head with it, but I left just in case."

Cole decided he believed the man about his aborted attempt to get Sunny in bed. "Did she introduce the two of you?"

"Maybe. I don't remember."

When Tessa failed to reply right away, Jim said, "Your sister told me about you. She said you were smart, ambitious and very successful. Driven was the word she used."

Tessa seemed to collect herself. She smoothed a non-existent wrinkle on the knee of her slacks. "I've always been the responsible one in my family, the person who picks up the pieces, which explains why I'm here today. One more question then we'll go."

Jim threw out his hands. "Shoot."

"Did you have unprotected sex with my sister?"

Jim erupted out of the chair. "What the hell kind of question is that? Are you telling me she's sick? Like AIDS or something?"

"No. But she did come back to Oregon pregnant. I'm trying to locate my nephew's birth father."

Jim crossed his arms and stared at her for a good ten seconds. "Well, I guess that explains how come Cole is with you. Rumor had it they were sorta close. I always thought that might be the reason behind Crystal's hurry to get divorced." He pointed his finger at Cole. "You're sure the boy isn't yours?"

Cole ignored the question. "You know why your daughter divorced me, Jim. The money. And the fact that I didn't want this life anymore. I was never going to be you, and we both knew it." He picked up a beaded pillow that had fallen on the floor. A thing. Probably picked out by some designer to evoke refinement and elegance, but despite the attention to detail, the house felt emptier to him than his unfurnished home. Any doubt he might have had over whether or not he'd made the right choice disappeared.

Tessa stood. "Mr. McNally, if you tell me you didn't have sex with my sister, I'll believe you." Her tone was calm and neutral. "There was nothing in Sunny's journal that implied you were Joey's father, but I have to hear that from you—since she can't tell me."

Jim stepped around the ornate coffee table to face her. "We were never intimate."

"Thank you. Now, if you'll excuse us, I need to get back to the hospital." She reached in her purse and pulled out a business card. "If by any chance you remember the name of the person who was with her that night, my cell number's at the bottom."

Cole mumbled a goodbye at the door and the two of them walked in silence to the truck. He opened the door for her and waited while she took off her jacket. "Do you think he was telling the truth?" she asked before getting in.

Did he? "Yeah. Jim's got a helluva poker face, but I don't think he'd lie about this. Brag maybe, but…no, I think he meant it."

"Are you okay? Finding out about your ex getting married again and everything?"

"I'm not upset," he said bluntly. "Any love we had for each other died a long time before our divorce. We got married blind. I thought she was one thing, and she obviously thought I was something else. I tried to be that person for a while, but when I lost the money I just didn't have it in me to try again."

"Where'd the money go?"

He opened the door wider until she got the hint and climbed in. One trip down memory lane was enough for one day. "Long story. Didn't you tell Jim you were in a hurry to get back to the hospital?"

She drew up her legs. Long, shapely legs. What was it about women in high heels that made men goofy? "I am, but I'll call Mom and June first. If there's no change and Joey is okay, I thought maybe you could show me the apartment complex Sunny managed. The long-haired guy might still live there."

He hurried around and got in. "That's been almost three years. Turnover in this particular complex has always been really high, and any records would be on the computer at the BJM offices."

"I didn't plan a full-fledged search, but it is Sunday afternoon. Maybe we could just walk the grounds and if we see anyone outside, we could ask if they know this guy."

"Some long-haired guitar player?"

"Who might be Sunny's G-man."

He let out a whistle. "I missed that, but it makes sense. No problem. Let's check it out."

He started the truck, driving slowly along the same street they'd traveled earlier. The houses were just as impressive the second time past, but Cole felt no desire to own one.

Tessa pulled out her phone. "Hi, June," she said a few seconds later. "It's me, Tessa. How's Joey?"

She suddenly sat forward. "What? But my phone didn't ring. Is it bad?"

They were just passing under the ornate portal of the gatehouse. He paused at the intersection. A left turn would take him to the L1604, the quickest way to the hospital. A right would lead them toward Rolling Oaks Mall, what locals called the Boob Mall. The apartment building Sunny had managed was only a few miles from it.

He leaned closer to hear what his mother was saying. Her words were clipped, but he got the message. "Sunny…surgery."

He turned left and stepped on the gas.

CHAPTER TEN

"YOUR DAUGHTER IS an amazingly strong and determined soul," the surgeon told Autumn when he finally emerged from the operating theater, nearly three hours after Cole had dropped Tessa at the hospital. He'd insisted on going back to the motel to help his mother entertain Joey so Tessa and Autumn could wait together.

"We found the bleed and were able to fix it. I think this might actually be a turning point for her. We'll know better in the next twenty-four hours, but I'm hopeful. Very hopeful. She's a fighter."

Autumn, who had spent most of the waiting time in a fugue state that Tessa couldn't penetrate, suddenly burst into tears. "Just like her father," she choked out.

"More like her mother," Tessa said firmly, hugging her mother's shoulders. She refused to compare Zeb's last months, struggling for every breath, to the battle her sister was waging. "Sunny won't give up."

The three of them talked a few minutes longer, then Autumn agreed to go back to the motel and rest while Tessa remained at the hospital. At least until Sunny was out of recovery and back to her room.

After her mother was gone, Tessa paced restlessly, made a few notes on her PDA, played a game of Sudoku in the back of some travel magazine and stared out the window at the growing dusk. Since they frowned on people using cell phones in the hospital—and she didn't really have anyone to call—she waited. And thought.

Not about her sister. Not about the G-man. Not about business. She thought about Cole.

She liked him. She had from the minute she'd seen him juggling cats in a Santa suit. And as long as she was being honest, she had to admit that she was attracted to him. Physically. Not romantically.

They were too different. He hadn't tried to hide his opinion of his ex-in-laws' home and lifestyle. But the refined elegance, obviously achieved with a designer's eye to detail, was exactly the kind of place she dreamed of owning someday.

Comfort, space and security. Did that make her pretentious? Possibly, but she was okay with that. If she used money that she'd earned, then wasn't she entitled to flaunt that to the world? Cole might be content to hide out in some remote, bare-bones cabin with a dog and his poker buddies, but that kind of lifestyle wasn't for her. No matter how damn handsome and kind he was.

She turned on her heel and started to pace, following the same path her mother had earlier. As she passed near a vent, a shiver ran down her spine. Why, she wondered, did they have to keep it so cold? If Cole had been there, she might have been tempted to turn to him for warmth.

There'd been a moment at his ex-in-laws' when she'd felt him lean close and take a deep breath. Knowing he was drawn to her scent had messed with her head—until Big Jim showed up.

She wondered where he was now. Halfway to River Bluff? She moved to a relatively warmer spot in the room where she and her mother had been sitting earlier, and pulled back the sleeve of her jacket to check the time.

"Are you late for a very important date?"

"Cole," she exclaimed. The heat she'd imagined earlier ran down her spine. "What are you doing here? I thought you were on duty at the North Pole tonight."

He walked across the room to her. "I am. Mom's in the truck. We'll go straight to the church. I just wanted to check on you first. Good news about Sunny, huh?"

He stopped an arm's length away.

"Yes. Great news. Your mother's prayers must be working."

He nodded. The harsh overhead lights made his thick wavy hair look almost silver. But he didn't look old, just venerable. Strong. Reliable.

"I don't think I thanked you for today. You definitely were my ticket in. I got the impression Big Jim wanted to see you."

He knit his brows together. "I doubt it. He was probably just curious about why I'd be calling after so long." He shrugged, dismissing the subject. "Anyway, one of the reasons I stopped by was to tell you I made a few calls while Joey was napping. One of the women I used to work with—Karen Hale, a real sweetheart and a true professional—was on duty at the office today. She did some investigating. I think we might have a lead on the G-man."

Tessa stepped closer. "You're kidding. Who? Where?"

"Karen talked to the current manager of the apartment building Sunny used to manage. According to this guy, there's a barbecue chain about half a mile from the complex that's popular with college kids—most of his renters are students. Anyway, he said this place has live music."

"The G-man plays there?"

"I don't know. Thought it might be worth a shot."

Her fingers were tingling, with excitement over finding a lead that could take them to Joey's father, she told herself. She stepped back and shoved her hands in her pockets. She suddenly felt like a foolish schoolgirl with her first crush. How absurd. "Um…great. Thanks. I'll check it out. Sometime."

Cole cleared the distance between them. Since her hands were stuck in her pockets, she couldn't stop him when he grabbed the lapels of her jacket and pulled her up flush with his chest. "I know I don't have a right…but I want in."

"I beg your pardon?" she asked, her lips just inches from his. His breath was warm on her face and smelled like peppermint again.

"We both know I'm not Joey's father, but I *am* Sunny's friend. And I care about what happens—to all of you. So, I'm coming with you when you look for the G-man."

That sounded a lot like an ultimatum. Nobody

invaded her space and started giving orders. "What about your big poker party?" she asked meekly.

"That's Wednesday. Mom's got a volunteer who can play Santa the rest of the week if I need him to, but he's a firefighter who works shifts. He goes back on nights Friday."

She tried to wiggle free, but that only succeeded in rubbing her chest against his. She felt her nipples pucker. The glint in his eyes told her he didn't mind one bit. She liked the sensation, too, but she didn't want to give him the wrong idea. She wasn't a practiced tease, like Big Jim had called Sunny.

"Okay. We'll look for him together. But no more of this."

"This?" His grin told her he was going to make her say it.

"You know. The sexual tension. Flirting. Whatever you want to call it. I need you to let go of my jacket and step back."

"Or what? You'll kiss me?"

That sounded an awful lot like a dare.

"Absolutely not."

At least that's what she'd intended to say. Instead, she pressed her lips to his. A quick, unexciting, barely puckered touch. Amateurish, at best.

But a second later, he did it the right way. His lips were warm and moist. Slightly sweet, tinged with that hint of peppermint. It lasted one, maybe two heartbeats, at most.

"Fine. I'm leaving," he said, breaking the contact. He

let go of her lapels and lightly brushed his hands down her chest—to smooth the leather, she supposed. "I'll call you later. No. Not tonight. You're going to be wiped out. In the morning when I'm on break, okay? But if anything changes with Sunny, you can call me. Anytime. Right?"

She nodded because her throat was too tight to get a word out.

With a smile—and just the tiniest of winks—he left. And with a groan Tessa collapsed in one of the hard, miserably uncomfortable waiting room chairs. "Damn."

"HOW IS SHE?"

Cole took his gaze off the road to glance at his mother in the passenger seat. They were about halfway home and they'd barely spoken. Mainly because Cole had been thinking about the kiss he'd shared with Tessa.

"I don't know. She wasn't back from surgery."

"I meant Tessa."

"Oh. Um, I think she's holding up reasonably well. She's a strong person."

His mother nodded. "I agree. She also strikes me as a woman who knows exactly what she wants in life, Cole. Not that there's anything wrong with that, but I don't think she's the right girl for you."

"Mom, we're working together toward finding Joey's birth father. That's it. Don't read something into this that isn't there."

She obviously didn't believe him. "You're only human, Cole. Today you spent time with a man you once regarded as a second father. He told you your ex-wife is getting married. Now you're sitting here thinking about Tessa. It's perfectly understandable to want to fill the void in your life, but not with Tessa. The two of you are too different."

"Like you and Dad?"

She made a small peep, and Cole knew he'd overstepped into that place his family never talked about. The Dad Zone.

"Sorry, Mom. Forget it. You're right. Tessa and I are oil and water. You should have seen her at Jim and Loretta's today. She made Retta look kinda dowdy." That brought a smile to his mother's face. "Yep, and I looked like the hired help. Or a traveling salesman."

She started to protest but he stopped her. "It's okay, Mom. I made myself fit into that world once and it nearly killed me. I don't plan to ever play that game again. And there isn't anyone—even Tessa—who can change that."

CHAPTER ELEVEN

"BUT WHAT IF what happened yesterday—the bleed in her brain—happens again? Doesn't she need to be in a hospital?"

The patient liaison had called the motel just after seven the next morning to set up a meeting between Autumn and Tessa and the doctor who was in charge of Sunny's case. Since they'd only been given an hour's notice, they'd been forced to bring Joey with them.

The child was fidgeting on Autumn's lap while Tessa tried to take notes.

"Mrs. Barnes, your daughter's condition is stable. We expect to see continued improvement, but there really isn't anything more we can do for her here." The doctor, a middle-aged man of Middle Eastern descent who spoke with a thick accent, seemed genuinely concerned about her sister's well-being. "Acute-care facilities serve one purpose. When we've done all we can do, we pass along the patient to others who are trained to specifically meet the needs of patients who are like your daughter—in transition."

He looked at Joey. "And in a smaller, less restricted setting, you'd be able to reintroduce her to her son."

Tessa was all for that. Last night, as she'd sat at her sister's bedside, she'd had the gut feeling that having Joey visit would help bring Sunny back to them. She'd pleaded her case with the nurses, and while sympathetic to her argument, they had a long list of reasons why he shouldn't come into the highly sterile setting. But once Sunny was moved…

"Where will she go? Could we take her home?" she asked.

He glanced at her chart. "You live in Oregon? No. That's not possible. An airplane ride…" He shook his head. "Mrs. Rodriguez with Patient Services will give you a list of facilities in the area. For now, I think you should stay close by. Is there anything else you want to ask me?"

Tessa couldn't think. She felt more drained and defeated than any other time in her life. Even when her family had been homeless and destitute. At least then they'd all been together. Now they were living out of a suitcase and Sunny was going wherever the vagaries of the health insurance system sent her.

They thanked him and walked to the elevator. Instead of going directly to the Patient Services floor, Tessa said, "Let's go outside and talk. I can't think in here."

Autumn nodded. Once outside the massive brick building, they followed the sidewalk that led to a courtyard near the multistory parking garage, pausing so Joey could watch a medical helicopter circle and land. As he chattered, they found a quiet spot and sat on an empty bench.

Her mother heaved a long, weary sigh. "I guess we should have seen this coming."

Tessa nodded.

Autumn's eyes filled with tears. "What if she doesn't…"

Tessa hugged her close and patted her back. "No. Don't even say it. This might be a great move. Less noise and chaos around her. Joey can visit. We'll get her back, Mom."

"Thank you, Tessa. For everything. I couldn't do this alone."

"That wouldn't happen."

"But what about when you have to go home? I know how important your business is to you."

Tessa faked a smile. "Hey, this is my month off, remember? Marci can handle things. That's what partners do."

Although Tessa was worried about that, too. The last couple of times she and Marci had talked, Tessa had sensed there was something her partner wasn't telling her.

They sat without talking for a few minutes, both lost in thought. Then Tessa's cell phone rang. She looked at the caller ID. A local number she didn't recognize. "Hello?"

"Tessa? This is Annie. Cole's sister. He told me about Sunny's surgery. Is she okay?"

"Yes, actually, she's doing better. In fact, they're planning to move her to another facility."

"That's great. I bet you're so relieved."

"We are, but this is new territory for us. You don't

know anything about convalescent hospitals in the area, do you?"

"No, but I know someone who does. My friend Becky is a nurse and she's got tons of connections. I'll call her as soon as we hang up and see what she has to say."

"Thanks, Annie. One of the key things we tell our clients is never go into a meeting blind."

"Sounds like good advice. Don't agree to anything until you hear from me."

She closed the phone and looked at her mother. "She's going to call me back with a couple of recommendations. Why don't we take a walk while we wait." She stood and held out her hand to her nephew, who still insisted on wearing his Davy Crockett cap.

The scruffy-looking hunk of fake fur made her think of Cole, not that he'd been far from her mind. She'd kissed him. Big mistake.

"Mom, I didn't mention this last night—you were too wiped out—but Cole has a lead on the G-Man. There's a chance he might be a singer–guitar player at a joint near where Sunny used to live."

"He's a musician?" she asked, stopping abruptly.

Joey looked at her curiously.

"Sounds that way. Hopefully, a better one than Zeb."

Autumn gave her a stern, reproachful glare. "Your stepfather was incredibly talented. He played five instruments. He should have—"

"I know, Mom. He should have been rich and famous, but he wasn't. He threw his life away on a dream and when he couldn't stand the reality of that, he escaped into drugs. Sunny and I both saw him shooting heroin." She shook her head. "I can't believe she'd get involved with a musician. I'm tempted to stop looking for him. None of us, especially Joey, needs another Zeb in our lives."

Autumn grabbed Tessa by the arm and shook her with a fierceness that surprised her. "That's not your decision to make, Tessa Jean. I was against this in the beginning, but now that you've started searching for this man, you can't just stop because you don't approve of what he does for a living."

Tessa started to argue, but her phone interrupted them. She brushed off her mother's hand and pulled the phone into view. "It's Annie."

"Hello?" She listened intently. "Really? That sounds impressive. I'll do my best. Tell your friend how much we appreciate her help. Thanks, Annie. I'll let you know what happens."

She closed the phone and looked at her mother. "The place we want is called Horizon."

"DID YOU HEAR the news?"

Cole craned his neck to look at his sister, who was peeking around the back of his throne. He'd been on duty for well over an hour and was already thinking the night would never end. "Um…no, what news?" he hissed, balancing a six-year-old girl named Brianna on his knee as she prattled without pausing to take a breath, naming toy after toy, as though she'd memorized the entire Toys 'R Us catalog.

"Becky got Sunny into Horizon."

"Becky Parker, I mean, Howard?" He had a bad habit of calling Becky by her maiden name since he'd known her in high school and hadn't ever warmed up to her ex-husband. In his opinion, his friend Luke really blew it when he let Becky get away.

"Of course Becky Howard. Who else do you know who's a nurse and has connections with the new crème de la crème health-care facility?"

He knew Becky was a nurse, but he also knew she wasn't the type to toot her own horn. How was he supposed to know she had an in at Horizon? Even though she was his sister's best friend, their busy lives seldom crossed. She had a son in high school and he hadn't been to any local games since he moved back.

"And I wan' three Bratz dolls," Brianna said, tugging on his fake beard. "Mommy says they're ugly but I want 'em anyway."

"Three. Got it. What else?" To Annie, he whispered, "So, Sunny's doing better? She must be if they want to move her. I tried Tessa's cell a couple of times today, but she didn't pick up and hadn't called me back before I got here."

"Not surprising. The paperwork was a nightmare from what Becky told me. And the co-pay is substantial, but Tessa did it. They got her moved, and Sunny is stable."

"And I wanna Barbie princess dress with crystal slippers that will make me taller."

He gave the child his full attention. "Why do you want to be taller?"

"So I can beat up Hogan. He's my brother. He fights with me. If I was taller, I could win him."

The bloodthirsty tone of her statement obviously required some Santaly response, but he wasn't sure what. "Um, you know, um, Brianna, Santa doesn't bring gifts to children who beat up their siblings."

Her bottom lip started to quiver. "He starts it."

Oh, crap, not a crier. "Well, just promise you won't hit him with your crystal shoes, okay?"

She nodded, but still looked about two seconds away from bawling.

"Good." He handed her a candy cane. "Smile for the camera."

She quickly slipped off his lap and raced to her mother, who would no doubt get an earful on the way home. He quickly motioned Melody over. "Can Santa take a quick break?"

"Sure," she said, lending a shoulder for him to hold on to as he stepped off the dais. "We've had an awesome night. The pictures are turning out great, Cole."

"Thanks to you," he told her. "You've really got all the ins and outs of that new camera down, haven't you?"

She looked pleased by his praise, and walked to the head of the line to break the news that Santa needed a breather.

He motioned for Annie to follow him, and once they were behind the curtain of the makeshift changing room, he removed his beard. He scratched his jaw and groaned in bliss. "This thing itches. I don't know how Ray stood it all these years."

"He has a big heart. Just like you," she said. "I'm doing a story for the paper and everybody has said good things about you. The kids seem to like you better than Ray."

Cole clutched at his chest as if gasping for breath. "No. Don't say that. Ray is a god. The man has buns of steel," he said, rubbing his tush.

She snickered softly. "Yours aren't that bad. I think Tessa likes them. She's here, you know."

"Tonight? You're kidding. Where are Joey and Autumn?"

"At Mom's. She invited them to stay with her. To be closer to Sunny and save the cost of a motel."

"What? When? Why wasn't I told?"

Annie shushed him. "Not so loud. There are children out there. I'm telling you now. I guess Mom figured she could have guests without getting your approval. After all, she had mine."

Her teasing didn't mitigate the nervous feeling in his chest. First, his mother warns him about getting too close to Tessa, then she invites the whole family to move in? He didn't get it. "For how long?"

Annie shrugged carelessly. "Why do you care? You don't visit all that often."

He didn't like the way she was staring at him. She could read him too easily. "I just don't want Mom to overdo it. You know how consuming the bazaar is. And I still don't know why nobody bothered telling me."

"Did you check your messages?"

He looked at the strip of twinkle lights above her

head. She'd left three on his phone but he hadn't listened to any because they weren't from Tessa.

"Well, there you go. If people listened to me more often, they'd know stuff. Like, Mom's excited to have a child in the house over the holidays. Plus, she said she felt a real connection with Autumn. You know, Mom could use a friend. I'm going to be busy with the baby, and you're wrapped up in all your projects…"

He wasn't sure he agreed. If the worst happened— if Sunny died—then these people would disappear out of their lives just as quickly as they'd appeared. His mother didn't need that kind of complication in her life. *Neither do I.*

"You're thinking too hard, Santa," his sister said, giving him a poke in the shoulder. "Mom says you're skipping out of Saint Nick duty to help Tessa look for Joey's papa. What about the big game? Is she invited?"

"That's Wednesday. And she already told me she doesn't play. I didn't write down the quote, but it went something like, 'Only a fool would risk losing his hard-earned money on a game of chance.'"

Annie's eyes opened wide. "Whoa. Not exactly a sentiment that would help her fit in around here, is it?"

"My point exactly. Now, I'd better get back outside."

He reapplied his beard and threw open the curtain. Tessa was standing less than a foot away. Same leather jacket, only this time it was tied around her waist. The sleeves of her white, crewneck sweater were pushed up and in her hand was the digital camera he'd seen that first night.

Had she overheard his conversation with his sister? What had he said? Anything stupid?

"Hi, Tessa," Annie said, pushing past him. "Are Autumn and Joey settled in?"

"Yes. Thanks to you and your mom. I was looking for her. She wasn't at the food booth." She took a step closer, and Cole could see how tired she looked.

Annie shook her head. "She's like a ringmaster of a circus when this bazaar is going on, isn't she, Cole? I can't keep up with her. I just dropped by to grab a couple of crowd shots for the paper. Gotta remind people to support the cause." She paused, staring at the camera in Tessa's hand. "Are you any good with that? We pay a pittance for freelance shots."

Tessa shook her head. "It's a hobby. I like photography, but it's not something you can make a living doing."

"Tell that to Annie Leibovitz—my hero, if not my namesake." She let out a sigh. "Ask Cole. He'll tell you. I'm lucky if the shot is in focus and everyone has their heads." With a laugh, she wiggled her fingers in "toodle-loo" fashion and walked away.

Out of the corner of his eye, he spotted Melody motioning for him. "I have to get back to work. Ho, ho, ho and all that. But…are you okay? You look almost as wiped out as you did the first night you were here." He touched her shoulder. Surely the costume's clumsy white felt gloves would keep him from feeling anything. He was wrong and immediately dropped his hand.

She stepped back, too. "I'm fine. Just too much

coffee today. Can't get my mind to shut off. I thought the fresh air and exercise would help."

He headed toward his dais in the roped-off area. "I'll be done in half an hour or so if you want me to walk you home. I know a shortcut."

"Okay. I'll tell you what I found out today about the bar where the G-man might be singing."

He signaled Melody to come help him up the steps—the combination of oversize boots and fuzzy beard obscuring his vision made the climb treacherous. Tessa jumped forward, lending her shoulder for support while placing a hand under his elbow to guide him.

Damn. She was wearing the same perfume. The one that made his mind go soft and fuzzy. "How'd you find the place?"

"MapQuest and luck. Big Bubba's Barbecue and Hoedown. Seems to fit the criteria, but I couldn't call because they're closed on Mondays and Tuesdays."

She led the way to his chair and moved aside so he could sit. A young mother was waiting—a plump pink bundle in her arms—at the foot of the steps. Tessa adroitly slipped away with a soft "I'll catch up with you later, Santa. Have fun."

To his surprise, he did. How much of that was because he'd see Tessa when his gig was over, he didn't want to think about.

CHAPTER TWELVE

"WELL, LOOK AT Y'ALL, Miss Holiday Spirit. Come on in."

Cole opened the door wide so Tessa could step into the spacious foyer. A Navajo-print rug that she hadn't noticed the last time she was there covered the tile almost from wall to wall. "Thanks. I can stay for a few minutes. Like I told you on the phone, your mother is filling in for someone at the refreshments booth and she needed me to deliver the food she made for your poker party."

That wasn't her only reason for agreeing to drive to Cole's house, but it was the only one she'd admit to. Privately, she planned to hang around long enough to sneak a few photos of Cole and his friends. If any turned out, she'd frame them as thank-you gifts for his and June's amazingly kind and generous hospitality.

"There's a big pot on the floor behind the driver's seat and a couple of bags of ice in the trunk," she told him as he closed the door.

"Great. I'll get them in a second. What have you got there? Can I help?"

She held up two plastic grocery bags. "Snacks. Your

sister said to get anything that was extra spicy and had plenty of hydrogenated oil. The unhealthier the better."

He let out a hoot and relieved her of her burden. "And what's that?"

She shifted the two-foot-tall cardboard box so she could hold it out to him with both hands. "A small, silly gift. I didn't see any holiday decorations around when I was here on Sunday so I picked this up at the bazaar last night. June brought it home so you wouldn't see it."

After bumping into Cole and Annie, she'd wandered through the booths. The little ceramic tree she purchased had reminded her of Cole, lonely but spunky.

"Really? Can I open it?"

She nodded. "That's the point. It won't do much good after Christmas."

He led the way to the kitchen. The place looked spotless and smelled like pine cleaner. Her ex-boyfriend had been a slob.

Cole slid the plastic bags to one side and used his fingernail to cut the tape on the top of the box. "Look at this. It's beautiful. And it plugs in," he added, waving the cord for emphasis.

The tree's creator had painted it a deep, authentic-looking green and added glittering gold ropes and brightly colored ornaments, while leaving holes at various increments to accomodate a strand of multicolored twinkle lights.

"She had another version that worked with tea candles, but you don't strike me as the tea-candle type."

"I'm not even going to ask why, but this is great. I've

been so busy it never crossed my mind to go to the storage unit and see if Crystal left me any of our ten thousand or so Christmas lights. Thank you." He leaned over and kissed her cheek. Friendly. Smart.

"You can hang up your coat if you want. I think I'll set this on the mantel. Add a little Christmas to the place."

She shrugged out of her coat and made the return trip to the foyer. She could see him carefully unraveling the cord, making sure the tree was secure before he plugged it in.

"Your mother sent a pot of something that smells so good I almost pulled over to taste it," she called, looking around for a closet. She didn't see a door nearby, but she spotted a three-dimensional wall sculpture shaped like a tree, with carved dowels sticking out. A cowboy hat occupied one spot. A faded wheat-colored work jacket another.

"A coat tree," she exclaimed. "That's so cool." Digging into her purse, she pulled out her camera and took several shots. "Where'd you get it?"

He joined her, hands in his back pockets. "I made it," he said nonchalantly. "Mostly out of scraps. The body is oak. I lost a couple trees when the excavators came through. Hated to waste the wood."

She turned the camera on him and snapped two shots in quick succession. "You're an artist."

He shook his head. "Just a carpenter." He reached for the doorknob. "I'll go get the beans. Excuse me."

Cole was grateful for the reason to leave. He wasn't an artist and he didn't like it when people suggested he was. He did a few creative things with wood, but his father had been a true master craftsman, fat lot of good it had done him. Cole wasn't like his father. He worked in the same profession, but that was it.

He stumbled over a break in the concrete walkway that he was still waiting for Ron to fix, but managed not to fall on his face with his mother's pot of beans in his hands. Tessa was waiting on the porch to open the door for him. She followed him in.

After he'd set the pot on the stove and turned on the burner, he opened the bags of chips. "How's Sunny doing?"

"Better than expected. The nurses are wonderful and very open to visitors. They play music for her and do lots of movement exercises so her muscles don't atrophy. They encouraged us to bring Joey in to see her. Now, *that* was scary. After all, how do you explain to a two-year-old that Mommy can't wake up?"

He had no idea. The image of Sunny, pale and lifeless, was imprinted on his brain. Poor Joey. "How'd it go?"

"It was intense," she said, ripping open one of the bags she'd brought. "I held him while he touched her face. I told Sunny he was there, and that he missed her very much. He threw a fit when we started to leave. That was hard, but we're going to take him back every day. I swear she sensed his presence."

"I'd like to see her again, if that's okay." He passed her an empty serving bowl for the chips then opened the refrigerator. "Can I get you something to drink?"

"Nothing yet, thanks. And, please, feel free to visit

anytime. Becky—who, by the way, is wonderful—believes the more contact with loved ones the better."

He stirred the beans one more time, even though they didn't need stirring. He wasn't sure why he was nervous around her. Maybe because he'd seen her naked the night before…in his dream.

"Have a seat. My boss's wife decided she wanted new bar stools to go with her new table, so he brought the old ones to work this morning. Hand-me-downs, but beggars can't be choosers. Are you sure I can't get you something to drink? How 'bout a beer? We have Shiner Bock and…Shiner Bock."

She laughed, but she also sat. "A beer sounds good, actually. What time will your guests arrive? I don't want to be in the way."

After snatching two bottles from the cooler—damn, he couldn't forget about the bags of ice in her trunk—he opened them then sat at a stool at the end of the bar so he could look at her. She seemed as relaxed as he'd ever seen her. "Cheers," he said, toasting his bottle against hers. "And thanks for bringing holiday cheer into my house."

"You're welcome. It's the least I could do." She opened a second bag and dumped the contents into another bowl, then passed it to him. "How many people will be here tonight?" she asked. "I only brought four bags of munchies."

Cole took a handful of corn nuts before answering. "Eight or ten. It varies."

"Are the three I met the other day coming?" she asked.

"Let me see if I can remember their names. Blake, your brother-in-law. Brady, the athlete. And…Luke, the army guy. Right?"

"Perfect. Do you have a photographic memory?"

"Not even close. Just something that comes in handy in business. But you probably know that from being in real estate."

He did, but putting names with faces had never been his strongest skill. "My boss is coming," he said, returning to the guest list. "And an old friend who was one of the original Wild Bunch."

"The one whose mother owned the bar where you used to have your games?"

He took a swallow of beer to wash down the corn nuts. "Yeah. Jake's uncle took over after Lola died. And slowly ran it into the ground. Now Verne's gone, too. And Jake's made it clear he plans to sell the place."

"Would you rather he didn't?"

Cole didn't know what he wanted. A part of him was relieved when Jake returned to town. Naturally, he was happy to see his best friend alive and well, but they had yet to have a real conversation. And the rumors kept flying about Jake's success. At this point, it was hard not to be pissed. "I don't think I have much say in the matter. But I can't blame Jake for hating River Bluff. People in small towns are quick to assign labels."

"People in big cities, too," she said softly.

He waited for her to elaborate but she didn't. Instead, she asked, "His mom ran a bar…. What did his father do?"

Cole shrugged, his hands palm up. "That depends on who you ask. Lola never told anybody his name. Gossip has always maintained it was Wade Barstow—one of the richest men in town—but they didn't have DNA testing back then."

"They do now," she said, patting her purse. The strap was hanging over the back of the stool.

He couldn't picture Jake rounding up the most likely suspects and asking for their spit. He shook his head. "Water under the bridge, as they say. Muddy water. I don't blame Jake for not wanting to move back, but the Wild Card is sitting on a nice piece of riverfront. If he fixed it up, he could make a lot of money on it. Plus, give us all a decent place to play cards."

Pooch gave a yip, which told him his guests were starting to arrive. There was one thing he wanted to pin down while they were alone. "Are we still on for tomorrow night?"

They'd discussed a tentative plan last night when he'd walked her home. "Yes. Did you call Big Bubba's?"

He nodded. "The owner was out of town, but I talked to the bartender. He said a guitar player works there off and on. First name Joel. Couldn't remember his last name, but he thought the guy lives in Helotes."

"Helotes?"

"A town you pass through on your way to River Bluff."

She sat forward, elbows on the bar. He could almost see her visualizing a map of the area.

"The bartender also told me this Joel guy plays at a cowboy bar in Bandera during the week. They get some good talent at the Eleventh Street and apparently he's the opening act."

"He could be playing there right now?"

He shook his head. "I called. The headliner canceled tonight, but they do have a fellow named Joel West scheduled to play tomorrow."

She looked at him but didn't say anything for a full minute. Her eyes shimmered with emotion. "He's the G-man, isn't he? I'm excited and thrilled—for Joey's sake—but also terrified."

They heard the sound of car doors slamming. His guests were here. He got up, but didn't walk away even though loud pounding on the door was followed by Ron's voice shouting, "Hey, open up. Where's the beer?" He wanted to be sure she wouldn't use her Internet skills to track this guy and see him while Cole was at work. "So we're on for tomorrow?"

She looked away and shrugged.

"Tessa?" He stepped back to her stool and made her look at him. "They'd call that a tell if you were playing poker. Are we going to Bandera to find this guy tomorrow night or not?"

A second round of pounding echoed through the empty living room. "Cole? Get off the john and open the door."

She glanced nervously over her shoulder. "Your guests are here."

"That's just Ron. He can wait. Something's going on. What?"

She swallowed. "Nothing to do with you. It's my

problem. My late stepfather played guitar in a couple of bands. It's a crappy life for a kid. Ever since I found out the G-man was a musician I started questioning whether or not I should contact him. Maybe Joey *is* better off not knowing his father."

"Hey, Lawry, what the hell? Have you got a woman in there?"

Cole rolled his eyes. "I'll be right back."

Ron's timing sucked, but then when didn't it? Cole let him in and greeted two men a few paces behind on the sidewalk. Ed Minor, Melody's dad, and Harold Knutson, Sally's husband. He assumed the two friends had driven out together. "Welcome, gentlemen. Food and drink in the kitchen. Make yourselves at home while we wait for the others."

In the distance, he could see two more sets of headlights approaching the turnoff to his driveway. It looked as if they were going to have a good crowd tonight. Too bad. All he wanted to do was talk to Tessa. He'd never seen her look as vulnerable and unsure of herself. Self-doubt was something he knew all about. The legacy of a loser father. But despite the mixed feelings he had for his father, he couldn't imagine what it would have been like never to have known Tim Lawry at all. He planned to tell her that…just as soon as he lost his stake.

TESSA STARTED playing hostess the minute the first guest entered the kitchen. Cole's boss. Ron Something. She took the initiative because moving around was far better than sitting on a stool being subtly scrutinized by a group of men who wanted to know how she fit in their friend's life.

"I don't," she would have told them if any had asked.

They didn't. Not even Ron, who seemed to have an opinion about everything. "Hey, I read about your sister in Annie's column. That sucks, man. How's she doing?" he asked between pulls on his beer.

"Better. We just moved her into Horizon."

He rubbed his thumb and first two fingers together. "Whoa. What bank did you have to rob? I heard that place is ex…pen…sive," he said, drawing out the word.

He was right. She already had a call into her bank to set up a line of credit on her condo. But she didn't tell him that. "It's her best chance of making a full recovery," she said before shifting her attention to two older men who walked in carrying beer to be added to the cooler and an interesting-looking dip.

"Hello, there. I'm Harold and this is Ed. My wife sent this—cream cheese with habañera jelly. Watch out. It's hot."

She thanked him and made room for the plate on the counter. A moment later, the clerk from the motel she and Joey had stayed at when they first came to town walked in. She couldn't remember his name, but when he tipped an imaginary hat in greeting, it came to her. Barney. Barney Fife to go with Ron Hayward. Welcome to Mayberry.

New arrivals continued to crowd in. Cole tried to stick by her to make introductions, but he was also busy setting up the game. After about half an hour of eating and chatting, the men started to filter into the dining room. The loud roar of a motorcycle engine announced the arrival of the last straggler. A man in black leather. The infamous Jake, she guessed.

He looked at her curiously but was called to the table before they could formally meet.

"Let's get this game goin'," Ron called. "I'm here to win some money."

Tessa declined Cole's invitation to join them. "Thanks, but I was warned in advance to keep my money in my pocket if I didn't want to lose it."

"Has my wife been spreading rumors?" Blake asked.

"There is such a thing as beginner's luck," Brady said. The football player. She remembered that from the other day.

Cole used one of his chips to tap on the table. "She's a spectator, Brady. Like your groupies in Vegas."

The table erupted into laughter. Gradually, the men seemed to lose interest in her as the game got under way. She was intrigued by each man's style and spatial requirements. None was exactly the same. Brady, she noticed, was held in high esteem by all of them. Whether that was because of his former fame or his poker skill, she didn't know.

The two older men—Harold and Ed—were both talkers who had no trouble keeping up—even when the spirited conversation turned risqué.

Blake was the one to bring them back on course. "The game is in play," he said more than once, and his authoritative tone seemed to catch everyone's attention.

Luke was the jokester, she decided, always ready with a quip or pun that sometimes had them all groaning. He was also steadily acquiring the biggest pile of poker chips.

None of the men seemed to eat or drink much—except Ron. His place at the table was marked by wet rings from the many beers he'd consumed, crumbs from his stack of corn chips and a mostly empty bowl that he'd refilled with soup at least twice. The man talked constantly to his seatmates on either side—Harold and Barney. Tessa had a feeling the seating arrangement wasn't an accident.

Cole was sitting next to Jake on the opposite side of the table. Tessa found it interesting that she hadn't seen the two men exchange more than a dozen words. She wondered if Cole was still nursing hurt feelings from being shut out of his friend's life. Tessa could sympathize. She'd never had a close friend other than her sister until she met Marci. Since the wedding last summer, their friendship had changed. Tessa had expected that, but she hadn't been prepared for the strange coolness she'd felt the last time she and Marci spoke. Marci had attributed her ennui to jet lag, but Tessa questioned that.

Since Marci and her husband, Matthew, had spent the month of November vacationing, and she'd returned to Portland the same day Tessa left for Texas, they hadn't seen each other face-to-face in over six weeks. That probably contributed to the strain on their relationship. Marci's text message that morning had read:

busy. tlk soon. best, M.

Instinct told her something was wrong, but she didn't have the energy to deal with long-distance problems. So, she focused on the images on her LCD screen. She tweaked the digital camera's settings to get just the right contrast between the sharp cut of Brady's jaw and the white of his shirt collar.

Click.

Nice. Cole's gonna like that one.

Next, she returned to Jake, whose turn it was to bet. The plain black Harley-Davidson T-shirt he was wearing showed off his sculpted muscles, but nothing about him invited you closer. Despite the fact he was movie-star handsome, he exuded a somber and impenetrable intensity.

She widened the frame to include Cole, who was joking about something with Luke. His easygoing smile seemed as warm and open as his friend's expression was cool and closed. Cole's oatmeal-colored Henley, with sleeves pulled back over his muscular forearms, hid little. The two were as different as black and white.

It struck her that the same applied to her and Cole.

"The bet's to you, Cole."

COLE HEARD HIS NAME but it took him a few seconds to pull his focus away from Tessa, who had been taking pictures since they all sat down at the table. The rest of the guys appeared to have blanked her out, but his powers of concentration seemed to fail him tonight. He couldn't stop following her with his gaze, inhaling her perfume when she came close and smiling at her when their eyes met. He was making a fool of himself and knew it. His friends would never let him live this down.

"Right. Thanks, Ed." He tossed two chips into the pile. "Call."

"Can I get anyone a beer?" Tessa asked. In addition to taking photos, she'd been playing hostess—something none of the regulars were used to.

"I'll take one," Harold chirped. He had one of the highest male voices Cole had ever heard.

Several others—Ron included—indicated they were ready for another, as well. Cole wasn't drinking. He was having a hard enough time staying focused as it was.

"So, Cole," Brady said after she left the room. "I heard Tessa and her family are staying with your mom. How's that working out?"

Cole shrugged, keeping his gaze on the cards as Ed flipped over the river. An ace. His heart rate went up a notch. He'd just filled a full house. Aces over queens. His first decent hand of the night. Unfortunately, he'd been too distracted to have even a wild guess at what anyone else had.

He slid his father's money clip over his hole cards. "You know Mom. She loves fussing over people. Which reminds me, has anyone heard anything about an anonymous donation? Annie said somebody set up a fund at the bank to help the family cover hospital costs."

Luke tugged on the brim of his cowboy hat and slouched lower in his chair. A sure tell. "Raise." But was the tell giving away a clue to his involvement in the donation or because he had a good hand?

Damn.

Brady's wide shoulders lifted and fell with a casual shrug. "I'm not that generous, which is why I'm out." He pushed his cards, facedown, into the pot.

It was Cole's bet. "I'll raise the raise."

Jake folded without comment and excused himself to use the john. Harold groaned and tossed in his cards.

"I knew I got out at the right time," Barney said, leaning back in his chair. "I think I'll get another bowl of beans. Damn, your mom can cook, Cole."

"Bring me one, man," Ron said, carelessly tossing in his hole cards.

After a minute of deliberation, Ed nudged the appropriate number of chips toward the middle. Blake called. Luke raised Cole's raise but didn't go all in.

Tessa returned with the drinks, which she passed out as unobtrusively as possible. "Thanks," Ron said, handing her a chip. "Here's your tip."

"Oh, no…I can't." She tried to give it back.

"Take it. I've been thinking we should hire a girl to work the party. You know, serve drinks, make sandwiches. Your daughter's about the right age, Ed. What do you say? Would you let her come to one of our games?"

Our games? Cole exchanged a look with his brother-in-law. Ron had already drunk a six-pack, and he was growing increasingly louder as his luck went sour.

"Hell, no," Ed said shortly. For an insurance salesman, he was surprisingly laconic.

"Why not?" Ron whined. "We're good guys."

"She's too busy. That reminds me," he said, looking at Cole, "her cheerleading squad was selected to be in Fort Worth for some big competition this weekend and the girl who was taking her place came down with mono. Melody wanted me to ask if you know anybody who could cover for her at the North Pole while she's gone. She doesn't want to let the squad down."

Everyone, even Jake, who was just returning to the room, looked at Tessa. Her beautiful eyes went wide and she discreetly hid her camera behind her back.

"Me? No…not me." She looked at Cole, pleading. "I usually shoot flowers and nature."

"Kids are nature," Ron said, slurring his words.

Ed grimaced. "Didn't mean to put you on the spot, miss. Just didn't want to forget to ask. M'wife says I'd forget to get up in the morning if she didn't wake me."

Tessa smiled. "It's okay. And after everything June has done for my family, I really shouldn't hesitate. I can't be there tomorrow night, but I could work on the weekend."

"That sounds good. She doesn't leave until after school on Friday. Let me give you her cell number so you two can figure out the details."

Luke rapped his knuckles on the table and said in a voice that no doubt made soldiers quake in their boots, "The game, people. We have a second raise. Cole, it's to you."

Cole took a deep breath and pushed in the correct amount of chips. "Call."

Five players had to show their cards. Cole's full house won.

"Oh, baby, that's the nuts," Ron said, cackling.

"You dog. I didn't see that coming." Luke's tone held both praise and surprise.

"Nice playing, Cole," Ed acknowledged. "That'll teach me to bet and talk at the same time. But at least Melody will be happy when I tell her I found a replacement."

Cole accepted the congratulations—and jeers—of his fellow players with equal aplomb. Mostly because his brain was stuck on the fact that Tessa had agreed to fill in at the North Pole the coming weekend. His luck appeared to be changing. But was it for the good?

CHAPTER THIRTEEN

"SO THIS IS BANDERA, huh?" Tessa said, looking out the window of Cole's truck as he turned off State Route 16 onto Main Street. "Your mother said it's called the Cowboy Capital of the World. It doesn't look that much different from River Bluff."

"Bandera has better PR."

She smiled, but it took effort. The day had been long and grueling. Sunny had run a fever in the night. Visitors had to don masks and protective clothing. Joey, who had a runny nose, had had to stay home.

Tessa had almost canceled, but she didn't want Cole to question her motives. Was she avoiding contact with this Joel guy because of his profession? She'd given herself a pep talk that afternoon. Just because Zeb had been a flake who couldn't handle a career in music didn't mean the G-man was a drug addict with no sense of responsibility. But the doubts remained.

"Actually," Cole said, "back in the days of the Western Trail, something like six million longhorns passed through here on their way to market. They hold an annual trail ride every year to commemorate the tradition—and drum up tourism."

To her right stood a handsome courthouse built from the same native limestone she'd had pointed out to her earlier. Its silver-topped dome beamed beneath some well-placed lights. "See that monument? It honors the national and world champion ropers who came from this county."

She glanced at it in passing. The butterflies in her stomach had started line dancing and she couldn't concentrate.

"I think parking will be at a premium if we get any closer," he said, turning down a side street to pull in to a space between two lifted pickup trucks that dwarfed his vehicle. "Good thing I'm a believer in the adage size doesn't matter."

"Unless maybe you're talking about hood ornaments, apparently," she said, pointing to the impressive embellishment affixed to the grille of the truck on the right.

"They don't call 'em longhorns for nothing."

Since the sidewalks in Bandera were on par with the ones in River Bluff, hit and miss, he offered his arm and they walked side by side in the direction of a noisy establishment partway up the next side street.

"I should warn you that people call this the bra bar."

"Do I want to know why?"

"You'll see."

They passed by a carved wooden cigar-store Indian as they approached the entrance to the Eleventh Street Cowboy Bar. A second gate had been set up for people going straight to the back for the entertainment, but Cole took her inside the small building, which looked right out of a western movie set.

The place was packed and the noise deafening but there was a geniality in the air that felt contagious. Cole caught her attention and pointed at the ten-foot ceiling. Several dozen bras dangled like multicolored flags—all colors, sizes and degrees of modesty.

"Oh, my…" Her exclamation was lost in the hum around them, so she was forced to lean closer to say, "What I want to know is who was the first woman to leave her bra behind—and why?"

Cole grinned and shrugged. "Come on. Let's go out back."

After paying the cover charge, they escaped some of the din, but probably not for long. Huge black speakers ringed a wooden dance floor where a dozen or so people were kicking up their heels to a jukebox tune.

"Beer?" he asked.

She nodded. Anything to take the edge off her nerves.

He bought them each a longneck bottle. "Where do you want to sit?"

"As close to the stage as my ears can take. Look at the size of those speakers."

She watched a couple of gals in tight jeans waltz by, giving Cole an appreciative look. She didn't blame them. In snug jeans and a crisply pressed white cotton shirt, he fit right in, even without a hat. She was wearing the same thing she'd had on two days earlier—black slacks, boots and her gray Dolce & Gabbana sweater. She'd never felt more like a city girl.

"There's an open table," he said. They headed in the direction he pointed, detouring slightly to check out a display selling T-shirts and mugs. She assumed the headliners had some merchandizing sideline, but when he pointed to a promotional flier at the very end of the table, her heart started pumping at double speed.

"Oh my God." She grabbed the black-and-white glossy. "This is him. Joel West."

Her knees suddenly felt wobbly. She must have swayed, because Cole grabbed her by the elbow and guided her to a stool at a tall table a few feet away. He pulled another stool up close.

"'Singer-songwriter Joel West hails from Tennessee but proudly claims to be an adopted son of Texas,'" he read aloud.

Tessa studied the face in the studio portrait. Dark sideburns. A ponytail, barely noticeable from the angle of his black Stetson. Wide-set eyes with wispy lashes just like Joey's. Thin eyebrows. Straight, medium-size nose. His smile reminded her of her nephew when he was trying to look innocent but knew he'd done something bad.

"Joey. Joel. Coincidence?" Cole asked. He shook his head.

She flipped over the photo. Printed on the back was contact information and scheduled appearances. Running her finger down the list, she paused on the date of her sister's accident. "She must have been on her way here when she crashed."

"Do you want to try to go backstage before—"

As if on cue, a man in a rhinestone-bedazzled western shirt walked to the microphone midstage and tapped it with his finger. "Is this good to go? Hot damn. Are y'all ready for some mighty fine country music?"

The bare limbs of the trees scattered about the open-air courtyard shook with the roar that went up from the audience. "Then let's get this party started. Our opening act is a fellow some of you have heard before on this stage. We keep asking him back because he's so damn good, and y'all like him so much. So put your hands together to welcome our adopted Texan son, Joel West."

People barely waited for the man to reach the microphone before they headed to the dance floor. Tessa sat up straight and squinted, trying to get a good look at him. The lights and moving bodies made it difficult to see his face.

His first song was a fast one. People were clapping and singing along with the refrain. Tessa thought the tune sounded familiar, but she was more interested in watching him sing than in trying to remember the song. "Let's get closer."

She hadn't danced in years, but something connected with her brain and she moved without conscious thought. Cole took her hand and gave her a quick twirl. She smiled, almost forgetting why she was there until the song stopped and the singer—the man she'd been searching for—stepped to the mic.

"Evenin', folks. I want to thank y'all for coming out." He slid his guitar to his back and tilted his hat back up so he could peer out, blinking against the lights. "I know you're looking forward to tonight's headliners, but it does my poor old heart proud to see this kind of crowd so early."

Tessa used the opening to move within a few steps of the stage. She could barely swallow, and her palms felt damp. Suddenly a pair of strong arms enveloped her. Cole's breath against the side of her neck helped calm her.

When Joel West lifted his chin, the spotlight gave the audience a clear view of his face. His slightly hollowed cheeks lent him a tortured-artist look that Tessa knew would appeal to her sister, but there were no obvious signs of drug or alcohol abuse that Tessa could see. He looked young and healthy, not dissipated and defeated.

"Those of you who have seen me before know that I write most of my own material, but I like to cover the lighter dance songs to keep the blood pumping. And the beer flowing," he added, nodding toward the bar.

"So, if you'll bear with me, here's a belly-rubbing slow dance for all you lovers and wannabe lovers on the dance floor." He seemed to be looking straight at Cole and Tessa when he grinned and nodded. "This one's called 'Someday Sunshine.'"

Tessa let out a gasp.

Joel West didn't hear her since he'd broken into a complicated riff on his guitar. He was talented, but Tessa knew it took more than raw talent to make a living in the music industry. It struck her again that Sunny might have chosen to leave Texas without telling Joel she was pregnant because she was afraid Joey's childhood would turn out like the one she and Tessa had known.

A memory assaulted her. She and Sunny sharing a sleeping bag near a thicket of bushes in a public park because her stepfather had used his share of the money from the band's gig to buy a fix instead of a motel room. The beer she'd sipped started to come back up. She looked around wildly for the restrooms.

"Are you okay?" Cole asked.

She shook her head. "I feel sick. Air. I need air."

Without a second's hesitation, he took her hand and started toward the exit. He grabbed their jackets on the way past. When the doorman insisted on stamping their hands, Cole asked when the next act would start.

"Forty minutes or so."

They didn't stop to put on their coats until they were half a block away. Tessa gulped in the night air, embarrassed and feeling foolish. "Sorry. I don't usually suffer from panic attacks, but I think this qualifies."

"Probably claustrophobia. A couple more beers might have helped," he said lightly. "The river's only about a block or two away. Wanna hang out there until his set is done?"

She nodded but kept her chin down—a sign he'd come to realize meant she was upset and didn't want to give anything away in her eyes. They walked in silence until the din of the bar was just white noise. Before long they could hear night sounds: chirping crickets and frogs, a few barking dogs.

A single streetlight illuminated their way as they approached the water's edge. No cars were parked beyond the entrance shack. No one seemed to be around.

"Very peaceful," she said with a sigh.

"I thought you'd like it. You should come back in the

daytime. The water is a peculiar shade of blue-green that doesn't seem quite real."

She turned abruptly to face him. "Hold me?"

The tremor in her voice that accompanied the question pierced his heart. He pulled her close, then turned their bodies so the breeze hit his back. It wasn't a cold night, but she was shaking. "What's wrong, Tessa?"

"Sunny and I had a big fight on the way to the airport. I thought she was vacillating about telling Joey's father he had a son. She said this was her life, her decision. I...I said that maybe if our mother had told *my* father about me, I wouldn't have had to grow up on the street using every spare penny to buy meds for *her* drug-addict father."

The words were so blunt, her tone so stark Cole wasn't sure what to say or how to respond so he just held her and waited.

"Are you shocked?"

He gently touched the side of her face. "You've met my older sister. She's never been shy about expressing her opinion. I know we've both said things we wished we could take back, and if she were the one in the hospital, I'd feel the same way."

Her eyes closed and she sighed. He didn't kiss her but he wanted to. He pulled her close again and rubbed his hand up and down the back of her soft leather coat. "Tessa, you're not to blame for Sunny's accident. And you said it was her decision to come back to confront the man who got her pregnant. Maybe she was hedging her bets in case she lost her nerve."

He looked at the shadowy reflection on the water's edge. The river flattened out here so there wasn't the slightest sound of trickling, just the occasional hollow rumble of a car crossing the bridge. She took a deep breath and let it out. "We should go back."

He dropped his arms, but waited until she looked at him to say, "Annie did a story on child abuse a while back. The doctor she interviewed said—"

She interrupted him. "I wasn't abused. Zeb was a sweet, likable failure. He probably would have gotten his act together eventually, but he was sick—HIV-positive—for the last ten years of his life. That meant less traveling with the band but more bills. Yes, we were on welfare, but Mom did her best. And I learned at an early age not to rely on someone else to get ahead."

She made a big production of adjusting the strap of her purse across her chest. "As for Joel West, he's exactly the kind of guy I'd expect my sister to fall for, but he's not Joey's daddy until *after* he passes the DNA test. Shall we go collect some saliva?"

They had to walk uphill…on uneven pavement. Even wrapped with an elastic bandage inside his boot, his ankle was throbbing by the time they reached the bar. They showed their stamped hands to the doorman and walked inside. The headliners hadn't started yet, but the DJ had cranked up "Boot Scootin' Boogie" to a fever pitch.

"There!" she shouted over the din.

Joel West was standing about twenty feet away at the walk-up bar with two adoring female fans on either side of him. He didn't seem too interested in either of them, in Cole's opinion.

Tessa picked her way through the growing throng to tap him on the shoulder. Cole couldn't hear what she said, but he watched the man's eyes widen. He pulled back, mouth slack, then he looked at her and said, "You're Sunny's sister? You're Tessa? Holy shit. Where is she?" He quickly looked around. "Do you have any idea how long I've been looking for her? She left without a word. Just like that. Gone. When I get my hands on her…"

He didn't complete the threat, but Cole could tell it was empty.

"Please tell me she's here. I gotta talk to her."

Tessa looked at Cole. "Where can we go that isn't so loud?"

He thought a moment. "There's an all-night truck stop on the way out of town. It's not fancy, but…"

Once she nodded, he gave the name of the place to Joel, who agreed to meet them there in fifteen minutes. The man obviously had a lot of questions, but Tessa wisely refused to say any more. They needed privacy for conversation—especially the kind she was about to have with Joel West.

THE QUESTIONS STARTED flying the minute the musician joined her and Cole at a quiet table well away from other diners. The waitress had left menus and three cups of coffee then disappeared. Tessa was far too nervous to drink anything, even water.

"Where is she? Why didn't she come herself? Who are you?" The last was directed at Cole.

"Cole Lawry. A friend."

"Lawry. I remember that name. You worked with Sunny at the real estate place. She said you helped her get the job. What's going on, man?"

Tessa sat forward, hands folded in front of her. "Cole's name was in Sunny's journal. He's where I started, and he's been kind enough to help me look for you."

Joel shook his head in confusion. "Look for me? Didn't Sunny tell you where to find me? She called me right after Thanksgiving. Said she wanted to talk, but then she never showed up. I didn't know what to think. Has something…happened?"

Cole explained about the car accident because Tessa couldn't get the words out.

"A c-coma? Oh my God, I've been so mad at her and all this time she's been in the hospital? I must be the biggest jerk in Texas. Where is she? I have to go there. Now."

Tessa reached out to stop him from leaving. She had a good feeling about this man. He truly seemed to care about Sunny, despite whatever made her leave in the first place.

"Can we talk first? Visiting hours are over, but I'll set something up in the morning. None of us will try to stop you from seeing her, but there's something I have to know—and I want the truth."

He sat back down and looked her straight in the eye. "Shoot."

"Why did she leave Texas without telling you she was pregnant?"

His jaw dropped open and he looked from her to Cole and back again. His brow wrinkled as he tried to grapple with the question. "Pregnant? Sunny was pregnant?" He drew in a ragged breath. "Did she…did she have the baby?"

Tessa nodded. "Yes. Joey. He's nineteen months old."

"Sh-she kept him?"

"Sunny and Joey have been living with our mother in Oregon. She got a part-time job at the same organic-seed farm where Mom works."

He sat back and closed his eyes. "A son. I have a son," he murmured softly.

His eyes looked misty when he opened them. "What happened between us—why she left—was all my fault." His speaking voice was just as fluid and rich as his singing voice. "I blew it. I just had no idea how badly."

She and Cole looked at each other a moment as they waited for him to explain.

"I've been writing songs most of my life. Selling a song and making money from it is like pissing on a wildfire, if you'll excuse the crude expression. Most songwriters go a lifetime without seeing one of their songs recorded and on the charts. Well, about a month after I met Sunny, I had my first big break. At least, it felt big at the time," he said ruefully. "I found an agent to represent me. He was all talk. Big talk. I was convinced it was only a matter of time before I was living in Nashville and raking in megadollars."

He shook his head. Without his hat, she could see his tightly curled hair that he kept slicked down and pulled into a ponytail at the base of his neck. Now she knew where Joey got his curls.

"About a week before she left, Sunny asked me how I felt about kids. I figured she was talking in general terms, and since I didn't want to be dragging a family all the way to Nashville, I told her I didn't want any."

He looked despondent. "Do you ever have a moment when you look back and wish you could cut out your tongue? God, I was an arrogant ass."

"The agent didn't come through for you?" Cole asked.

"The agent was a fraud. I figured that out when he asked me for a thousand dollars to hire some 'professionals' to record my song. I may not be Hank Williams, but I am a professional. And if my voice won't sell my song, neither will someone else's."

He drank from his cup. "After she left, I went off on a bender. Hitchhiked back East to my folks. Sat around feeling miserable and misunderstood until they finally kicked my sorry ass out the door. I decided to give Nashville a try anyway. Got invited to play with a band. Stayed with them about a year. They had a recording contract and tested out one of my songs. Believe it or not, it's on the album. But the band broke up. The lead singer wanted a solo career. He wasn't interested in my kind of music. I get a few bucks now and then in royalties. I learned a lot, and I decided I like Texas. So, I came back."

"You never looked for Sunny?"

"I did. I don't know that much about the Internet, but I tried. There's no Sunny Barnes listed in Portland. I even typed in Tessa Barnes. No luck. You're unlisted?"

"Mom and Sunny don't live in Portland. The farm is about thirty miles away. Closer to the coast. And Sunny and I had different fathers. My last name is Jamison."

"Oh, sure. I think I knew that. So, where does that leave us? Do I get to see your sister and my son or are we going to have a pissing contest?"

She pulled a business card the Horizon administrator had given her out of her purse. "Visiting hours start at ten. I'll put your name on the visitors' list."

"Ten. I'll be there."

"If Mom agrees, I'll bring Joey along to meet you, but she's very protective of him and hasn't been that thrilled by my attempts to find his father. She might want to wait until after we get the DNA results back."

He stared at the card, his hand trembling slightly. "DNA. Saliva, right? Can they do it at the hospital? How long does it take? If he's mine, I want to know."

Tessa looked at Cole, and was rewarded with a nod that told her her quest was over. She opened her purse and took out the plastic bag that had originally held three kits. Two remained. "My gut says you're Joey's father, but this will put a lot of minds at ease. Cole, you're my witness."

Joel swabbed the inside of his cheek, then they sealed and labeled the sample. "There's an express drop-off by the post office in River Bluff," Cole told them. "We can swing by on the way home."

Tessa was strangely reluctant to leave, but she was certain she'd see Joel West in the morning. Maybe, she told herself, he'd be the one to get through to her sister. Like Sleeping Beauty and the Prince.

CHAPTER FOURTEEN

TESSA STOOD AT the island counter of June Lawry's small but homey kitchen to scrutinize the glossy prints she'd picked up an hour earlier. She'd been delighted to discover that River Bluff's lone grocery store–slash–pharmacy had a digital-processing lab. She'd planned to edit and print once she got home, but by deleting shots and transferring many to a CD, she was able to free up space on the camera's memory card for her volunteer "job" that night.

Not bad, she thought, thumbing through the prints. Several were definitely frameworthy.

She paused to look at the shot of Joey on Santa's lap. Had it really been only eight days since she met Cole? So much had happened in such a short time. She wondered if she'd have talked herself out of contacting Joel West if Cole hadn't been at her side. Distinctly possible.

She stacked the shots like a dealer with a deck of cards and glanced at the clock on the wall. Nearly five. Cole was due to pick her up in forty-five minutes. The North Pole opened at six, and she wanted to get some test shots to figure out where to stand and which setting worked best, given the lighting.

Since her clothing options were limited, she'd dressed in her standard black jeans, boots and a red sweater she'd borrowed from her mother. June had handed her a cheerful green-and-white-striped apron and a green felt elf hat to wear on the job. And dangly earrings made of tiny silver bells.

She shook her head and smiled at the sound. Joey had loved them, so she was sure the other children visiting Santa tonight would, too.

Joey was in the living room watching a Christmas video that June had brought home from the library. Tessa assumed Autumn was nearby, as well. She'd barely let Joey out of her sight after agreeing to introduce him to Joel West. Or Westerfield, as he'd been christened. "Fewer syllables sell better," he'd explained.

Tessa liked him. She gave Sunny credit for choosing a decent guy with a good head on his shoulders—even if it had been temporarily swollen with promises of fame and fortune.

She pictured their meeting that morning at Horizon. He'd been waiting when she arrived. She'd added his name to the visitors' list and led him down the hall to Sunny's private room.

He'd dropped to his knees at her bedside, gripping her hand as he wept.

Tessa hadn't stuck around to see more. Instead, she'd called her mother to set up a meeting between Joey and Joel. She'd expected Autumn to argue with her and insist they wait for the DNA results, but instead her mother agreed that Joel should follow Tessa back to June's. When introduced for the first time, Joey had acted shy, as he usually did around men he didn't know, but after about ten minutes his curiosity won out. Before long, father and son were playing tag amongst the outdoor Christmas decorations in June's yard.

Joel had only stayed about an hour. He'd admitted to feeling conflicted about where he needed to be and had asked permission to visit Sunny again on his way back to San Antonio. He had a gig that weekend he couldn't cancel. "Especially now," he'd added. "If I have a family to take care of, I'm gonna need the money."

Her mother walked into the kitchen. She looked tired, but at least the dark circles under her eyes had disappeared. "Are you nervous?"

"Does it show?"

Autumn poured herself a cup of coffee from the insulated pot June left on the counter. "Of course not, but I know you."

Tessa didn't argue the point.

Autumn thumbed through the photos with one hand, pausing to take a hard look at several. She pulled out the group shot of Cole and his buddies at the poker table. It was one of Tessa's favorites. "Are these the Wild Bunch?"

Tessa stepped closer and pointed out each man by name, recalling what she could of their jobs and backgrounds.

"And most of them have been friends since elementary school, June said." Autumn sighed wistfully. "I wish you and Sunny could have had that kind of childhood, instead of traveling with the band, always on the move. You don't think Joel West is like that, do you? Like Zeb. Always looking for his big break."

Or next score. "No. Joel doesn't remind me of Zeb in any way." She tried to keep her tone flat. They'd been down this road too many times.

Her mom looked at her sharply. "Don't say his name like that. Zeb loved you and Sunny with all his heart, and it wasn't all bad. You got to see the country. And meet a lot of interesting people. Do you remember when the band opened for Alice Cooper?"

"*No.*" *But I remember eating cold pizza for breakfast when Zeb was too hungover to get up and you were hassling with the other band members over his share of the receipts.* Somebody always withheld something to cover Zeb's most recent drug buy.

Tessa hesitated a moment then walked to the round oak table under the window. Twilight was falling but the Christmas lights tacked up outside glowed through the curtains. She motioned for her mother to sit with her. "Mom, this probably isn't the time or place, but all this talk about paternity issues has made me wonder. Are you sure you can't remember anything about my father?"

Mom rested her cheek on her hand and sighed. She was still a beautiful woman despite the gray in her hair, which she refused to color. Petite, like Sunny, with small, fine-boned features. A free-spirited hippie chick, who'd spent her youth flitting from one guy to the next.

"You have no idea how badly I wish I knew, but I was so young and mixed-up. I was sixteen when I ran away from the group home the court placed me in after my mother died. My dad hadn't been around for years. Dead? Or just gone? Mama never said. Then this rock band came through town and I turned into a teenage groupie."

While she admired her mother's courage, she still wanted to shake her. "What was the name of the band?"

"I told you, Tess, it doesn't matter. I didn't stay with them for long. I was young and not unattractive. Guys would ask me to come with their band and I'd go. A few weeks, a month, a whole tour. Depended."

"On the quality and quantity of the drugs," Tessa murmured.

Mom touched her arm. "I'm not proud of any of this, but I stopped cold turkey when I found out I was pregnant with you. I got a job working for a booking agent and I made a home for us."

"Until you met Zeb." Tessa glanced at her watch. "I shouldn't have brought it up. Like I said, the DNA thing got me thinking. Don't worry about it."

"I'm sorry, Tessa. I really am. But I'm glad you went looking for Joel. It was the right thing to do—for everyone's sake."

"Thanks."

Neither spoke for several minutes.

Tessa finally picked up her camera—her most dependable escape route.

"You'll do a wonderful job," Autumn said. "Zeb always thought you'd make a great photographer."

Tessa stood and reached for her purse. Anger seethed just beneath the surface of her skin. How easy her mother made that sound. "Forget about business, Tessie," Zeb had said over and over. "You have an artist's soul. You come alive when you have a camera in your hand."

"Photography is my hobby," she said stiffly. "That's all it will ever be, Mom. You can't make a living at it."

"How do you know? Have you ever tried? You're so wrapped up in your company you barely have time to take pictures of Joey."

"Because if I didn't, what would we do about health insurance, car payments and taxes?"

"Of course, you're right. Where would Sunshine be now if you…"

Tessa could see she was too choked up to go on. She patted her mother's shoulder. "Sorry. I appreciate the compliment, but one thing I learned from Zeb was how difficult it is to make a living in the arts. It's a nice dream, and maybe I'll make enough to retire early, but in the meantime, I have to work."

She squeezed her mom's shoulder and smiled. "What are you and Joey doing tonight? Want to bring him down to see Santa again?"

"Actually, Joel asked if he could take Joey and me to dinner on Sunday then go to the bazaar. He thought it would be fun to see Joey with Santa."

Tessa's hand shook slightly when she took her jacket

from the back of the chair. "That was nice of him. Are you going?"

Autumn looked undecided. "This probably sounds selfish, but I'm worried about what will happen if…if Sunny doesn't wake up."

"Mom, no. That isn't—"

"Let me finish. I know you can't stay here indefinitely. You have a business to run. June said Joey and I can keep living with her. She even volunteered to help babysit. But I'm afraid if you're not here, Joel will try to take him away."

Tessa dropped her coat on the table next to the photos. "Mom, none of us know Joel yet. But he seems like a decent guy. He made a mistake in his relationship with Sunny, but he's trying to do the right thing now. Just take it slow and get to know him before you start questioning his intentions, okay?"

Her mother nodded. "You're right. We'll go with him on Sunday. Have you thought any more about when you're leaving?"

Tessa had gone online to check for plane fares today. She was still on schedule to meet with Marci the day after Christmas—unless something happened. Something… An image of Cole Lawry popped into her head.

Wrong something. Definitely wrong.

"Nothing's finalized."

Autumn got up and walked to the door of the living room. "Oh, good, Joey's fallen asleep. He's been a handful lately. Maybe having a father will calm him down."

It never did much for me, but…Tessa kept the thought

to herself. And she was glad when a second later, the kitchen door opened and a familiar blond head popped in.

"Ho, ho, ho. Where's Santa's helper?"

She put a finger to her lips to shush Cole, then she kissed her mother on the cheek and turned to leave.

"Watch who you're calling a ho, mister," she said under her breath, "or you'll be taking your own pictures tonight."

Cole's muffled laugh followed her out the door. Suddenly, she was looking forward to an evening at the North Pole.

"DID WE SURVIVE?" Cole asked, after the last child in line toddled through the candy-cane arches. He slumped down in the wicked chair, although some kind soul had thoughtfully provided a thick seat cushion that had probably saved his life. "How many were there?"

"I lost count," Tessa answered from her post by the printer. "But, thanks to you, our donation box is stuffed. And look at all the toys people brought."

He turned his head to look at her. Damn, that elf hat was sexy. How come he'd never noticed that when Melody was taking pictures?

Maybe it was the sparkle of humor in Tessa's eyes when she set the next baby, toddler or child on his lap and smoothed down his fake beard. Her touch had set off most un-Santa-like thoughts. Scary, actually. She was so off-limits. Hell, he didn't even like her some of the time. He already had one bossy, opinionated woman in his life; he didn't need another.

Plus, this one is leaving.

Another reason to keep his mind on his job and off her perfectly sculpted behind, he reminded himself.

"Do you need my help getting down," she asked, appearing at the edge of the dais.

He sat up and started to remove his beard, but she yelped, "Wait." She picked up her camera.

"Tell me you're kidding," he said with a voluminous groan. "We're done, aren't we?"

"Officially. This is for me. The metamorphosis. Santa to Cole. I already documented your mom helping you into the costume."

He didn't bother trying to argue. He'd discovered she could be forceful and assertive when she was on an artistic mission. With a grouchy sigh, he pushed to his feet. "Okay, but I'm not doing a striptease where everybody can see, even if there aren't any kids around."

"You're too modest."

"Damn right."

He nearly stumbled when his overly large boot caught on the carpeting, but Tessa was there to anchor him. And help guide him down the steps.

Once he was safely behind the curtain his mother had rigged, he removed his hat and beard. "Step one," he said, staring directly into the camera.

Click. "Got it."

He tossed both items on the card table someone had set up. He unbuttoned the hook at the back of his neck.

"Um…belt first, right?"

He rolled his eyes. "Critics all. Fine. Belt first."

Knowing her viewfinder was trained at his waist made his fingers feel thick and clumsy. The well-used patent-leather just wouldn't cooperate.

"Let me help," she said, clearly enjoying this.

"I can do it."

"I know you can, but if Auntie Tessa helps we'll get home before dawn."

Cole threw his hands up. "I'm all yours."

She snapped another shot. Hopefully, he looked resigned, not annoyed. She let the camera hang by its strap against her chest as she squatted beside him. "All this extra padding probably makes it hard to see. And your mom said the suit is due for a few new accoutrements next year."

He couldn't actually feel her touch—she was right about the layers of padding—but he smelled her perfume and sensed her closeness on a primitive level. He closed his fingers into a fist to keep from doing something stupid. Like pulling her into his arms and kissing her.

"There," she chirped triumphantly. "You can pull it off, if you want." She hopped back and held up the camera. "If you hum a little strip music, I'll turn this into a video clip to post on YouTube."

"Do and I'll make sure Santa leaves a lump of something other than coal in your stocking." He whisked the belt through its loops.

She laughed. "No pun intended, I'm sure."

"That's Luke's department. Can I take off the shirt now?"

"Be my guest."

He tried not to think about her atypically flirtatious tone as he went through the steps his mother usually helped him with. Since it was her costume, June liked to make sure he didn't accidentally rip something. "Where's Mom?"

Buttons first.

"Don't know. Haven't seen her."

Then the heavy velvet jacket.

"How 'bout Annie?"

He sloughed the suspenders off each shoulder and gave the Velcro straps holding the pads in place a pull.

"No idea."

He scratched his stomach through his white undershirt, relieved to be free of the hot, restrictive costume. Using the table for support, he kicked off his giant boots.

"I feel like a clown," he said, looking down at his stocking feet before letting go of the oversize pants.

When he glanced up, Tessa was staring at him, camera lowered. Something passed between them that made his pulse speed up. The answer to a question he didn't intend to ask.

He stepped toward her. The pavement was chilly through his stockings but he barely felt it. "Are you coming home with me tonight?"

She swallowed, then nodded. "I think I am."

He didn't want to risk any questions like why or for how long. He kept his mind blank as he located his boots and keys. He quickly stuffed the suit in the bag for his mother while Tessa did the things she needed to do to close up shop. They hurried away from the North Pole without stopping to talk to anyone—or exchanging another word with each other.

"Oh, no," Tessa said, stopping suddenly. "I rode with you." She looked around the parking lot in obvious surprise.

"Is that a problem?"

"I...um...I wasn't planning on staying. Overnight. Too many people to answer to in the morning."

He opened the passenger door for her and waited until she was seated before saying, "Got it. I'll drop you at Mom's, and give her the Santa suit. Then, you can follow me home. If anyone asks, we're going to the Scoot 'n Boot for a drink."

She tilted her head. He could tell she was smiling. "I bet that ability to think on your feet served you well when you were a Realtor." Half a second later, she added, "Works for me."

He closed her door and hurried to the other side. If she wanted to talk in real estate terms, then he'd make use of one of the oldest adages around—he'd strike while the iron was hot.

CHAPTER FIFTEEN

"YOU'RE NOT AN impulsive person and this is an impulse you're going to regret," Tessa said to herself as she watched the taillights of Cole's truck turn off half an hour later.

She was *not* in love with Cole Lawry. She couldn't love a man she didn't respect.

Not that Cole wasn't admirable in many ways, but he was the first to admit he'd abandoned his goals and his ambition when things got tough in the big city. This proved he wasn't the right man for her.

They wanted different things out of life. No big deal. He was a handsome, sexy man with a killer smile and a sweet nature. He didn't play the guitar or do drugs. Another plus. And the fact this was just for one night made him almost perfect.

His face appeared outside her window. "Change your mind?"

She turned off the engine and picked up her purse, which contained the condoms she'd bought when she got her photos printed. A small package. Not a huge investment.

"No," she said, opening the door. "Although I do feel guilty. Sunny's lying in a hospital bed and I'm out having fun. Is this wrong? Am I a bad sister?"

He helped her to stand and closed the door with a slam. Putting his arms around her, he leaned in so their bodies pressed against the car. His breath was warm and smelled of mint.

I'm going to take a dozen candy canes home with me, she thought, bringing her lips to his.

"You're a fabulous sister. Didn't you read Annie's article? I believe her exact words were 'devoted' and 'selfless.'"

Horny and *selfish,* you mean.

He kissed her, taking away the opportunity—and inclination—to speak. He wasn't aggressive or in any hurry, and Tessa felt herself relax. She began to enjoy the coaxing nibbles that invited more. She opened to him, needing to taste him. Sweet yet tingly.

He tilted his head to deepen the kiss and she moaned something that meant yes, but the sound seemed to echo and transform into an odd whine.

She pulled back and blinked. "What was that?"

He was grinning. "My bloodthirsty watchdog." Nodding toward the porch, he whistled, "Come here, Pooch. You remember Tessa, don't you?"

The dog poked its nose out from behind a potted plant, then cleared the distance in four great leaps and wiggled in bliss at being greeted by his master. Tessa used the diversion as a chance to regain her composure. Thank goodness we're in the country, where his nearest neighbor would need a telescope to see us, she thought, straightening her shoulders.

After petting Pooch extravagantly, Cole took her hand and led the way toward the welcoming circle of light cast on the porch. The dog bounded ahead.

"Watch your step," he said, guiding her around a rough patch of ground. "Broken water line before I moved in. Ron keeps telling me he's responsible for fixing it, but he hasn't gotten around to it."

"That's right. You said he was the contractor who built your house. I suppose it's tricky being a client and an employee."

"Exactly. He's a decent boss, don't get me wrong, but his customer follow-through is his weakness. He knows it. The other day I suggested he let me supervise post-production on his new construction jobs, but he said no. He has some control issues."

Tessa understood. She was the same way. She and Marci had had a similar discussion over their duties since the beginning of their partnership. Tessa had learned to back off and give Marci space to do her job without constant supervision, but it hadn't been easy. Tessa felt she'd improved where her sister and mother were concerned, too, but was that true? She'd kept digging until she found Joel. Would Sunny thank her or curse her when she woke up? *If...*

"Kiss me again," she said.

He swept her backward into a flamboyant dip and kissed her until her purse fell off her shoulder, which made them tip over a bit too far. He jerked sideways with a grunt. He righted them without a problem, but had to hop on one foot to the steps and sit down. "Damn."

"I'm sorry. I'm too heavy. I hurt your back."

He shook his head. "Not your fault. Back's fine. It's my ankle. I screwed it up when I was a kid and it never healed right." He yanked off his boot and rubbed it furiously.

"Hey," she said, sitting beside him. "Don't make it worse. Do you need an ice pack?"

He shook his head. She could tell he was upset. She put her hand over his. "Cole."

He stopped torturing his ankle and let out a sigh. Their heads touched. "It'll be fine in a minute or two…especially if I keep my weight off it. Lying down would probably help." He waggled his brows lecherously.

She batted his arm. "Maybe short-term, but in the long run you should see an orthopedist and get it fixed."

He shrugged. "Saw one. When I was living in San Antonio. He said I'd be flat on my back for three weeks after surgery and would need to walk with crutches another month after that. I had too many deals going to take that kind of time off."

"So what's stopping you now?"

He snickered. "Ron doesn't offer health insurance for his employees."

She knew how costly the premiums were but she couldn't imagine being without some kind of coverage. His complacent attitude was one more example of how different they were. Unless…

"How did you say you hurt your ankle?"

He stood and pulled her to her feet. "Stepped in a gopher hole."

"How old were you?"

"Eleven. Can we talk about something else? I'm not an invalid. A bit gimpy, but nothing an aspirin and hot sex can't cure."

She sensed there was more to this story, but he turned away before she could ask. He walked unevenly, but his limp could have been because he was missing a boot. As she followed him inside, her gaze was drawn to the Christmas tree she'd bought him. The multicolored lights made the skimpily furnished room seem more cheerful and festive.

They stood together silently a few heartbeats. Tessa felt her nerves build. She hated this awkward moment, when you knew what you wanted but there didn't seem to be a graceful way to get to the bedroom.

She looked down and saw her opening. "Ice pack. Do you have one?"

"It's in the master bath."

"I was hoping you'd say that."

His smile told her he felt the same way. "Follow me."

He pulled off his other boot and tossed it under the coat tree to join the one he'd dropped when they came in. His stocking feet made a whispering sound against the matte finish of the earthen-colored tile. As they walked down the hallway, Tessa pictured a few of the photos she'd taken, framed and on the walls.

The bedroom door was open, and the outdoor lighting made it easy to see the switches. She stepped inside and looked around. She hadn't noticed much about the room the first time she'd been there talking to his mother.

It was big. Even a computer desk and chair, bed with nightstands and two dressers—one with a TV on top of it—barely made an impression in the space. The bed caught her eye.

She started across the room. "That headboard is unusual. Where'd you get it?"

He followed her and sat on the mattress that was covered in a simple, dark brown corduroy spread. The only other place to sit was an ergonomic chair by the desk. That's where Tessa set her purse before investigating the headboard.

Obviously handmade, it resembled an intricate puzzle composed of two kinds of wood winding in a complex labyrinth. "This is incredible. Did you make it?"

"My dad."

She ran her fingertips over the polished wood. Up close, the detail was truly amazing. "This must have taken him years to make."

"Two. Between the time Annie was born and when I came along. This was his gift to Mom, for giving him children."

She looked at Cole. "He was a true artist."

He didn't meet her gaze. Instead, he sat sort of hunched over, his damaged ankle resting on his left knee. He seemed lost in thought. She had a feeling he didn't even realize he was rubbing his ankle again.

"How'd he die?"

His chin came up. "Committed suicide." His mouth

pulled to one side in a sardonic, no-big-deal expression. "Kinda strange how a guy who cared enough to build something like this would off himself a few years later, huh?"

His words and tone were too blasé for the subject, but Tessa understood. Nonchalance was an effective defense against pity. "If he loved your mother this much, then he must have been in terrible mental anguish to do something that would separate him from her forever."

He didn't say anything for a moment. "That's one way of looking at it."

She sat down beside him. "My mother and I had a talk this afternoon. She pointed out that not every minute of my childhood was lousy. When Zeb and Mom first married and Sunny was a baby, we did some fun, family kind of things. It wasn't until later…when Zeb got sick and things got tough that I started bugging Mom about telling me who my *real* father was." *And when no heroic figure on a white horse swooped in to rescue me, I decided it was up to me to change the situation.*

"Autumn didn't want to tell you?"

"She couldn't. Too many men."

"Maybe you're better off not knowing. What if he was like my dad? Moody and distant most of the time. He'd come home from work and close himself up in his shop. You never knew if it was safe to approach him. Then, one day you'd come from school and he was packing the car to take the family to Six Flags. And then a few months later, right before Christmas, you come home from playing with your friends after school and there's a sheriff's car in your driveway."

"What did you do?"

He went still. "I saw Annie sitting on the porch crying, and I knew—before anybody told me. So, I took off running. Maybe I thought if I never heard the words it wouldn't be true."

She rubbed his back in small, comforting circles. "Is that when you hurt your ankle?"

He seemed startled by her question. "Yeah. Dumb, huh?"

She leaned closer and kissed him. He returned the kiss with an urgency that matched her own. He touched her breast, and she realized just how aroused she was. So fast, so not like her.

Slow down, she started to say, but instead she lifted her arms to help him take off her sweater.

"You, too," she murmured, snaking her palms upward under his shirt, thumbs brushing his nipples.

They fell back against the mattress and turned on the bed to face each other.

Cole had known for days—since their conversation on the banks of the Medina at the very least—that this was going to happen. He thought he was prepared for a carefree sexual encounter between two adults who were attracted to each other even though they had nothing in common. Their lives were still worlds apart, but they did share one thing. They both knew what it was like to have someone you loved and trusted fail you.

He still wanted to make love with her—God only knew how badly—but he wanted more than sex. He wanted her.

"You are so beautiful."

She didn't seem comfortable with the compliment, which struck him as odd since she always came off as so self-assured. Maybe her expensive, name-brand clothes provided some of the confidence. Like body armor. *Interesting*.

Levering up on one elbow, he looked into her eyes and said, "Before we go any further, we have to agree on two things. Number one, you're the most spectacular woman I've ever held in my arms. And number two, I'm the most amazing lover you've ever had."

He could tell she was fighting to keep from laughing. "I have to agree on that *before* we make love?"

He nodded. "Yes. Takes away any pressure on your part to look perfect—you're perfect in my eyes," he added, meaning it. "And I won't worry about performance anxiety. It's been a while for me and it takes practice to figure out exactly what pleases a woman."

A sweet shade of gold crept into her eyes. "Cole, you've already made me happier than my last boyfriend did during the entire time we dated." She ran her fingers through his hair, pulled his face closer to hers. "Can we start practicing now?"

"Good idea," he whispered as he nuzzled her neck, planting tiny kisses along her jaw.

When he removed her bra, she folded her arms across her chest. "Rule number one," he said gently, taking hold of her wrists. He pinned her arms over her head and looked at her body. Her nipples were small and pointed, the areolae a darker shade of brown. He released his hold and scooted downward. Instead of touching her, as he wanted, he used the tip of his tongue to tease, first one, then the other nipple. He licked and, finally, took her into his mouth with a long draw that made her moan and open beneath him like a rosebud.

He fought to keep his wits about him, but when he trailed his hand down her belly and dipped his finger into the warm folds of her body, he nearly lost it. Her soft cry and the way she lifted her hips against his hand urged him to hurry.

Her lashes quivered against her cheekbones as he explored and teased her most sensitive spot. Her breathing grew fast and shallow, and she responded with an uninhibited passion that fed his need. He barely had the willpower to sheath himself with a condom before giving in to her.

"Now, Cole. I need you now," she demanded, her nails sinking into his back.

Once he entered her, there was no thought of pacing. Instinct took over as they made that mutual climb to the peak of release. Lights exploded behind his eyes. He dimly heard her triumphant shout, echoing his.

Seconds later, he collapsed against her, chest heaving like a sprinter after a qualifying heat. She was breathing just as hard. She licked her lips and through slatted eyes said, "You were right about rule number two."

He laughed from his gut, reminding him that they

were still joined together most intimately. His depleted juices were recharging.

Her eyes opened wide. "Why, Santa, do you have another present for me?"

"Only if you're prepared to be a bad little girl."

She put her finger in her mouth and slowly pulled it out. "I think that can be arranged."

The elaborate headboard protested when she rolled them over so she could be on top, but Cole didn't complain at all.

CHAPTER SIXTEEN

COLE WAS SPRAWLED on his back in what Tessa would have named the Satiated Man Pose…if she'd had enough energy to take his picture.

She was sitting with her back against the lovely headboard, wearing a T-shirt Cole had given her. It bore the San Antonio Spurs logo. Not because she was self-conscious about being naked in his presence, but because the air temperature was cool.

Their lovemaking had been amazing. Better than anything she'd ever known with Alan, who had all the right moves but never seemed to connect with her. Cole seemed to sense what she wanted before she did.

"You aren't going to ambush me with your camera, are you?"

His voice was a huskier bass than normal. "Maybe," she said. "But would it be wise to blackmail Santa? I've already been warned about getting a lump of…something in my stocking."

"That was *before* you made Santa so happy," he said with a lascivious chuckle.

It struck her that she was happy, too. And comfortable. Maybe too comfortable. Regardless of what happened with her sister, she couldn't see herself returning to Texas on a regular basis. Great sex wasn't enough. She planned to be a millionaire before she turned forty.

She glanced at the clock radio on the bedside table. A few minutes past midnight, time for her to go. But she didn't make any effort to move.

"Did Mom mention the big holiday program her church puts on the last Sunday before Christmas?"

"You mean the one where they bless the sick or injured? Yes. She asked if she could put Sunny's name on the program."

"Will you still be in town?"

She should have felt relieved that he still accepted her intention to leave, but the question threw her. She needed to go home, and with Joel in the picture and everyone so willing to help, there wasn't any practical reason for her to stick around, yet...

"This is a terrible time of year to travel. Unless I want to go standby, the soonest I could get a confirmed seat was on the twenty-fourth."

"Christmas Eve? You and Santa would both be in the air at the same time?"

She drew her knees to her chest, drawing the covers up over his torso. "I guess."

"Damn. That sucks. Christmas Eve in River Bluff involves meat, drink and games."

"Poker?"

He shook his head. "No. Clue. That was Annie's

and my favorite game when we were kids. I always fancied myself a much younger and more debonair Colonel Mustard."

She could see that, too. "And Annie was Miss Scarlet."

"Of course."

Suddenly, she felt sad. And scared. She had no idea what was happening with her family. How long would Sunny be hospitalized? Would she ever recover? What about Joey and Joel? What would happen once the paternity results came back?

"I should go."

"Just like that? Was it something I said? You want to be Colonel Mustard?"

She leaned over and kissed his forehead. "It's late. I have a toddler with his own agenda, who loves to pounce on me at dawn every morning." She got out of bed and picked up her clothes, strewn about the floor. "I'll be right back. Stay in bed. Rest your ankle."

Cole watched her walk to the bathroom. He wasn't sure at what point exactly the reality had hit him, but he knew without a doubt that Tessa was more than just an uncomplicated sexual encounter. There'd even been moments when he could picture her in his bed in this house for the rest of his days.

He muttered an expletive and yanked the covers up over his head. *What a damn fool.* He could almost hear Annie giving him crap. "Only you could fall in love with a woman whose ambition is on par with Big Jim's. Your current income wouldn't cover the cost of Tessa's annual footwear budget."

A sharp-toned chirp—like the sound of a prairie dog sounding an alarm—made him flip back the covers. "Tessa? I think your phone is beeping," he called, climbing out of bed. He paused long enough to tug on his jeans.

On the floor a foot or so away, partially hidden beneath his desk chair, he saw her bright-red phone.

He picked it up and looked at the display. "Two missed calls."

She stepped out of the bathroom, dressed except for her boots. Her hair was brushed and tucked behind her ears. She looked ready to leave.

"I turned the phone on vibrate while I was taking photos at the North Pole. Guess I forgot to check it." She took it from him and sat on the end of the bed. "They're both from Mom."

She quickly dialed, despite the late hour. His mother's house, he assumed. "Mom? What's going on?" She looked at Cole, her jaw dropping. "Are you serious? They gave her a sleeping pill and she woke up? That doesn't make any sense."

Cole's heart started racing. Sunny woke up from her coma? It sure sounded that way. He yanked on his shirt.

"Mom…mom…slow down. I can't understand you. I'll call Horizon next. Do you want me to pick you up? Can June stay with Joey?" She listened a minute longer. "Okay. Fine. I'll meet you there. Drive carefully."

She closed her phone and looked at Cole. "It might be a false alarm, but Mom said the doctors prescribed a sleep aid if Sunny got restless, and half an hour after giving it to her, the nurse noticed she had her eyes open and appeared to be trying to speak. Mom was just on her way out the door. She's got your mother's car."

Cole finished pulling on his socks then shot to his feet. "Let's go. I'll drive."

She looked at him blankly. "Why?"

He was a bit peeved that she didn't automatically assume—especially after what they'd just shared—that he'd insist on going along. "It's late and I know a shortcut. Go start your car. I'll be right there."

She looked as though she might argue with him, but instead she palmed her phone and headed for the door. "I'll call the hospital. If this is a reaction to some medication, it might not last. One of the nurses told me a coma patient's recovery is usually gradual. The person may only be awake for a few minutes the first day then they slowly become more and more alert for longer periods."

"What a great Christmas present it would be for your family if she's on the road to recovery," he said. But Tessa had already left the room.

CHAPTER SEVENTEEN

A CHRISTMAS MIRACLE.

Cole tried to ignore the headline of the article Annie had written about Sunny's recovery as he opened the door of his mother's refrigerator. The clipping had been hanging there—bracketed by candy-cane magnets—for the past two weeks.

He was glad Sunny was getting better, but he was damn tired of fielding questions about her progress, and it seemed as though no one could stop talking about the medical anomaly that apparently made the comatose woman wake up.

"Bring me one, too, Cole," Annie called.

He'd stopped by his mother's to talk to Tessa, but she was gone. Delivering flowers for the Christmas program that evening, Autumn had said on her way out the door. "She should be back any minute."

He'd decided to wait. They needed to talk, and the past two weeks had given them practically no opportunity. Unfortunately, instead of Tessa, his sister had shown up.

"Coke or Shiner Bock?"

"Very funny."

He grabbed himself a beer and poked through the impressive array of food until he found a can of lemonade, her beverage of choice recently.

"Are you going to the service tonight?" Annie asked when he walked back into the living room. She was sitting on the sofa, reading a Christmas newsletter from some distant relative. "Rumor has it one of the news affiliates might send a camera crew."

"Are you serious?"

"It's a tug-on-the-heartstrings story. Especially this time of year."

Tessa hadn't returned to her role as photographer at the North Pole because once word got out about Sunny's reaction to the sleeping pills she'd been given, the media had swarmed. Even Annie had had to field phone calls from reporters. Cole had seen Tessa on TV twice. From what his mother said, money was pouring into the trust fund that had been opened for the family at the local bank.

But apparently none of that had changed Tessa's plans to leave. He walked to the picture window and looked out. Dusk had fallen. He made a mental note to plug in his mother's Christmas display on the lawn.

"What's going on, Coley-boy? Blake said you've turned into a hermit. Didn't even play poker last week. Is that true?"

"Cash-flow issues," he lied.

She snorted in disgust. "When are you going to hit up that cheap son of a gun for a raise? I understood why you agreed to start out at a low salary when you were just getting back into the trade, but you're better than most of Ron's experienced crew members now. Maybe you should go out on your own. You deserve better."

He'd been thinking the same thing, but not for the same reason. *Maybe Tessa would stick around if I were bringing in the kind of money she makes.* The idea pissed him off. "Why? So I can work seven days a week hustling jobs to keep my underpaid crew employed?"

She cocked her head and looked at him but didn't answer.

"For what? Enough money to fund my retirement account…which could get wiped out by another Enron fiasco? Or the chance to work with home owners like me and Crystal who break up halfway through a project and screw up the builder's schedule?"

"Well, since you put it that way—"

He pounded his fist on the table, making the Mr. and Mrs. Claus figurines wobble. "I don't have to prove anything to Tessa. I have a good life. I'm never going to be rich, but guess what? Rich is highly overrated. It comes with sleep disorders and ulcers. And depression."

She sat forward. "Are you yelling at me because you're mad at Tessa?"

He took a deep breath. "I'm not mad at her. She has her way of looking at things and I have mine. Hers is all about ambition and money and showing the world that she's not a victim. I get it. I've been there, done that, burned the T-shirt."

"But you love her and she's leaving and you don't know what to do."

He put the icy-cold bottle to his forehead. "I'm doing exactly what Tessa wants. Nothing. Can we talk about something else?"

"Sure. No problem. But in your present mood, I'd say it's a good thing the holiday bazaar ended when it did. Ho, ho, bite the poor kid's head off. Where's Tessa? You two really need to talk."

"That's why I'm here. She's helping Mom deliver the lilies. They should be done by now."

She tossed up her hands. "And what if she decides to stay for the service without coming back here first? Take the shortcut and go meet her."

She had a point. The service was due to start in fifteen minutes, and knowing Tessa she'd probably pitch in to help. "What about you?"

She stood and pushed him toward the door. "I'm running late because my pants don't fit anymore and I had to go home to change. Blake should be here any minute. He volunteered to pick up Sunny and the gang, including Joel, at Horizon on his way back from San Antonio. Our giant beast of a car can handle Sunny's wheelchair. Go. Go now. And don't be such a guy about everything. Tessa's a successful, highly motivated businesswoman. You could do worse." She put one hand to her lips and pretended to look shocked. "Oh, wait, you already have."

Cole was still growling on his way out the door. But he was smiling, too.

TESSA MISSED COLE.

There, she'd admitted it. She'd spent two weeks trying not to think about him, about their night together, about all those things that made her crazy about him.

She wasn't in love with him. What she felt for him was a serious case of like…with lust overtones. And the fact that she was leaving the next day shouldn't be a problem for someone in like with someone else. But it was.

"Are you ready?" June asked, walking up to where Tessa was standing beside the trunk of her car, wool-gathering.

"Oh. Sorry. I should have had this open. Did you find out where they want us to put the flowers?"

Three dozen individual white lilies to be handed out to those on the congregation's prayer chain. Sunny had definitely been on that list and, while she couldn't walk unassisted, she'd made steady progress in the past two weeks and was looking forward to participating in the service that evening.

Afterward, friends and family would gather at June's. Tessa assumed Cole would be there, although they hadn't discussed it. They hadn't talked in days.

"Um, June, do you know if all of Cole's poker friends will be at your house tonight?"

June looked lovely in a red wool dress with black pumps and pearls. Tessa—like usual—felt under-dressed. She planned to burn her black slacks and red sweater when she got home. She couldn't wait to get back to her lovely, fashionably current wardrobe. "I think so. Maybe not Jake, but the others usually drop in."

Good. She'd splurged and framed photos for

everyone who had helped her family—including the Wild Bunch. She was certain the boys had made unbelievably generous donations to the fund set up in Sunny's name.

Tessa opened the trunk. The oblong white cardboard boxes weren't heavy, but they were awkward to handle, so they each took one and started toward the church. Tessa had never visited the gothic-looking building during the day. She'd only seen it from the vantage point of the holiday bazaar, which had been dismantled a week earlier.

The steep roof and narrow stained glass windows made the building seem austere, but the people she'd come to know who were members of the church had been nothing but warm and welcoming.

June was leading the way up the handicap ramp. "Did I tell you I took a couple of Annie's prematernity outfits to your sister this morning? Sally Knutson, a local hairdresser, was there. She'd talked Sunny into cutting her hair—to blend in with the shaved part. It's just darling. Wait till you see her."

"Sunny used to say she'd never cut her hair, but the good thing about a faulty memory is she doesn't know that."

They shared a smile.

Tessa had been told that Sunny would require months of physical and occupational therapy, and that portions of her memory might never return, but she'd shown steady improvement since her miraculous awakening.

An Internet search had revealed that Sunny wasn't the first comatose patient to wake up after being given a prescription sleep aid, but no one seemed to know for certain why the drug worked for some brain-damaged patients and did nothing for others. Tessa was just happy Sunny was one of the lucky ones.

Tessa hurried past June to open the door. The church was far from empty. A dozen or more parishioners were busy preparing for that evening's service.

"Pastor John said to put them on one of the rear pews, out of the way," June said, skirting a group of men setting up low bleachers for the children's choir.

Tessa followed, but her attention was drawn to two older men carrying the high-backed chair Cole had used at the North Pole to an elaborately carved lectern.

"Wasn't that wonderful news about Joel's paternity test?" June asked, setting down her box on the dark blue padded cushion. "Not that he didn't seem committed to Sunny and Joey even before you got the results, but this certainly makes it official."

Tessa placed her box beside June's. "Joel's a decent guy. I'm not crazy about his career, but that's my problem."

They headed back to the car. She'd given a lot of thought to the conversation she'd had with her mother about the past. There was no denying that Zeb's personal problems and subsequent choices had made a tremendous impact on her life and her decisions, but as an adult, she had the power to change that. But did she want to? She liked her life.

They returned to the car for the remaining box.

"Parking is always hard to find on holidays," June said, stopping Tessa from following her. "Would you mind terribly driving home and walking back? I'll take this box in and make sure the flowers get set out. You have plenty of time if you take the shortcut."

"Sure. No problem. Save me a seat."

After parking behind Cole's Forerunner a few minutes later, Tessa dashed inside to freshen up then slipped out the kitchen door and cut through the backyard. She carefully picked her way along the side of the detached garage. She'd been through here several times, but usually with a flashlight, which she'd forgotten to bring with her.

She was just passing Mrs. Vanderswan's rose bed when she heard a low groan. She froze. "Hello?"

"Tessa?"

She dashed around the corner of the patio to find Cole sitting on Mrs. Vanderswan's weathered flagstone retaining wall.

"Cole. Your ankle again?"

He let out a muttered grumble that included a curse or two and hopped to one foot. "Just stepped wrong. Old lady Vanderswan needs to do some work on this place before she winds up with a lawsuit."

"She could probably argue that you were trespassing."

"Whose side are you on?"

As she came closer, he could see her smile. Tender and sweet. The way she looked at Joey when he was being difficult. "Yours. Here. Lean on me. Can you make it to your mom's?"

He looked at his watch. "We don't have time. You'll miss—"

"I'm not going to watch you sit through three choir performances in agony. Come on."

He gave in, even though his ego was hurting more than his ankle at that moment. He didn't actually need her support. If he watched how he placed his foot, he barely noticed the pain, but her nearness was a gift he couldn't pass up.

They entered the house through the side door. Her white Toyota Camry was in the driveway behind his truck. Obviously, Tessa had dropped his mother off then returned home.

"Sit," she ordered, pulling out a chair at the table. "I saw one of those cold wraps in the freezer. Take off your boot."

"Could you grab me a couple of aspirin? Mom keeps a bottle in the pantry. Top shelf."

She returned a few seconds later with a flexible wrap he'd used many times in the past, three white pills and a glass of water. After securing the icy bandage around his ankle, she sat down across from him. "I'm sorry for your pain, but I'm glad we have a few minutes alone. It's going to be hectic around here after the service."

"I know."

"I'm leaving tomorrow."

He gulped down an extra swallow of water to dislodge the bitter pill that had stuck in his throat.

He hadn't heard that. The finality in her tone made him want to hit something. "You're going to miss Christmas."

Her shoulders stiffened. Probably in reaction to his judgmental tone. "My partner and I have a standing date to meet on the twenty-sixth. We plan our agenda and budget for the coming year. It's a tradition, not particularly holidayish, but one I don't plan to skip."

"And your partner is so anal she can't wait a day or two?"

She jumped to her feet and poked her chest with her index finger. "I'm the one who's anal, remember? Focused. Driven. And I grabbed the first flight I could get a seat on because I think something is seriously wrong with Marci, my partner. She says she's fine, the business is fine, but…she's lying."

He didn't ask for details—he didn't need them. He could tell by the bags under her eyes and lines of tension around her mouth that she was under a lot of pressure. Self-imposed, but pressure nonetheless. He'd experienced his share of similar crises. The last one had cost him nearly everything he'd worked so hard to get.

He sat forward and rested his elbows on the table. "Tessa, whatever is going on in your partner's life isn't going to change if you arrive back in Portland a day— a week—late. Your business isn't going to get flushed down the tubes overnight. But if that did happen there's probably nothing you could have done to save it anyway. I know this from experience."

"Maybe your business wasn't as important to you as mine is to me."

He wanted to argue with her, but she was right. He knew that now. "Tessa, am I alone here in thinking we had something pretty damn good the other night? Doesn't that kind of passion deserve a second look? What if it's the real deal? I know this is fast, but I was hoping I could talk you into staying…with me. One thing I know from poker is you can't win if you're not in the game."

She stared at him just long enough for Cole to know he wasn't going to like her answer. "You're forgetting something, Cole. I'm not a gambler. I wish I were. I'd call Marci and say, 'Sorry, pal, I don't know what your problem is but I'm moving to Texas. You're on your own.' But I can't do that."

"Why?" He knew the answer, but he had to ask.

"Because without me paying the premiums on my sister's health insurance, Sunny never would have been able to afford Horizon. Mom wouldn't have any kind of retirement fund to look forward to. Joey wouldn't have a dime saved when he's ready to go to college. It isn't all about me, Cole."

"I never thought it was, Tessa. I admire how dedicated you are. I agree with what Annie called you in her article—selfless and devoted. But you don't have to do it alone. What if I came to Oregon? They probably need carpenters in Portland, right?"

Her eyes went wide and she inhaled sharply.

She didn't jump at his offer. In fact, he could see by the way she pressed her lips together that said she planned to say, *Thanks, but no thanks*. He'd been a salesman too long not to be able to sense when a sale turned sour.

She walked back to where he was sitting and pulled up a chair so she could face him. "Cole…there are a million reasons for me to say yes. All of them selfish. But the harsh reality is no matter what happens with Marci, I have to get back to work. This trip has tapped all my reserves. Thankfully the donations that have come in will help Sunny and Joey, but I still need to work. I definitely won't have time for a social life."

Social life. Not exactly the declaration of love he'd been hoping for.

"Okay," he said, shaking the ice pack off his leg. "We call that going 'all-in' in poker terms. You didn't call my declaration of love. I get to keep my chips."

When he leaned over to pull on his boot, she touched his cheek. "You get to keep your life without me screwing it up. Believe me. That makes you the winner."

They walked back to the church in silence. Not the companionable silence she'd once enjoyed with him. More of a chilly detachment that told her she'd hurt him, despite her best efforts to be practical.

She refused to feel guilty. He'd asked her to stay; she'd said no. That's how it was. After tomorrow, she could put this strange, convoluted affair behind her and resume her life. The one she'd worked damn hard to make from scratch.

The children's choir had evidently finished its program, Tessa gathered by the general hubbub that greeted them when Cole opened the church door. Small bodies in their best Christmas outfits were filing out one corridor, while adults in shimmering gold gowns took their places.

Tessa spotted her mother motioning them to the front pew. Cole followed her a step or two behind. Tessa knew it was her imagination, but she swore she could feel the entire congregation's gaze on her. Did they guess she'd just broken River Bluff's favorite son's heart?

Autumn and the others scooted to the left, opening up two spaces beside Sunny's wheelchair. Tessa let Cole go first so she could sit next to her sister.

She'd barely caught her breath when the minister, a man in his early forties, she guessed, approached the pulpit. He had a microphone clipped to his collar, so his voice filled the cathedral. "After that wonderful performance—recorded for posterity by at least fifty parental camcorders—let us move to the part of the service we've all come to cherish. And tonight we are blessed with the presence of one of God's angels, returned to us from the entrance of the heavenly gates by the collective prayers of her friends and family. Her name is Sunny Barnes, and she wanted to join us tonight in person so y'all could see what power your prayers enacted in her life."

Tessa reached out and squeezed her sister's hand. From the pew directly behind them, Joel stood up. He handed Sunny the lily he'd been holding for her, and then pushed her wheelchair to the altar. A microphone had been set up on a stand. Joel adjusted it with a practiced hand to the right height for a seated person, then slipped to one side, squatting out of sight in case she needed him.

The overhead lights made Sunny's short, wispy locks

glow like a halo. The elegant white flower wavered slightly in her unsteady grip, but she managed to place it in the vase the pastor held for her. "I...want...to...thank you," she said haltingly. "I haven't met most of you...at least I don't think I have." She blushed sweetly, causing a twitter in the audience. "But I know you in my heart. And I will always a-appreciate what you've done for me and my family."

The roar of applause was so loud Joey put his hands over his ears and scrunched down beside his grandmother. Autumn didn't make any attempt to wipe away her tears. Tessa cried, too, but for so many reasons, she couldn't say if they were tears of joy...or despair.

CHAPTER EIGHTEEN

COLE KNEW THAT the only way not to dwell on his disappointment was by working. Although today was Monday, it was also Christmas Eve, and Ron had given all his employees the day off. Unpaid. That meant Cole had no choice but to dive into one of the many unfinished projects around his house.

He'd be expected at his mother's around dinner, but that left plenty of time to paint the guest bathroom.

He was tackling the trim when Pooch gave his single-alarm bark. Cole's heart went haywire for a few seconds until his rational mind set it straight. "She's gone. Get a life."

Tessa was in San Antonio by now, dropping off her rental car, he figured. She was the type to give herself plenty of lead time. Practical. Organized.

Anal.

He felt guilty when the thought darted through his mind. He didn't consider her that way at all. She'd used the word, not him.

And he hadn't said a thing in her defense. What kind of man didn't defend his woman when someone was picking on her? Especially if she was picking on herself. He sucked. No wonder she left.

"Anybody home?" a man called.

Blake. "Not Annie, too," he said under his breath. He loved his sister; he just wasn't ready to face her.

"In here. If you don't mind paint fumes."

"Beats that nasty cigar your boss smoked at the last game," his brother-in-law said when he appeared at the doorway. "Nice color."

"Thanks."

Ever since Annie had brought up Ron's miserly tendencies, Cole had been giving serious thought to quitting Makin' Hay Construction. No job, no feeling obligated to invite Ron to their poker games.

"What's up? I figured you'd be doing your last-minute shopping," Cole said, setting his brush on the top of the open paint can.

"My reputation precedes me, I see. Nope. Got it done yesterday. Bought a football and a white teddy bear. Since Annie won't let the doctor tell us what the baby's sex is, I had to get either/or gifts."

"She's tough."

"I know, but my life's about as perfect as yours is screwed up, so I'm here to help."

"Great. Here's a paintbrush."

"Not what I had in mind. The guys are outside. I picked them up—along with a case of longnecks." Blake put his fingers to his lips and whistled.

The sound of boots on the deck made Cole groan. He looked around the bathroom door to see Brady, Luke and Jake approaching. *Jake, too?* He shook his head. "Give me a minute to wash out this brush."

He took his time. There wasn't anything to talk about. Tessa had made her decision. She wasn't looking for a relationship right now. How much clearer could she make it? But his friends didn't know that. They cared about him, and he appreciated the gesture.

They wound up sitting on the porch because the sun was trying to shine and the smell of paint was giving Cole a headache.

Blake was the first to get away from small talk. "She left, huh? Going back to Oregon on the red-eye."

"Yep," Brady said. "That's what I heard. And I have to say, Cole, you let me down. Cost me twenty bucks."

"Huh? You bet on whether or not Tessa would stay?"

Luke shook his head. "Naw. We all figured she'd leave eventually. Brady thought you'd go with her. I said you're a Texan first. You'd wilt in the Northwest." He chuckled. "But Brady's a romantic at heart."

Brady slugged him.

Blake ignored the ensuing tussle. "We all thought you had something going with her, Cole. Something…good. You've been different since she got here. More up."

"Parts of him, anyway," Luke wheezed from under the neck squeeze Brady had on him.

Blake's sigh was part indulgent, part annoyed. "We're worried about you, bud. We don't want to see you moping again."

Brady let go of Luke. "Yeah, you were a real hermit

for a while. If it weren't for poker, we never would have seen you. Hey," he said, pointing at Jake, "that reminds me. Jake's giving us all a Christmas present. He's gonna let us start playing at the Card again."

"Until the property sells," Jake added in a hurry. He hooked his thumb over his shoulder in the direction of Cole's dining room. "No offense, Cole, but that table is jinxed. I think Ron's wife put a curse on it. Only way to explain how a drunk could be that lucky."

"You're fixin' up the Wild Card?"

"Bare necessities. Nothing fancy. I'm sick of living in a hovel, and everyone says it'll sell better with a new roof and a coat of paint."

Cole agreed. He started to ask for details, but his brother-in-law cut him off.

"Why are you here, Cole?"

Cole looked around. "Is that one of those philosophy questions, a-tree-falling-in-the-forest thing?"

Luke grinned and gave him a high five.

Blake sighed as if he were a teacher surrounded by juvenile delinquents. "Annie says Tessa is the one, Cole. Your sister knows you better than anyone. And she's pregnant, which means she's ultrasensitive to the feelings of the people around her." Luke sounded like he was choking, but Blake ignored him. "She says you're in love with Tessa, and Tessa is in love with you. Is that true?"

Cole slammed down his beer bottle. "That's my business."

Brady hunched forward. "We're your village, man. We care. And we think you made a mistake letting her go."

Jake nodded. "Just say the word. Luke can…um…*borrow* his brother's chopper and we'll get you to the San Antonio airport before her plane takes off. Even if we have to set down on the tarmac."

They all nodded in a guy way.

"You're my village idiots, you meant to say," Cole told them. "I have three words for you—nine, one, one. You mess with a planeful of people and you're looking at jail time."

That cooled their enthusiasm.

"My buddy runs one of the rental-car lots. He'd let us set down there," Luke said. "He's even got those golf cart thingies we could borrow to shoot over to the terminal."

"I can run faster than those, and I have a bad knee," Brady pointed out.

"But Cole can't. If his ankle goes, we're screwed," Jake said soberly.

"Stop. Time out. This is nuts. You'd never get past security, and even if you somehow talked your way through without a boarding pass, the bottom line is Tessa doesn't want to be with me. I asked, and she said no."

There, his humiliation was complete. He took a long guzzle of beer.

Nobody spoke for a few minutes. "How do you mean, no?" Brady finally asked. "Was it an I'd-rather-be-married-to-a-guy-on-death-row-than-date-you kind of no?"

"Or a you're-a-great-guy-but-I-don't-think-about-you-in-that-way kind of no?" Luke volunteered.

"Or the familiar standby 'It's not you, it's me. I need my space to find out who I am,'" Jake added.

Cole found each of their suggestions revealing, but before he could answer, Blake said, "Maybe there just wasn't any chemistry between them."

"There was enough chemistry to burn down the freaking lab. And she definitely—we definitely—felt that way about each other. There isn't another guy, on death row or anywhere else. And she knows who she is. A person who takes care of other people first. She went back to honor the commitment she has with her business partner. No business, no income. No income, no way of taking care of her mother or helping her sister and nephew if things don't work out with Joel. Which is exactly what any of us would do."

His friends exchanged looks that would have blown any bluff at the table. Did they feel freakin' sorry for him? Crap. Pity was the last thing he needed.

He stood up. "Hey, listen, thanks for coming. I know you care about what happens to me—you need my money every week. But don't worry. I'm okay. I'm not going to kill myself just because the woman I love isn't ready to say 'I do.' I'm a grown-up. I can handle rejection. I might even be an expert at it."

Brady popped to his feet, ever the athlete. He shook Cole's hand. "Are you going to the Circle C tomorrow? Luke's mom told me she counts on you keep the rest of us from getting out of hand. She calls you the sweet one."

"No, that's what she calls me," Luke said, getting up more slowly.

"When you were three, maybe."

Luke snarled at Brady, then cuffed Cole lightly on the shoulder. "The bird is at your disposal, Cole. Anytime. Just say the word."

Cole pulled him into a quick guy-hug, pounding his back. He knew how much Luke hated asking his older brother for anything—especially the helicopter. It only served to remind Luke that he'd been grounded from the military after the crash that permanently affected his vision.

Jake was the last to approach. He stared at his Harley-Davidson boots for a good minute. "I know you're busy, but if you have some extra time, I could use your help at the Wild Card."

A peace offering. No explanation about why he never contacted Cole over the years, never told him about his success upon his return to River Bluff. But it was a start.

"Sure, man."

The three ambled toward Blake's black SUV, but his brother-in-law stayed behind after the others left.

"Listen, Cole. We all like Tessa. Those framed photos she gave us last night were awesome. And they said a lot about how much she cares for you. You don't let a woman like that just walk out of your life. Look at me and Annie. We came so close to losing everything. Now I wake up every day thanking God I got a second chance to be with her. Not everybody's that lucky. If Tessa's the one, don't blow it."

Blake swung himself down the steps then paused to look back. "You know, Annie and I could dog-sit if something came up and you needed to be away for any extended length of time."

Cole got the hint. "Thanks. I'll remember that. See you at Mom's tonight?"

"I'll be there. I wish you weren't, but unlike your sister, I know when to shut up and let you make your own mistakes."

My own mistakes.

The words followed him as he walked back inside. He stopped in front of the framed portrait he'd unwrapped at his mother's the night before. He'd hung it in the foyer where everyone could see the black-and-white of Cole and his friends huddled around Brady, who was seated at the poker table. She'd somehow captured each guy's personality in one split second.

He knew without being told that Tessa had chosen that photo for a reason. It represented an idealized image of friends, continuity and community. All things she'd never really known...and maybe subconsciously didn't think she deserved.

Like I don't deserve to get my ankle fixed?

A shiver ran down his spine.

He closed the door and walked into the living room. As he looked around, he was suddenly struck by the emptiness of his home, his life. Why hadn't he bought new furniture? If this was where he planned to spend the rest of his days, why had he made such a miserly effort to make his house a home?

No wonder Tessa had turned him down. Instead of spurning the workaholic lifestyle that had nearly killed him, he'd downsized his life to the point that he looked like a poverty-stricken charity case. The last thing in the world Tessa needed.

He strode into the kitchen, where his cell phone was charging. He didn't know if he and Tessa could work out all their differences, but they sure as hell couldn't even start building something together when they were half a country apart.

He quickly jotted down a list of things to do:

Call Ron and quit.
Make arrangements for Pooch.
Book a flight to Oregon.

TESSA FOUND her gate without any trouble, but one glance at her watch confirmed that she'd given herself way too much extra time. Dropping off her car hadn't taken as long as she'd expected, and the shuttle to the terminal had been ready to leave the minute the clerk had handed her the credit card receipt. To her surprise, the lines television reports had told her to expect appeared concentrated at airlines flying toward the northeast. Hers moved with inordinate speed.

Too restless to sit, she walked to a food-service court and bought a soda. That killed a whopping ten minutes. She wandered into a gift shop where the clerk was setting out New Year's items. Candy, sparkly crowns and beads in purple, silver and green. Colors she asso-ciated with Mardi Gras.

She perused the paperback-book display but couldn't

find a title that interested her. There were several coffee-table books dealing with the Alamo, San Antonio's colorful history and Texas, in general. She thumbed through a pictorial history of Bandera County, but quickly put it down. The images reminded her of the shots she'd taken and given away the night before.

Everyone had been very complimentary. June had cried when she unwrapped the triptych of flowers Tessa had found while exploring River Bluff on foot.

She wished the clerk a merry Christmas then returned to the waiting area near to her gate. She sat down and took her camera out of her purse. The three-inch screen on the back was bright and easy to see—even through her tears.

The most recent shots were taken at Horizon that morning when she stopped to tell her sister goodbye. Joey on his mother's lap. Sunny holding up the nightshirt Tessa had given her. The colorful text said Good in bed.

The best image was of Sunny, bracketed on either side by Joel and Autumn as they perused the photo album Tessa had put together of her sister's amazing journey.

She kept clicking until she found a shot of Cole. A kind, generous man who knew who he was and what he wanted out of life. What was so bad about that? True, his house wasn't as big and fancy as his ex-father-in-law's, but it was a blank palette that someone could turn into a lovely home. Someone who wasn't afraid to gamble—just a bit—now and then.

Tessa turned off her camera, tossed it in her bag and

grabbed her phone. She walked to the far corner of the uncrowded waiting room and hit speed dial.

"Hello?"

"Hi, Marci, it's me. I'm at the airport, but before I get on the plane I need to know what's going on. There's something you're not telling me, and my imagination has been working overtime. Are we getting sued? Did the office burn down? What's wrong?"

Marci made an atypical whining sound. "I wanted to tell you in person, so I could see your face. I need to know how you feel about this, and I know you, Tessa. You fake happy when you think that's what someone you care about wants to see."

"I do?"

"Yeah. Like when I got married."

"Marci, I *am* happy for you. No one could be happier."

"I know. When I first told you, you smiled and hugged me, but deep down I knew you were worried about what that would mean to our business."

"I'm a worrier, I admit it. But everything turned out great. Business is wonderful and you've proved to everyone that you can have it all. You're my inspiration."

"Tess. I'm pregnant."

The words hit Tessa like a punch to the gut. Her soda started coming back up but she swallowed harshly. "Oh my gosh. That's wonderful. I'm so excited for you. Congratulations."

Marci didn't say anything for a moment. "I knew you'd say that. This is why I wanted to tell you in person. You're upset."

"I'm not. You'll make a wonderful mother."

"Oh, come off it, Tessa. I'm a control freak who has to be right. I'll probably screw up this kid so badly he or she will sue me someday, but fortunately, after working with you, I've learned to be a team player when the situation calls for it. So, I'm hoping Matthew and I can handle one kid between us."

"Of course you can. You're the most focused, highly motivated person I know."

"Thank you. You're not bad yourself. Look how great you've been with Joey. He adored you even before all this happened. He knew instinctively he could trust you not to let him down."

Tessa's vision clouded with tears. "I'm going to miss him so much. Sunny can't travel. She has months of rehab ahead of her, and Joel—Joey's daddy—just got a job managing a bar in Bandera, so they probably won't ever come back to Oregon."

"What about your mom?"

Tessa shrugged. "I don't know. She and Cole's mother have become good friends. They're talking about taking a bus trip to Branson this spring."

"So, you're going to be here alone."

I've always been alone.

But now there was someone who wanted to be a part of her life on a permanent basis. "Cole said he wanted us to be together and he'd be willing to move to Oregon."

Marci let out a high-pitched squeal that made several travelers turn their heads to look at Tessa. "Did you say yes?"

"I'm in the airport and he's not. What does that tell you?"

Marci went quiet. "Tessa, you and I are pragmatists. If we'd hired A.R.E. Consulting to do an analysis of our business given the changes that we've both experienced recently, what do you think our verdict would be?"

Tessa thought a moment then answered truthfully. "We'd suggest the owners dissolve the partnership equably while they still valued each other and their friendship."

"Exactly."

The bald reality was scary, yet oddly liberating.

"Matthew and I have been talking about this for days. He went over our books and crunched all the numbers taking into account what each of us produced last year. Tessa, he's certain you can do just as well on your own and still afford to hire a part-time assistant—me."

"Are you serious?"

"Think about it, Tess. You'd save the overhead cost of renting an office we barely use. The changes to our Web site would be minor. And I could do the stuff you hate— reports, billing and…dealing with our accountant."

Tessa chuckled as her initial trepidation was edged out by curiosity. "You honestly believe I could do this on my own?"

"Why not? Between the two of us, we have enough leads to keep A.R.E. Consulting busy for six months. Even if some of the deals fell through because the client wanted us sooner, other jobs would pop up. They always have. Sure, going out on your own is a gamble, but not a big one."

But I don't gamble.

"And you know the best part?" Marci asked.

"What?"

"You'll be working from home. And you get to decide where that is. Portland…Texas…Timbuktu."

Gooseflesh skittered across her arms and tears filled her eyes. Home. Where was that?

The answer came through loud and clear. Anywhere Cole was.

She wiped her eyes with the back of her hand and took a deep breath. "You're an amazingly smart, perceptive friend, Mars. Does Matthew know how lucky he is?"

Marci chuckled. "Some of this was his idea. He knew I felt guilty about abandoning you, but he was terrified that if I kept working the way I have been I'd deliver our baby out of state."

"You never would have let that happen, Marci. You're far too good at scheduling. And I'm going to count on that when you're working for me."

They talked about how to make a smooth transition at A.R.E., but Tessa's mind couldn't stay focused. There was nothing stopping her from moving her operation to River Bluff. She and Cole could be together. If he still wanted her…

At that moment a voice over the speaker announced the preboarding for her flight to Portland. "They just called my flight, Mars. I gotta go."

"Why?"

The question stopped her.

Why, indeed? She was her own boss now. She didn't have to make a standing meeting on the day after Christmas. She and Marci could get together whenever Tessa returned to Portland. Whenever… "I knew there was a reason I chose you to be my partner, Marci. You're a genius who thinks outside the box. I love you, my friend."

"Does that mean you're staying?"

"Yes. But don't worry. I'll catch a flight in a day or two. Ask Matthew to put together a list of our joint assets and we'll divide things up when I get back."

"No problem. He already mentioned a way we could donate the desks and chairs to a nonprofit group and save on our taxes."

Leave it to Matthew to think like an IRS attorney.

"You're going back to River Bluff, right? Are you going to call first or just show up and surprise everybody?"

Tessa glanced at her watch. By the time she got her hands on another rental car and drove to River Bluff the festivities at June's house would probably be over. "Actually, I think I'll go straight to Cole's, although there's a good chance he's not speaking to me. I sorta blew off his proposal last night."

"Santa asked you to marry him and you said no?"

The dismay in her friend's tone clearly said Marci thought she'd messed up—big-time. Cole had probably discussed it with his family and friends. Maybe they'd convinced him he was better off without her.

"What if I'm too late, Mars?"

Marci didn't answer right away. "Do you have phone numbers for any of his friends? Not his sister," she stressed. "She's going to be a hard sell. But you said these Wild guys have been friends forever, right? They could tell you where you stand."

Poll the Wild Bunch? Tessa swallowed. She wouldn't blame them for hating her.

Oh, well, she thought, when had life ever been easy?

"I gotta go, Mars. Other people will be dining on turkey and ham tonight, but it looks like my menu consists of barbecued crow."

She glanced at the gate where the last of the passengers on her flight had queued up, then she grabbed the handle of her carry-on suitcase and started back down the brightly lit corridor toward a customer service sign. "Have a merry Christmas, Marci. I love you."

"Me, too, Tessa. Good luck. Let me know what happens."

They said their goodbyes as Tessa sprinted to the help desk to explain her situation. The woman behind the counter obviously would have preferred to be home with her family than helping some indecisive traveler who didn't know if she was coming or going. Tessa tried to be patient, but now that she'd made her decision, she couldn't wait to tell Cole. Something that needed to be done face-to-face.

Forty minutes later, she was still in San Antonio. Still without wheels. "I'll take anything," she begged the clerk at the rental-car agency.

The young man behind the counter acted as though she was asking for a sleigh and eight tiny reindeer. "I don't have anything, ma'am. I told you when you called from the desk at the terminal that I'm expecting a return but it has to be cleaned and—"

"I don't care if it's clean."

"It's our policy."

"I'll sign a waiver."

"Wait over there." He pointed toward a bench well to the back of the line.

She swallowed her frustration and sat down. At least she could follow Marci's suggestion. She found Luke's card in her purse and punched in his cell number. He picked up on the second ring.

"Luke Chisum."

There was a lot of noise in the background. Probably the family party he'd mentioned last night, she realized.

"Hi, Luke. It's Tessa Jamison. I'm still in San Antonio."

"Did you miss your flight?"

"Um, yes. On purpose. I've, um, had a change of heart. I decided to stay."

"For good?"

"That depends on Cole. You haven't talked to him recently, have you?"

"Had a beer at his house this afternoon."

A distinct chill in his tone told her she'd been a topic of discussion. "Is he okay?"

"Kinda down, but he's a survivor. What made you change your mind?"

She wasn't sure how to put into words the sense of

relief she'd felt after she made the decision to stay. "You know how they say a picture is worth a thousand words? Well, I have six hundred shots on my camera and five hundred are of Cole. And not just as Santa Claus. I figure my subconscious mind was trying to tell me something. I just wasn't listening."

"But now you are?"

"Yes. I'm actively listening for my name to be called by a seventeen-year-old rental-car clerk with attitude," she said, leaning back in her chair to avoid getting stomped on by yet another wave of customers. Not surprisingly, the clerk wasn't beaming with holiday cheer. Did everyone plan as poorly as she had? "At this rate, I won't get to River Bluff before morning."

"You need a ride?"

She hesitated. Was it her imagination or had his voice changed? She thought she heard a John Wayne twang for a second. "I need a car."

"Would a helicopter do?"

Definitely John Wayne. "I beg your pardon?"

"Sit tight, little lady. I think I can help you out, but I gotta make a few calls."

The connection went dead. "Did he just call me 'little lady'?" She shrugged, put her chin in her hand and let out a sigh. This might well be the longest Christmas Eve on record.

CHAPTER NINETEEN

"I KNOW WE USUALLY open our presents in the morning—after Santa has come, but I want you to open this one from me now, Cole," June said, carrying a colorfully wrapped package the size of a toaster oven. Too light for a toaster, though.

Autumn had retired a few moments earlier, after relaying that Joey had finally settled down and was sound asleep. The toddler had been the center of attention since his grandmother let him open his gift from Cole. A plastic, snap-together train set specifically designed for toddlers.

"Thanks," he said. "But if it's not a train set, I'm going to have to exchange it. After playing with Joey's, Blake and I decided we want our own."

His mother laughed softly and sat beside him on the couch. She looked at the toy, still spread out in front of the illuminated Christmas tree. The dozens of other wrapped boxes and gift bags had been pushed to one side. "Do you think I should put the train away or leave it? He'll get more toys in the morning."

"I'd planned to put it back in the box before I leave.

Joel said he'd like to take a few things along when they visit Sunny in the morning."

She smiled. "Okay. Good. Isn't it wonderful how fast she's improving?"

Cole agreed. He was happy for Sunny and her family.

"And with Joel finding a job in Bandera, it seems like everything is falling into place."

For everyone else.

"Open your present. It's getting late. Are you sure you don't want to sleep on the couch so you're here first thing in the morning when Joey wakes up?"

He shifted and a spring made a squeaking sound. "No thanks. I'm always up before six. As wiped out as he was, I'd be surprised if Joey opens his eyes before eight." Which was why Cole was seriously considering stopping at Annie's on the way over in the morning to use her computer to check flights to Portland.

His mother laughed. "Oh, Cole, you have so much to learn as a parent. But your day will come."

Would it? He certainly hoped so. Hanging out with Joey—and all the kids he'd seen while playing Santa—had made him yearn for a family in a way he never had when he was married to Crystal.

"Was I the first one up on Christmas morning or Annie?"

"You. Always you. Your father started putting a bell on your doorknob on Christmas Eve so we'd hear you. Otherwise, you'd sneak a peek under the wrapping paper."

"Me?" he asked, shaking his head. "No way. You always tell people what a good kid I was."

"And still are," she said, squeezing his shoulder. "But you had a lot of your dad in you. Curious. Impatient. You wanted it all right now."

A lot like your dad. How much like his dad? What if he flew to Oregon and Tessa still closed him out? Would he be so depressed he'd be tempted to end it all like his father had?

His ankle started to throb. "Mom, do you think I could have inherited whatever made Dad do it?"

Her gasp told him she hadn't expected the question. "No, absolutely not. Neither you nor your sister are manic-depressive. That's not what they call it now, but that's what your father's doctor said he was suffering from back then. Tim Lawry was the love of my life, Cole, but he was also ill. Physically. Mentally. Metabolically ill." She took a deep breath and closed her eyes a moment. "I didn't understand then that your father's highs and the lows were due to something happening inside his body. I blamed myself—especially after he died."

He could see the torment in her face even now.

"I know how you hurt your ankle, Cole."

"You do?"

"Annie told me. People do impulsive things when they're upset, especially eleven-year-old boys. That doesn't make you bipolar. You're the most levelheaded person I've ever met. Now, open your present."

He laughed to mask his sudden emotion. Two quick rips and the wrapping paper was on the floor. He shook the cardboard box to see if the object inside matched the picture on the label. "A suitcase?"

He opened the top flap and yanked on a sturdy handle to pull out a sage-green weekender. "It's great, Mom. I can use it when I go to Oregon." He looked at her, willing her to understand and support his decision even if it meant a change that would separate his family. "I have to at least try."

She put her hand over his. "That's what I figured."

"Thanks, Mom. Thanks for everything. I'm going home to pack, but I'll be back in the morning to see what Santa brings Joey."

"I have a feeling he's bringing you something special, too," she said. "You were an awfully good boy this year."

Cole was still chuckling as he tossed his new suitcase onto the seat beside him. The only present he wanted was on a plane for Oregon. But, he thought, with a little luck, I'll be right behind her.

BY NINE THAT EVENING, Tessa was ready to give up and call a cab to take her to a nearby motel for the night. Or she would have if her darn cell phone battery hadn't given up the ghost. She hadn't heard back from Luke before it died, so she had no way of knowing if he'd put together some kind of transportation for her. The young man behind the rental-car desk—Jeremiah—wasn't as heartless and unfeeling as she'd thought, merely new to his job and unskilled. If there had been a car available on the lot at any point in the evening, there wasn't one now. And he'd just apologetically informed her that he needed to close up so he could return home to his mother's house in Gruene.

"I'm really sorry," Jeremiah said for the eleventh time.

Tessa grabbed the handle of her suitcase and turned to leave. "Thanks for trying. Merry Christmas."

She'd hike back to the terminal and grab a cab.

She'd only taken two steps when his phone rang. She stopped, curious to see if he'd answer it. He looked at her and groaned. "I hate this job."

She wasn't surprised. "It might be Santa calling."

As he gave the spiel she'd heard a hundred times that night, she resumed walking. Suddenly, Jeremiah yelled, "Wait!"

She turned. He mumbled something into the phone before hanging up the receiver. He raced to the window that faced the empty parking lot, motioning for her to follow.

"What's going on?" Not rain, she hoped.

"I…um…think your ride's here. That was my boss. He's got a friend who's got a friend who, well, look."

She heard a loud noise but couldn't place the sound. Following Jeremiah's lead, she put her hands on either side of her face and looked outside. "Did that helicopter just land there?"

"Yep."

A door opened and two men in Santa hats got out.

Jeremiah looked at her with awe on his face. "Man, you have friends in high places."

"I do?"

Too stunned to move, she watched as Brady and Jake charged toward the building, their jaunty red plush hats bouncing with each step.

"Holy cripes, that's Brady Carrick," Jeremiah yelped when the two men burst through the door.

Brady acknowledged the boy with a brief nod but his focus was on Tessa.

She gulped loudly. "Hi. What are you doing here?"

Jake picked up her suitcase. "Luke's calling it Operation Santa Fix." He gave her a sardonic look and motioned for her to come with them. "The chopper is his brother's. Luke didn't tell him he was borrowing it, so we have to be fast."

Tessa sputtered. "You're taking me back in a stolen helicopter?"

"Don't worry," Brady said, taking her by the elbow. "Luke's flown thousands of missions under enemy fire. He can handle his brother."

She dug in her heels. "Why would you do this? Not for me."

A third person—sans Santa cap—appeared in the doorway, probably sent to check on what was taking them so long. Blake. He answered her question. "We're flying around in a hot copter on Christmas Eve because Cole is our friend. And Cole loves you. That makes you our friend, too. So, can we go now? I'm not sure we actually have clearance to land this close to the airport."

"Oh," Tessa said. "Let's go."

She waved goodbye to a stunned-looking Jeremiah and rushed outside, running headfirst into the wash from the rotors. Everything happened so fast after that she didn't have time to figure out how she got strapped to a tiny bench in the back of a helicopter with two of Cole's closest friends, but a few seconds later the noisy beast took off.

Tears sprang to her eyes. She couldn't reach her purse, which along with her suitcase, was tucked under the bench seat beneath Brady. She dug in her pocket for a tissue but couldn't find one. She was about to use her sleeve to wipe her nose, when Jake, who was seated on her left, handed her a handkerchief.

"Thanks," she said, mopping up her tears.

He cupped his hands around his ears, indicating he couldn't hear her.

"Thanks," she shouted. "I can't believe you did this. I really can't. I've never known friends like you."

Jake and Brady, the bulky body across from her, looked at each other. "Cole's…Cole," Brady said. "He'd do the same for any of us. And he deserves a break. Especially where love is concerned."

Love.

The idea made her dizzy and sort of queasy, but she told herself that was from flying in a helicopter. She was terrified to look around, but more afraid of what would happen when they landed. Would Cole take her back? She should have called. She shouldn't have left in the first place. Was it too late to jump?

Blake, who occupied the copilot's seat up front, turned to look over his shoulder. She couldn't read his face in the dim light, but she saw him give her a thumbs-up signal. Blake. Smart, calm, grounded.

She took a deep breath and let it out. She could do this. She'd play the hand that was dealt to her and this time she'd win.

COLE WAS SITTING on the side of his bed, trying to remember how to change the setting on his alarm clock when he heard the unmistakable sound of a helicopter. Many of the well-to-do ranchers in the area used helicopters to get around. But he'd never known them to fly at this time of night.

As the noise grew louder, he jumped to his feet and walked to the window. Pooch let out a mortified whimper, so Cole opened the door to let him in. "It's okay, boy. Maybe Santa's upgraded from reindeer. You stay here. I'll check this out."

He was in stocking feet, so instead of walking to the middle of the yard to see, he leaned over the railing and looked up. The running lights told him the bird was close and preparing to land in the cleared space where Cole had once planned to build a barn and workshop. He dashed back inside to turn on the exterior lights. They didn't help much but they might keep the pilot from setting down on his house.

The prominent logo on the side of the aircraft told him Luke was behind the controls. Why? Had the Wild Bunch gotten restless and decided to give Santa some competition?

The bouncing white glow from three flashlights alerted him to his visitors' approach. Sure enough, Brady, Jake and Blake appeared at a quick clip. Brady and Jake were wearing Santa hats, just like the one Cole had recently retired.

And they had another person with them. Tessa.

She took off running as soon as they reached the perimeter of light from his porch. Brady and Jake stopped. Blake, who was carrying a suitcase in one hand and Coach purse in the other, kept walking.

"Cole," Tessa cried breathlessly, sailing up the steps. "Your friends brought me back because I don't want a big house in the city. I don't need designer clothes to prove who I am. And I…I want you to teach me how to play poker."

He knew what he wanted those things to mean, but he couldn't be sure until he asked—even if that meant going all in with no idea where he stood in relation to the pot. "Will you marry me?"

She took a deep breath then said, "Yes."

His face felt like it might crack in half from his grin. "Works for me." Then he pulled her into his arms and kissed her.

Blake dropped Tessa's bags on the bottom step, then coughed. "The hats were Brady's idea. The rescue mission was Luke's. Jake and I went along because it would have killed us not to. Now, I have to get back to my wife before she kills me. Good night and Merry Christmas."

Tessa wriggled one arm free. "Merry Christmas!" she cried, waving like a madwoman. "And thank you. I love you all."

Once the three men were back aboard and the helicopter lifted off, she turned to Cole and hugged him fiercely. "I had no idea that love could be so big."

"This is Texas, remember? Everything is bigger here. But…" He made himself slow things down. He knew better than to assume anything. "I know that you can't just walk away from your life in Oregon, so my bag is packed. I'm ready to go whenever you are."

She touched his face—his sweet, generous, forgiving face. "How does never sound?" His eyes went wide. "Well, I have to go back to close things up, but Marci and I talked. She's pregnant. We're dissolving the partnership, which means I can do my job from home. And this is where I want to live, Cole. With you. For the rest of my life."

He caught his breath and it took him a few seconds to respond. When he did, he looked upward and smiled. "What do you know? There really is a Santa Claus." Then his chin dropped and his grin widened as he stared into the eyes of the woman he loved. "'Cause you're exactly what I asked for."

* * * * *

*Don't miss the Wild Bunch heroes when they
deal out their* TEXAS HOLD'EM *hands
next month—and up the ante again!
Look for Jake's story
GOING FOR BROKE (SR #1458)
by Linda Style in December 2007,
wherever Harlequin books are sold.
Turn the page for a sneak peek....*

SHE FELT CHILLED, and her hands shook. She was more scared than she realized. She placed both hands against her cheeks. "I guess I should go back upstairs."

"Are you okay?"

"Just a little shook up."

He stood, reached out and pulled her into his arms as if it was the most natural thing in the world.

"Maybe a glass of wine will soothe your nerves."

As far as she was concerned, standing here with his arms around her was more soothing than a glass of wine could ever be. "That sounds good."

He pushed back, gave her a quick pat, like a friend would, then walked to the fridge. "Nothing fancy, just a bottle of wine one of the guys brought over last night."

She grinned. "Wine at a poker game?"

"A housewarming-slash-renovation gift. Sally Knutson sent it with Harold."

"That was nice of her." Maybe not everyone in town wanted Jake gone.

He got out two glasses, found a corkscrew, opened the bottle, poured them each a half glass, then handed her one. She moved closer and raised her glass to his. "Here's to a successful renovation."

Looking at her, his expression seemed to soften. Then he clicked his glass against hers. "To success, whatever that may be."

They sipped together and then just stood there, his gaze never leaving hers.

She felt like an amoeba under a microscope. "What are your plans once the bar is finished? Will you stay and run the place?"

He scowled, then gave a wry laugh. "I'd never live here again."

"Then why renovate?"

A wicked smile curved his lips. "Because I can."

"And why hire me, of all people?"

She couldn't read his expression. "You needed a job."

"That's very kind of you. Everything you've done is more than I'd have expected." She pursed her lips. "Considering."

"One might think that," he said, edging closer until he was standing mere inches from her, so close she could feel his body heat. "Or, one might think I have other motives."

Her heartbeat quickened. Her palms got sweaty. He didn't mean… Was that how he planned to get even? The idea made her blood rush. She pulled herself up. "Do you?" Her breathing became heavy and suddenly she didn't give a damn about any of it and she wanted to kiss him in the worst way. "Have other motives?" she breathed.

His gaze had locked on her mouth, and he seemed

to be inching closer and closer. It didn't matter. She leaned forward and kissed him, soft at first, then quickly she brought her arms around his neck, deepening the kiss with a passion she didn't know she had for him. His lips still on hers, he lifted her, kissing her back as passionately as she was kissing him. She felt his muscular shoulders under her fingers, his hard body pressed against hers, his obvious need. She wanted to touch him, all of him, and just as her hands dropped lower on his back, he pulled away.

Her lips throbbed and she might've felt stupid if he hadn't responded as he did and if he didn't still have his hands on her.

"This is a bad idea," he said, his breathing labored.

Her first response was hurt, but her body said something entirely different. "Oh, I beg to differ," she said, her voice sounding husky and not her own. "I think it's a wonderful idea."

He dropped his arms and took a step back. "Uh…as nice as that was, sex wasn't my motivation for hiring you."

Her face warmed. Was there sarcasm in his voice? No. She'd seen the heat in his eyes. But maybe he had no intention to do anything about it. And she'd forced him into it. The idea made her want him even more. In that instant, she decided she was going to make him want her as much as she wanted him.

She walked slowly around him, then picked up the wine bottle and poured some more in her glass. She took a slow sip and, looking directly into his eyes, she said, "No? I'm not sure I believe that. You could've hired any number of people with my skills."

A slow smile just barely lifted the corners of his mouth.

"Maybe you only think you hired me for my skills— and other altruistic reasons," she added. "Helping a woman with a baby and all that."

He dragged his gaze from her head to her toes, then back again. He crossed his arms. "Or maybe I hired you because you were always so unattainable and now you need me."

SPECIAL EDITION®

LIFE, LOVE AND FAMILY

*These contemporary romances will strike a chord
with you as heroines juggle life
and relationships on their way to true love.*

New York Times *bestselling author*
Linda Lael Miller brings you a
BRAND-NEW contemporary story
featuring her fan-favorite McKettrick family.

Meg McKettrick is surprised to be reunited with
her high school flame, Brad O'Ballivan. After
enjoying a career as a country-and-western singer,
Brad aches for a home and family…and seeing
Meg again makes him realize he still loves her. But
their pride manages to interfere with love…until
an unexpected matchmaker gets involved.

Turn the page for a sneak preview of
THE McKETTRICK WAY
by Linda Lael Miller.
On sale November 20,
wherever books are sold.

Brad shoved the truck into gear and drove to the bottom of the hill, where the road forked. Turn left, and he'd be home in five minutes. Turn right, and he was headed for Indian Rock.

He had no damn business going to Indian Rock.

He had nothing to say to Meg McKettrick, and if he never set eyes on the woman again, it would be two weeks too soon.

He turned right.

He couldn't have said why.

He just drove straight to the Dixie Dog Drive-In.

Back in the day, he and Meg used to meet at the Dixie Dog, by tacit agreement, when either of them had been away. It had been some kind of universe thing, purely intuitive.

Passing familiar landmarks, Brad told himself he ought to turn around. The old days were gone. Things had ended badly between him and Meg anyhow, and she wasn't going to be at the Dixie Dog.

He kept driving.

He rounded a bend, and there was the Dixie Dog. Its

big neon sign, a giant hot dog, was all lit up and going through its corny sequence—first it was covered in red squiggles of light, meant to suggest ketchup, and then yellow, for mustard.

Brad pulled into one of the slots next to a speaker, rolled down the truck window and ordered.

A girl roller-skated out with the order about five minutes later.

When she wheeled up to the driver's window, smiling, her eyes went wide with recognition, and she dropped the tray with a clatter.

Silently Brad swore. Damn if he hadn't forgotten he was a famous country singer.

The girl, a skinny thing wearing too much eye makeup, immediately started to cry. "I'm sorry!" she sobbed, squatting to gather up the mess.

"It's okay," Brad answered quietly, leaning to look down at her, catching a glimpse of her plastic name tag. "It's okay, Mandy. No harm done."

"I'll get you another dog and a shake right away, Mr. O'Ballivan!"

"Mandy?"

She stared up at him pitifully, sniffling. Thanks to the copious tears, most of the goop on her eyes had slid south. "Yes?"

"When you go back inside, could you not mention seeing me?"

"But you're Brad O'Ballivan!"

"Yeah," he answered, suppressing a sigh. "I know."

She rolled a little closer. "You wouldn't happen to have a picture you could autograph for me, would you?"

"Not with me," Brad answered.

"You could sign this napkin, though," Mandy said. "It's only got a little chocolate on the corner."

Brad took the paper napkin and her order pen, and scrawled his name. Handed both items back through the window.

She turned and whizzed back toward the side entrance to the Dixie Dog.

Brad waited, marveling that he hadn't considered incidents like this one before he'd decided to come back home. In retrospect, it seemed shortsighted, to say the least, but the truth was, he'd expected to be—Brad O'Ballivan.

Presently Mandy skated back out again, and this time she managed to hold on to the tray.

"I didn't tell a soul!" she whispered. "But Heather and Darlene *both* asked me why my mascara was all smeared." Efficiently she hooked the tray onto the bottom edge of the window.

Brad extended payment, but Mandy shook her head.

"The boss said it's on the house, since I dumped your first order on the ground."

He smiled. "Okay, then. Thanks."

Mandy retreated, and Brad was just reaching for the food when a bright red Blazer whipped into the space beside his. The driver's door sprang open, crashing into the metal speaker, and somebody got out in a hurry.

Something quickened inside Brad.

And in the next moment Meg McKettrick was standing practically on his running board, her blue eyes blazing.

Brad grinned. "I guess you're not over me after all," he said.

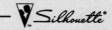

SPECIAL EDITION™

**brings you a heartwarming
new McKettrick's story from**

NEW YORK TIMES BESTSELLING AUTHOR

LINDA LAEL MILLER

THE
McKETTRICK
Way

Meg McKettrick is surprised to be reunited
with her high school flame, Brad O'Ballivan,
who has returned home to his family's
neighboring ranch. After seeing Meg again,
Brad realizes he still loves her. But the pride
of both manage to interfere with love...until
an unexpected matchmaker gets involved.

—— McKettrick Women ——

Available December wherever you buy books.

THE ITALIAN BILLIONAIRE'S CHRISTMAS MIRACLE
by *Catherine Spencer*
Book #: 2688

Domenico Silvaggio d'Avalos knows that beautiful,
unworldly Arlene Russell isn't mistress material—
but might she be suitable as his wife?

HIS CHRISTMAS BRIDE
by *Helen Brooks*
Book #: 2689

Powerful billionaire Zak Hamilton understood
Blossom's vulnerabilities, and he had to have her.
What was more, he'd make sure he claimed her
as his bride—by Christmas!

Be sure not to miss out on these two fabulous
Christmas stories available December 2007,
brought to you by Harlequin Presents!

REQUEST YOUR FREE BOOKS!

2 FREE NOVELS PLUS 2 FREE GIFTS!

HARLEQUIN®

Super Romance®

Exciting, emotional, unexpected!

YES! Please send me 2 FREE Harlequin Superromance® novels and my 2 FREE gifts. After receiving them, if I don't wish to receive any more books, I can return the shipping statement marked "cancel." If I don't cancel, I will receive 6 brand-new novels every month and be billed just $4.69 per book in the U.S., or $5.24 per book in Canada, plus 25¢ shipping and handling per book and applicable taxes, if any*. That's a savings of close to 15% off the cover price! I understand that accepting the 2 free books and gifts places me under no obligation to buy anything. I can always return a shipment and cancel at any time. Even if I never buy another book from Harlequin, the two free books and gifts are mine to keep forever.   135 HDN EEX7   336 HDN EEYK

Name	(PLEASE PRINT)	
Address		Apt.
City	State/Prov.	Zip/Postal Code

Signature (if under 18, a parent or guardian must sign)

Mail to the **Harlequin Reader Service®**:
IN U.S.A.: P.O. Box 1867, Buffalo, NY 14240-1867
IN CANADA: P.O. Box 609, Fort Erie, Ontario L2A 5X3

Not valid to current Harlequin Superromance subscribers.

Want to try two free books from another line?
Call 1-800-873-8635 or visit www.morefreebooks.com.

* Terms and prices subject to change without notice. NY residents add applicable sales tax. Canadian residents will be charged applicable provincial taxes and GST. This offer is limited to one order per household. All orders subject to approval. Credit or debit balances in a customer's account(s) may be offset by any other outstanding balance owed by or to the customer. Please allow 4 to 6 weeks for delivery.

Your Privacy: Harlequin is committed to protecting your privacy. Our Privacy Policy is available online at www.eHarlequin.com or upon request from the Reader Service. From time to time we make our lists of customers available to reputable firms who may have a product or service of interest to you. If you would prefer we not share your name and address, please check here. ☐

HSR07

Inside ROMANCE

Stay up-to-date on all your romance reading news!

Inside Romance is a FREE quarterly newsletter highlighting our upcoming series releases and promotions.

Visit

www.eHarlequin.com/InsideRomance

to sign up to receive our complimentary newsletter today!

Get ready to meet

THREE WISE WOMEN

with stories by

DONNA BIRDSELL, LISA CHILDS

and

SUSAN CROSBY.

Don't miss these three unforgettable stories about modern-day women and the love and new lives they find on Christmas.

Look for *Three Wise Women*
Available December wherever you buy books.

HARLEQUIN®
NeXt™

TheNextNovel.com

HN88147